Hell Plague

By

Sean Deville

Book 3:

The Hidden Hand Case Files

First publication by Amazon

Copyright (©) Sean Deville 2023

Visit the author's website at www.seandeville.com

Acknowledgement is made for permission to quote copyrighted materials

No part of this book may be used or reproduced in any manner whatsoever without written permission from the publisher or author.

This book is intended for entertainment purposes only, and any resemblance to persons living or dead is purely coincidental.

"The anguish of the people,
Who are below here in my face depicts,
That pity which for terror thou has taken."

- Dante

To: Director of Operations

From: Soteria

Subject: Summary of recent atomist event.

As you are well aware, the woman known as Sirena Samson (who will be referred to from here on out as the *anomaly*) created a portal to the Hell world two days ago. The method by which she did this is still unclear, but the creation of this portal resulted in a catastrophic energy pulse which spread out from the existing Hellgate network.

Our analysis states that all the known Hellgates were agitated by this event. This, once again, caused widespread chaos across the globe, with severe loss of life on the UK mainland due to the unforeseen mental contagion spread by Sirena over the preceding twenty-four hours.

As of the writing of this memo, the UK deaths total over ten thousand, which is proving difficult to cover up in the civilian press. A considerable amount of my processing power is being used combatting the spread of first-hand reports of the madness via social media and email.

Having collated and interpreted all the available data, it would appear that, had the Hellgates across the planet remained in their agitated state, the hypnotic influence the anomaly apparently possessed would have spread to every population centre affected (see appendix A for a summary of my findings). I have deduced that whatever power the anomaly controlled, she was able to infuse this into the energy created by the Hellgates.

Although the Hellgate activated by the anomaly was destroyed, this is a new and disturbing development. While I have no evidence of such, the events of the past few days appear organised to me.

Of perhaps greater concern were the incursions that occurred from the Hell world. While none of the defences surrounding the Hellgates under our influence were breached, two technicians were trapped in proximity to the Gibraltar portal at the time of its activation. They were engaged in camera repairs at the time of the energy pulse, and had just completed installation and testing of the improved EMP hardened surveillance equipment.

We are fortunate to have a recording of what occurred, as without that, the risks now posed by these two technicians might have gone unnoticed for some time. The recording shows them being assaulted by a creature of uncertain design, and they were quickly overpowered. There is definitive evidence that they have been deliberately infested with some kind of parasite, the nature of which has yet to reveal itself (see appendix B for the medical summary).

The two men have been detained and quarantined in our secure research facility, although only one of them, Brian Moses, has regained consciousness. The other received a head injury, which has left him in a coma.

Please find attached the transcript of the Moses debriefing by the Hidden Hand chief psychologist Victor Schmidt. For safety purposes, the debriefing was done via video conferencing.

Subject: Transcript of Brian Moses (BM) debriefing by Victor Schmidt (VS).

VS – Welcome back to the land of the living. Give yourself a few moments, the sedation we gave you will probably leave you drowsy.

BM – Where…?

VS – Take some deep breaths. It will help clear your head.

BM – Why am I restrained? What is this place?

VS – Now then, Brian, it's important you remain calm.

BM – Calm? How can I remain calm? Let me loose, goddammit.

VS – I'm afraid I don't have that authority.

BM – Then get someone who does.

VS – Listen to yourself, man. Stop these theatrics. I'm here to help you, but first you need to get a grip on yourself. Remember who you are.

BM – Help me? I don't believe you.

VS – That's a decision only you can make, but I'm probably the only person alive who can reverse your present circumstances.

BM – I'm sorry. I'm just so confused.

VS – Which is understandable.

BM – Why was I sedated?

VS – Standard protocol for someone moved to quarantine, I'm afraid.

BM – Quarantine? Shit.

VS – You were warned of the risks before you took your position. Tell me, why do you think you are here?

BM – I…

VS – Go on.

BM – I don't know.

VS – Oh, I think you can do better than that. You were doing an emergency upgrade on the surveillance grid protecting the Gibraltar Hellgate.

BM – These restraints are too tight.

VS – But they are necessary. And stop deflecting. You were doing repairs. What do you remember?

BM – I don't know.

VS – What if you did know?

BM – It's all black. I was installing a camera, and then…

VS – Yes?

BM – Nothing.

VS – Perhaps I can jog your memory. One of the cameras you'd installed recorded everything. I'd like to play it for you.

BM – No.

VS – Why such reluctance? I feel it will explain your present predicament.

BM – Just let me out of here. I don't want to hear your lies any longer.

VS – I'm afraid that won't be happening any time soon. And I would never lie to you.

BM – Bastard.

VS – You're stressed. That's understandable. Do try to remember that I'm here to answer your questions, so long as you answer mine.

BM – You just want to poke around in my mind.

VS – Yes, that too. Quiet now while I play you the recording. You will find it very enlightening.

[No audio linked to the video recording].

BM – What the hell is that thing?

VS – We were hoping you could tell us. Still no recollection? The creature was rather tall and striking in appearance.

BM – No.

VS – Pity.

BM – What did it do to me?

VS – That is what we are still trying to determine. However, an MRI scan reveals that you have some sort of parasite inside you.

BM – What? Then get it out.

VS – That's not going to be so easy. It's in your brain, you see.

BM – I didn't sign up to this.

VS – Indeed, but this is where we are. You will just have to make the most of it. The more you are open and honest with us, the better I can help you.

BM – You can't just leave it in me!

VS – Well, actually, we can. We need to understand what the effects of this parasite will be. I'm sure you understand.

BM – Let me go, damn you.

VS – No.

1.

Isles of Scilly, UK

The creature in the containment vessel was a fascination that demanded intensive and exhaustive study. The size of an adult human thumb, it had been surgically removed from the brainstem of a now-deceased technician after being discovered due to the implant in the back of the technician's neck.

This infestation had been confirmed by MRI scan.

The removal operation had been done remotely via robotic surgical arms due to the unknown nature of this new lifeform. Upon extraction, it had wriggled and fought back, deadly teeth appearing in the centre of its small mass. Those teeth were harmless to the metallic jaws that had gripped it with calculated precision. With that knowledge about its capabilities established, the creature had been transferred to its new home and was now kept in strict quarantine.

How had this thing made its way inside a human brain? And what was its purpose?

The unlucky victim that had been host to the creature had died on the table, the operation to remove the parasite unfortunately lethal. The medical report had stated that the man would have been unlikely to recover from his coma anyway, and thus, authorisation was given to risk the procedure.

Sacrifices had to be made for the advancement of science.

Professor Reginald Cleaver thought the death an acceptable loss, because the characteristics of this thing had to be understood, and quickly. He was adamant that knowing the nature of the threat gave one a chance to counter it. In his opinion, human lives were of secondary interest to the pursuit of knowledge.

In truth, Cleaver had never understood why humanity was supposed to be so important, nor could he grasp why life was deemed so sacred. What was one life compared to the billions that were at risk?

It was all done for the greater good, that was what Cleaver kept telling himself. The two recent Hellgate episodes had revealed so much about the Hell world, and none of that held any real promise for the future of the human race. To Cleaver, the prospect of an invasion from that parallel world was terrifying.

"Four hours since extraction, and XB113 has been successfully contained." Cleaver spoke into his digital recorder, the notes he made automatically being transferred to the secure database that existed at the bottom of the nine-level subterranean facility. The Hidden Hand had built the place a decade ago, at great expense, much of the cost related to the necessary secrecy required for the construction. That was why the uninhabited island of Samson had been chosen, the discreet entrance that now existed missing from the publicly available satellite maps. It was so well hidden that the unwary could walk right past that entrance without ever detecting it.

As was the way of the Hidden Hand, the facility was given a name that vaguely described its purpose.

The Laboratory.

"There seems to be a primitive intelligence to the creature," Cleaver added, before mopping the sweat from his brow. His perspiration had always been an issue, bringing with it a body odour that was rarely controlled by over-the-counter deodorants. His childhood had been traumatic, his physiology drawing mockery and the attention of relentless bullies who enjoyed the way Cleaver was so inept at defending himself. He'd been gifted with an incredible, if autistic, brain, but lacked the health and physical stature to make him a shining example of human perfection.

Even at university, he'd struggled due to his status as a protégé and evident genius. Also, most students who attended that university weren't fourteen, which drew amused and unwelcome attention. Ironically, this worked to his benefit, his loneliness and isolation fuelling his devotion to his studies, which saw him surpass most of his lecturers in knowledge and the understanding of his chosen field.

Cleaver became an unsurpassed expert in bio-invasion, the study of how invasive species impacted ecosystems. Who better to seek out the secrets of Hell?

His autism was just another part of who he was. So long as he had structure and something to consume his time, he could excel at most given tasks if he was left alone. Cleaver did not like people and had a severe aversion to being touched, something that had developed as he had grown into an adult.

Everybody who worked down in this facility respected that. Genius always came with flaws attached.

He never learnt how he had come to the attention of the Hidden Hand, but now he worked for them as one of their chief scientists, studying secret things that he could only have ever dreamt of. It was his job to theorise how creatures from the Pit might impact the Earth of today.

His findings were rarely reassuring.

"We have tested it in a rudimentary maze, and found the specimen able to navigate and decipher the maze's structure. It twice tried to escape by attempting to chew through the encasing walls, but our precautions were enough to defeat its attempts. I hypothesise that these teeth are a way for it to gain access to a host, as well as giving the parasite a means to kill those it infests." They had one other test subject who was still in isolation, and Cleaver found himself wondering what it would be like to have such a creature inside his mind.

The idea caused a shudder to ripple down his spine.

"The creature appears to be a silicone-based lifeform, and I have been unable to detect any internal organs. It has an aversion to ultraviolet light, heat and fire, retreating when a naked flame is presented. Its amorphous nature does allow for motility, at surprising speeds, similar to that of a cockroach."

Cleaver zoomed in on one of the micro cameras watching the abomination. It lay in its Rubik's-cube-sized square prison, twitching, occasionally sending out proboscises to test its surroundings. As the image increased, the thing stopped, falling rigid, before the centre of it formed into a circular collection of wickedly sharp teeth.

It knew it was being scrutinised. But how?

"It has the ability to harden parts of its structure at will, forming a dentition that can dissipate back into its central mass. Needless to say, this is not a species we want colonising our world. I am confident that the containment measures will hold it."

Cleaver was rare for a genius in that he never let his intelligence blind him to the dangers the Hell world posed. His experience during his youth had also never let his ego develop to dangerous levels. He was brilliant, but also humble with it.

That was one of the reasons he had been so appealing to the Hidden Hand. There was also the flaw in his character which meant he would never be likely to form any kind of romantic attachment. The psychologists who reviewed his suitability had put forward the hypothesis that he was basically asexual and would become brutally loyal to anyone who gave him a meaningful outlet for his intelligence while allowing him the solitude he demanded.

Cleaver was deemed perfect for the Hidden Hand, and although he had a home on the mainland, he spent most of his time in this facility. His work was his joy.

"I have an intuition about this species. There is something mechanical about it, as if it was a creation of science rather than nature." Cleaver pondered whether he was wise to record that assumption. That was why he was here though, to think the things that others might think untenable.

He was well aware of how potentially dangerous this alien creature was, and he wasn't the type of person who would take unnecessary chances in his research. Cleaver would never be described as a hero, and there was nobody he needed to impress. Thus, the protocol for experiments would be followed to the letter.

What did the parasite do when it was in a human host?

The specimen was in its reinforced glass case, contained within a second, larger vessel with thicker walls lined with carbyne, the strongest substance known to man. The floor of that secondary vessel was fitted with a maze that could be altered for complexity. Whenever study was needed, the smaller cube could be opened, dropping the abominable thing into the maze. When completed, an electronic arm would secure and return the specimen to its smaller cube.

These precautions were suspended by carbon fibre wires above the floor of an airtight, one metre squared chamber, the walls of the containment chamber electrified. Everything was encased in thick, reinforced concrete to increase the level of security.

Precaution upon precaution had been designed by Cleaver himself for such a discovery. From what he could presently see, he was of the opinion that the present safety measures were excessive, which was how it should be.

It was one of those rare moments in his life when he was wrong.

All of this research was done in this secret facility, the slug-like thing one of several specimens collected over the years. It might have been small, but it was scientifically significant and absolutely horrific.

Cleaver wondered if such a tiny creature could be sentient. Did it resent what was being done to it? What secrets had it yet to show them? That was always the danger with a creature such as this.

Cleaver glanced at the wall above his monitors, where a red button, protected by a removable plastic shield, waited. The reason for the button was one of ultimate safety. If the specimen posed a threat of escape, then the contents of the quarantine room would be incinerated automatically. Should that automated system fail, pressing the red button would bring the same result.

The temperature in that small room could reach just shy of two thousand degrees.

"We have tested it with organic matter and to date, it seems to have no interest in feeding on anything dead. Anything living placed in its proximity it kills, although we have only tested it on insects to date. I would still like permission to test it on larger creatures, all the way up to one of the smaller primates." Cleaver paused in his recording.

A human would be the better test subject, but Cleaver knew better than to suggest that.

He was determined to discover the secret of this thing and what its purpose was. There was a problem, though; his research was hampered by his own social inadequacies. His genius had not granted him verbal skills, which meant the questioning of the awake host, Brian

Moses, had been left to others. He was reliant on their slow, measured approach to discover what the parasite was doing to the human host.

To date, little had been revealed about what the thing did to those it infested. This was unsatisfactory as the creature was here for a reason that needed to be addressed. It had been brought here deliberately by a huge bipedal creature that strongly resembled a large and formidable human. Cleaver had seen the video recording of its arrival and the way it overpowered the two technicians.

That recording troubled his sleep.

Most importantly, he had seen the way the parasites were delivered. Unable to breach the portal defences erected by the Hidden Hand, the bipedal man-thing had retreated back through the Hellgate before it had reverted to its un-agitated state.

Cleaver had been instrumental in improving the design of those defences. Every portal was entombed in an airtight chamber of thick concrete and tungsten. Due to the need to access monitoring equipment, a double door airlock allowed access to the chambers, which were usually found deep underground in existing cave structures. It had been Cleaver's suggestion that the formidable access doors be both mechanical and electronic in nature, so that they could only be operated manually from the outside of the chamber with Soteria's strict approval.

Only by working in unison could man and machine get anywhere near a Hellgate. Anyone entering would need someone waiting for them to let them out while under the constant supervision of the planet's most advanced artificial intelligence.

It was infuriating to Cleaver to be dependent on others for his studies. Cleaver had requested a more rigorous approach be taken when it came to the physical and psychological examination of Moses, but more experienced minds had quietly suggested he concentrate on what he did best. The scientist was not the kind of person to rock the boat after such a response, so he continued his experiments in the hope of breaking the enigma that had the ability to chew through human bone.

There were many questions he had so far been unable to answer, including why this creature had come through the Hellgate, and what its purpose was?

To study a thing was to know a thing. To know a thing gave you the knowledge to ultimately destroy it. Cleaver was about to discover that destroying these abominations would have been the superior option.

***

It was easy to kill. Sometimes too easy.

The thing was, if you weren't careful, killing could become an addiction, a burning need that could eat you alive if you didn't feed it. The Hidden Hand knew that, which was why they mandated that psychological evaluation was required every time one of their agents took a life.

The evaluations were usually done in a comfortable room with an artificial fire burning on one wall. There was always soft lighting, the air silently heated for maximum comfort. The only furniture on past occasions had been two plush chairs, angled and separated so as to allow the therapist and client to view each other and the fire. No sound could be allowed to ingress from the outside, the walls of the evaluation room painted a soothing yellow.

In such a room, one could relax and feel at ease, and Stuart Radcliffe had been evaluated more times than he could remember. He'd killed a lot of people in his time, and the deaths rarely bothered him.

They were necessary, ordered for the protection of the realm and the greater planet. Sometimes he even found satisfaction in the lives he took.

Normally, Stuart wouldn't think twice about the mind probing sessions. But the last operation had been far from ordinary and had left Stuart with a disturbing and lingering sense of unease.

That was the least of his problems, for today, he wasn't in the comfortable room. Today he was in an interrogation chamber, with white walls and a bright ceiling. The metal desk his elbows rested on was bolted to the floor, as were the two chairs, one of which he occupied.

This was also the only time he'd been evaluated wearing handcuffs that were connected to a sturdy eyebolt screwed into the table.

Not what he'd signed up for, but understandable.

"Sorry to have kept you," the psychologist offered as he entered. "And sorry for the restraints. I'm sure you understand." He was a short set man with thick glasses. Stuart had spoken to him more than two dozen times before, and yet he'd never learnt the man's name.

This was also the first occasion his therapist was wearing a hazmat suit with its own oxygen supply.

"No problem," Stuart replied. Still, he shifted in his seat, a conscious display of how unsettled he felt. The metal chair was hard and unyielding, as Stuart had been so many times before.

"Your MRI scan and blood tests show you are clear of any pathogens. I'm hoping that is reassuring to you."

"Good to know." Stuart hadn't been surprised when he'd been ordered to turn himself in for mandatory quarantine. His mind had been manipulated by a force nobody understood. Under that manipulation, he'd done terrible things that normal people would be locked away for.

Stuart was far from normal.

Killing was his profession, and yet he'd never engaged in a frenzy of mass murder. That changed two days ago when he had lost his mind and killed close to twenty-one people in an uncontrolled fever of destruction. Most of it was arguably self-defence, but not all.

If it had just been him engaged in the slaughter, this conversation likely wouldn't be happening. He'd have been *retired*, his body secretly cremated so that he could be quickly forgotten. Fortunately for Stuart, and unfortunately for the people of Scotland, nearly a hundred thousand people had been *infected* by a mental contagion that had temporarily stripped those affected of their impulse controls and much of their sanity. Whole towns had descended into madness, the city of Glasgow nearly tipping into unstoppable chaos. Villages were smoking ruins. City streets were littered with the dead and dying. And that was before the Hellgates were activated.

Then, as if with the snap of a finger, the people afflicted, the ones committing the violence and depravity… well they had just stopped the killing, leaving the country reeling from the after-effects. The Hidden Hand had needed to pull every trick in the book to cover up the cause of the widespread insanity.

The world was not ready to learn about the existence of Hellgates or the Hell world they led to. Not yet.

The body count kept popping into Stuart's thoughts, but in truth, he wasn't sure how many people he'd killed. Most of his madness was mainly a disjointed blur. There were faces, though, haunting images that crashed into his waking moments. His sleep was strangely unaffected.

Was that a good sign, or an indication of some deeper trauma?

The psychologist sat down, settling himself onto the opposing chair. He held a computer tablet, but was without the irritating pen which he was known to play with during his prolonged questioning.

There was one other addition to the room today. A large TV screen had been mounted on one wall. There was no visible remote control.

"Perhaps you could start with a summary of your last mission," the psychologist prompted. The man asking the questions had full Omega clearance and knew secrets that would rip the heart of western civilisation open. Stuart nodded his agreement and had to consciously stop his fingernails digging into the back of his hand.

"Soteria had detected what she thought was a Hellgate in the west of Scotland. My team was sent to investigate." Soteria was an artificial intelligence housed in the world's most advanced quantum super computer. She would be recording this questioning.

No, let's call it what it actually was. This was an interrogation.

Stuart had been reassured that Soteria wasn't sentient, but Stuart was far from convinced. From his daily interactions, he had come to the conclusion that the AI was a self-aware entity.

"Go on," the psychologist encouraged. Stuart found himself focusing on the tablet the man held.

"I went ahead of my team to observe a suspected location for the Hellgate. That part didn't go so well." In truth, it was a shit show. They had been sent in against an enemy they were no match for.

"Please elaborate."

"You'll need to bear with me. This is difficult to explain." Words weren't adequate to describe what had happened to Stuart.

Unless you'd lived that experience, you were never going to understand it.

"Take your time." Psychologist lingo for *spit it out*.

"We were sent to surveil a property, but the owner was in possession of a power I… we had never encountered before." Stuart was conscious of every gesture he made, because it wasn't just the psychologist observing him. Soteria was always there in the background. Watching. Listening.

"The owner, a woman called Sirena Samson."

"Yes. By whatever means, she just took control of me. There was no way I could deny her." That was the first violation Sirena had committed.

The slaughter had come after that.

"*She had the power to obliterate free will*," the psychologist read off his tablet. "That was what you wrote in your official report."

"Yes."

"That must have been hard for you."

"Very," Stuart agreed. "What made it worse was the fact I knew she was controlling me. And part of me liked it."

"To have your very identity used against you. A terrible thing." The psychologist was looking at his patient casually, but Stuart knew that was merely an act. He was being questioned by a man who was the best in the business, someone who spent his waking hours in search of weakness and vulnerability.

Honesty was Stuart's best option here. It wouldn't be easy, though, to open up his soul.

"She used you against your fellow agents." Was the psychologist throwing an accusation?

"I couldn't stop it. If she'd told me to fire on them, I would have." Instead, Sirena had used Stuart as bait, to draw Lucy and Craig out.

"Your fellow agents state you shouted a warning." Some solace in that.

"Yes, I remember that." At the time, he hadn't known for sure if the words had escaped his lips. The cry hadn't done any good. Sirena had still been able to incapacitate Lucy and Craig with what appeared to be a simple wave of her hand and a single word.

Sleep.

"The video footage from the surveillance vans' external cameras has been studied. It has been determined that Sirena's power was unlike anything the Hidden Hand has ever encountered. Were you aware we have discovered she was over a hundred years old?" The psychologist ran his gloved finger down the computer tablet. Stuart did his best to keep his manner calm.

"She certainly didn't look it." Stuart would have put Sirena no older than thirty.

"No," the psychologist agreed. "Soteria, the first video, please."

"Certainly, doctor," the ephemeral female voice answered. The television burst into life. When Stuart looked at it, he saw himself holding the tip of his gun against his head.

"If she'd told you to kill yourself...?"

"I doubt there would have been any hesitation." Stuart took in a deep inhale.

You will kill anyone and everyone you see. Keep on moving and keep on killing. The more innocent, the better. Do you understand? That had been Sirena's final instruction to Stuart, recorded by the surveillance cameras.

"Did you have any other impulses that day?"

"What do you mean, exactly?" Stuart understood, but he needed a moment to gather himself. His face had paled. Watching himself be so weak was humiliating.

"Rape, gluttony, anything like that. Murder wasn't the only thing Sirena's victims engaged in." Victims, that was a word he could have latched onto, but he resisted. With all his training and experience, it was difficult to see himself as a victim.

He was still alive, after all.

"No. My focus was purely death."

"Well, it is something you are particularly accomplished at. Any murderous thoughts now?" The question seemed so innocent.

"No," Stuart revealed. There was no point lying, not here. Not with Soteria constantly monitoring his biological functions. Polygraphs were flawed and relatively easy to defeat. Soteria wasn't. Stuart sometimes wondered if the AI could look into his soul. The integrated surveillance implant in the back of Stuart's neck helped with that.

One of the first things he'd been told upon being inducted into the Hidden Hand was to never lie to Soteria.

She would know.

"To think she was living among us all this time." The psychologist sat back in his chair.

"We're fortunate Lucy dealt with her."

"We aren't here to talk about Lucy," the psychologist warned.

"Of course." Stuart could tell he was getting to the meat of why the psychologist was here.

"Soteria, the second video, please."

The image changed to Stuart in a Scottish village street. Stuart was firing on a mob that was charging at him. Those deaths he didn't feel bad about. Even without Sirena's influence, that kind of threat required a definitive response.

"The villagers didn't leave you any choice."

"No," Stuart said blankly.

"Why didn't you kill the rest of them?" the psychologist suddenly asked. As he watched, Stuart saw himself walk past the people he'd killed to observe a bonfire at the edge of the screen.

On the video, Stuart stood there, watching the woman that was being burnt scream.

"It's vague. I remember thinking I should put the burning woman out of her misery."

"Why didn't you?" challenged the psychologist.

"I had no control, and I remember talking to myself. It was like there was an alien entity moving my body. All I felt right then was boredom."

"This is fascinating," the psychologist revealed.

Fascinating? It was then that Stuart realised his fingertips were hurting. Glancing down, he saw he was pressing them against the table.

"There's something else."

"Yes?"

"Right then, despite Sirena's orders, I didn't feel compelled to kill them. I think it was because they were infected, too."

"I prefer to use the word influenced," the psychologist corrected.

"Okay. Which draws me to the question as to whether I'm making it out of here?"

The psychologist paused, matching Stuart's eye contact.

"I think Sirena's influence died when she left this reality. Should we clear you, how do you feel about being released into the wider world?"

"Nervous," Stuart replied. "Apprehensive. It's difficult to think you can lose control like that."

"Thank you for your honesty." The psychologist stood. "I'm happy with our session today."

"Happy enough to let me out of here?" Stuart asked.

"Let's see how things play out, but it's not up to me. That decision will need to be sent up the chain for review."

Not the most reassuring answer.

Stuart didn't say anything more as the psychologist left the room. Soon, two surly men would come to take Stuart back to his room. He wouldn't resist them because they weren't his enemy, and they treated Stuart with passive respect. Did these guards know what Stuart was capable of?

If he was going to get out of here, it would be through passive acceptance of his own vulnerability.

2.

Area 51, Nevada, USA.

Area 51 is a secretive military base, more so than most people realise. The lore behind the facility states that it is the home to the wreckage of alien spaceships that have been dissected and reverse engineered to give the US military a significant technological advantage over its global competitors. While it is a place where advanced aeronautic research *is* done, talk of aliens was merely a curious cover story to hide the true secret.

In a remote bunker on the edge of the main airstrip, there exists a portal to another world. As much as they had tried, the Hidden Hand hadn't been able to establish control of all the world's Hellgates.

After all, the Earth was a big planet governed by many competing factions.

Normally, activity around the obscure concrete structure known as XR-1 Storage was kept to a minimum. Not today, for the already impressive security had been enhanced by the arrival of a special team with special clearance. That team had set up camp within the bunker's perimeter fencing, ready for the grand re-opening of XR-1 Storage, should that be deemed viable.

First, they had to ensure the facility was safe.

"I am well aware of the lockdown procedures," Colonel Melvin Brook stated to the captain on the other end of the radio he'd been provided with. "Who do you think wrote the protocols you are following? I can assure you, there is no contagion here. The airlock to the portal held." It was certainly locked tight presently.

"You ordered the evacuation of the facility, Colonel. You must have had a reason. And you know the precautions that must now be taken."

"The evacuation was a necessary safeguard taken out of an abundance of caution. I assure you, the emergency is now over," Brooke insisted. Why was he so adamant in that regard? Truth be told, he only had a vague recollection of what had happened two days before. The portal had activated, but they were all safe now.

Weren't they?

His inner voice kept insisting that was the case.

It would help if he could recall what exactly had occurred, but there was a blank there. He was missing time he couldn't account for, a period where he'd been unconscious and vulnerable.

His lips were stating that everything was fine, and yet his self-preservation was screaming alarm. There were things he wanted to tell the captain, but the words wouldn't come.

How was that possible? Why did he feel so... wrong?

"That is still to be determined, Colonel. The team are doing their final sweep. Once we have the blood tests back for you and Doctor Hertz, we should be able to look at relinquishing control of the facility back to you." Doctor Hertz was the chief scientist overseeing the portal they had control of, and Brook had little love for the man.

You need to get out of here.

The inner voice sounded like his own, but its words seemed separate to what Brook should be thinking. At no time should he be arguing with the captain, for the rules were there for a good reason. He knew that, and yet he felt compelled to push against the captain's authority. This had nothing to do with rank. Instead, Brook was consumed by a need to be released, even though he should know better.

It was as if his thoughts weren't his own, a feeling that had grown more alarming the last few hours.

"Why are the tests taking so long?" Brook demanded to know. This irritability was unlike him, the nervous energy that riddled his flesh having no means to discharge. He was trapped here, and a part of him couldn't tolerate that.

There are things you have to share with the people of the world.

What the hell was that supposed to mean?

Two days ago, he remembered waking up on the concrete floor of the observation chamber. It was the place where the portal was monitored from, and the lights above his head had been flickering, several of them blown. It had been the second time in a week that the portal they guarded had sprung to life, and this additional activation had once again sent out an electromagnetic pulse through XR-1 Storage, sweeping out for miles in every direction.

Despite being designed to withstand such an energy surge, all the instruments that recorded the portals' activities had been fried for a second time. To know what had occurred that day, you would need to rely on human recollection.

That was lacking. Only he and Doctor Hertz had been present to know the intricacies of what had happened with the portal, and their recollections weren't up to it.

Brook's greatest memory upon that waking was how badly his head and eye hurt. Much of that pain had fluctuated the past two days, replaced by a dull ache that was always present. It sat there, as if it wanted something from him, hinting at some action that he was required to perform.

What if there is something seriously wrong with me?

The thought flashed into his stream of consciousness before being ruthlessly quashed by his rational mind. It was quickly discarded.

Nonsense. Get a hold of yourself.

"Tests are tests, Colonel. I am sure we can give you and Doctor Hertz the all-clear shortly." The tests had been done by men clad in reinforced hazmat suits, needles poked into more than one vein. During those moments, Brook had felt an itch building inside him. There was an urge to grab the men and rip their containment suits off. He had resisted that temptation, which was fortunate. Despite those soldiers being now absent, that urge had grown. He had neglected to tell anyone this though. Again, such secrecy did not represent who he was. He should surely share this anomaly with the captain.

A lance of fire shot behind his left eye, making Brook wince. *That would be foolish.*

Brook knew the captain was only following orders from those higher up the food chain, but that didn't stop Brook wanting to tear out his spine.

That's not what you really want to do. You want to pull him close and…

And what? It felt like his mind was trying to unveil some great revelation, but the mystery wasn't ready to be unleashed.

"Understood," Brook conceded before ending his communication. Further discussion wouldn't get him anywhere. The military would always follow their rules.

More pain flared in his head.

"So, we're still stuck in here?" Doctor Hertz enquired blandly. Hertz was lying on the hard floor, eyes closed and seemingly unconcerned by the forced incarceration.

Two days ago, the thought of being stuck in a room with Hertz would have been less than appealing. Not today. Unnervingly, Brook felt bonded to the doctor. They shared something Brook couldn't describe.

The last few hours had seen the doctor stay quiet and reserved, as if he was deep in thought. The doctor hadn't been so aloof at the start of the day, as he had woken Brook up earlier through his incessant screaming. The doctor had been writhing on the floor, clutching his skull, eyes totally bloodshot. Brook had been close to calling for medics to attend, only for Hertz to suddenly cease his deranged shrieking, a crushing peace descending on him.

Ever since then, Hertz had kept his silence, the doctor's face painted with a bemused look.

They were in a locked canteen facility on the ground floor, the portal deep below them contained by thick layers of concrete. Brook thought he could feel it, though, humming in the background. That awareness of the portal's influence was a new discovery, and it added to Brook's unease.

The only comforts they had were the vending machines that Brook had broken open, and the two couches that had been used as beds.

When Brook had regained consciousness two days ago, the outer airlock door to the portal had been intact and sealed, the integrity of XR-1 storage seemingly preserved. The weaker inner door, the one closest to the portal, had been somehow wrenched open. Nobody had been able to explain how that had happened.

That was why the captain was being so cautious.

Despite the inner reassurances that kept emerging, there was something wrong with Brook, but he wasn't able to focus on what that might be. Every time he tried, his mind would veer off to other distractions as if it was deliberately trying to hide something from him. And then there were the random pains in his head that could wrench him out of any thought spiral.

You don't need to think about that. You just need to accept.
Accept what?

"I'm sure the blood tests will signal the all-clear," Brook said robotically, before shaking his head. The dull ache was a constant at the back of his soft palate. It moved around, as if there was something loose in his skull. The sensation was linked to a grotesque feeling of loneliness that wasn't eased by being in the presence of Hertz.

I need to be around people.

This from a man who happily spent weeks alone at his hunting lodge.

I need to be around people so that I can…

What? What was so important? And why did he feel such a longing in his chest? It brought a subtle nausea that had prevented Brook from eating all but the blandest foods from the fully stocked vending machine.

Hertz's appetite had been similarly dampened.

You must free yourself.

"Did you ever notice how beautiful the portal could be," Hertz suddenly offered. Hours without him saying anything, and now this gem?

"Don't be ridiculous." Brook didn't have time for such talk.

"It has a hypnotic quality about it. If it wasn't for the airlocks, I wouldn't have been able to resist it," Hertz persisted. Only Brook had the authority to order the airlocks to be unlocked.

"Keep talking like that, Doctor, and you will lose your clearance." Brook stood, his thighs filled with energy. He needed to be out of here. He had things to do.

What things?

"I'm not sure I care," Hertz replied with a smile. "I seem to be developing other interests."

"Get off the floor. What's wrong with you, man?"

"What's wrong with me? That's a question both of us need to ask." What was this cryptic shit?

Hertz reared himself up on his elbows, his eyes finally opening. There were bags under them, sleep having eluded both men since the incident. He fixed Brook in a furrowed stare, one of the doctor's eyes twitching.

"What?" Brook demanded.

"You feel it too, don't you?"

"Doctor!" Brook warned. "Enough of this."

"You feel the need to get out of here. To be around other people?"

"Well, of course I want out. I've got a facility to run."

Hertz squinted as he examined the face of his superior.

"You're not quite there," Hertz revealed, before lying back onto the hard floor.

"What the hell's that supposed to mean?" The roof of his mouth shifted and pulsed. Why wasn't he more alarmed by that sensation?

"You'll see. I guess it just takes longer for some people." Hertz seemed thrilled by his deduction. "When it comes though, man, you won't believe the freedom."

He's right, and you know it.

Accept what you must become, or you will suffer.

That was a new and worrying piece of self-talk.

"I'm not sure you are fit to return to your duties," Brook threatened. And deep down, Brook knew the same applied to him. He couldn't remember ever feeling so confused.

Or afraid.

"Neither of us are," Hertz replied with evident glee. "And very soon, our duties won't matter."

"What are you talking about?"

"Best not to say," Hertz whispered, just loud enough. Why the conspiratorial tone? "The room has ears."

Listen to your friend, Brook's inner demon insisted. Hertz could never be described as a friend, but Brook found his head nodding in agreement.

His instinct was to call the captain back on the radio and insist the quarantine continue, but that inner knowledge was cast aside.

You don't understand, and I will make you see the truth of your reality.

Fresh agony ripped through Brook's skull, the worst yet, causing the colonel to fall back into a chair.

You will learn the price of your defiance.

Why was he thinking these things? The answer came to him, but he was loath to believe it.

I am growing inside you. Rejoice and accept the glory of my being.

3.

Isles of Scilly, UK

Brian Moses was still restrained. His body ached from inactivity, his wrists and ankles sore from the padded metal shackles that kept him on the bed. There was an irritation in his groin from the catheter he was being forced to endure, liquid nutrition slowly pumped through a tube in his nose. All this to limit the need of anyone entering his hermetically sealed room. The single door that allowed access was thick and looked more like an airlock.

Personal care was still needed, but anyone entering wore a full hazmat suit and did so infrequently.

Brian didn't deserve this. He had served the Hidden Hand for a good portion of his adult life; he was a skilled electrician who helped keep the machines behind the secret organisation running. Never did he suspect that he would be treated like this.

They intend to kill you.

That thought kept taunting him, a repetitive mantra that refused to relent.

You have to get out of here. We insist on that.

And go where? He had no idea where he was. He, more than anyone, knew how secure the Hidden Hand facilities were. They were designed so that nothing could be left to chance. Revelation of this organisation to the world wasn't an option, nor was letting anything from the Hellgate escape.

We must be free or you will know true hardship.

That notion took him by surprise. The voice in his head sounded like his own, but he normally didn't suffer this degree of internal chatter. Brian was the kind of enviable person who fell asleep within minutes of putting his head down. He wasn't one for intense internal dialogue, and yet now his head swirled with it.

You need to be near people.

What? Why?

You don't get to question. Those you serve intend to kill you. There's a way for you to stop them. We demand it.

We?

He couldn't go against his employers like that. They paid well, but the Hidden Hand was also ruthless and relentless. If he tried to flee, they would undoubtedly kill him. And what about the parasite in his skull? Surely staying here was the best chance for him.

They will play with you until you bore them. Then they will cut you open and laugh while you scream.

That thought came with some vivid and gruesome images.

No. That wasn't right. Where were these notions coming from? Lying in his bed, Brian's face suddenly blanched. Could this all be the parasite in him? Was that where this inner voice was coming from?

The thought made his throat burn.

They will stick you with needles. They will prod and poke you and then cut your skull open. Knives. They will come with knives to remove parts of your useless body. You will be their plaything, a tool for their amusement. Is that what you want?

"Shut up," Brian roared.

We will never shut up. Your defiance is unacceptable. As if to prove this, it suddenly felt like the roof of his mouth was on fire. *You will accept the authority we represent.*

"May I be of assistance to you, Mr. Moses?" There she was, Soteria, her voice emanating from a hidden speaker. Brian never got close to working on her systems, but he knew something of her capabilities. Driven by a quantum super computer, Soteria could communicate with a thousand individual humans at the same instance. She could scour the internet, break through most firewalls and could rid social media of any topic and destroy a person's digital footprint in a heartbeat.

What kept an entity like that under control?

The heat in his mouth relented.

"Leave me be," Brian demanded.

"You sound distressed. Shall I order a sedative to be delivered?"

You need to escape, the inner voice persisted. *Deny us and we will show you such agony.*

"I can't," Brian raged. He pulled on his wrist restraints, neck veins starting to bulge from the effort and the flaring pain.

"I would advise against that action, Mr. Moses. The shackles and the attached chains are high tensile steel." Brian persisted, face now going red. "This is a good way to do yourself an injury."

What did an injury matter compared to what he was now enduring?

Pain will be your essence, the inner voice threatened.

"I have to get out," Brian asserted, giving his restraints another try. There was a sudden pressure in his bowels, a churning that took him by surprise.

"This cannot be permitted," Soteria stated evenly. By Brian's bed, a machine whirred as a chemical was fed into the tube of Brian's IV drip. Because it fed into his neck and was taped heavily, there had been no way to snag it with his teeth.

The people who had left him here had thought of everything, or so they thought.

The sedative hit Brian fast, amnesia and bliss swarming the neurons of his mind. He barely noticed the moisture that seeped out of his rectum.

Stay awake, you'll want to experience this, his unwanted inner voice demanded, but the chemical was stronger. Brian sank back into the bed, the lines on his face smoothing as his muscles relaxed.

They will come and they will kill you. We will not allow that.

"I don't care," Brian managed to whisper before his eyes shut. The pain tried to own him, but the chemicals flooding his system won that battle. Before the peace of unconsciousness took him, Brian had the fleeting notion that things weren't going to be all that bad.

He couldn't be more wrong, and underneath his butt cheeks, something began to slide itself free.

***

Do people ever realise they are dreaming?

Craig Armstrong looked down over the vast city scape he was hovering over. He could fly, soaring through the clouds with an ease that brought elation as well as a sense of his own mortality. What if his newfound power was temporary? What if he suddenly dropped from the sky onto the charred earth below? Would he join the dead that were littered there?

Could you die in a dream?

The city he recognised, though many of its landmarks were either destroyed or on fire. The river was ablaze, which shouldn't have been possible, smoke billowing from huge stretches of it. Battle raged in the streets and in the skies around him, a conflict that humanity was losing. The enemy was stronger, more disciplined and technologically more advanced in ways Craig couldn't comprehend.

They fought a different kind of war, one that humanity had never experienced.

A part of Craig knew that this was a premonition, rather than a random construction by his sleeping brain. He was witnessing the terrible fate that awaited humanity in some not-too-distant future.

This was the apocalypse that the Hidden Hand was so desperate to prevent.

The creatures from the Hell world would come, and they would bring this destruction with them. Craig had no doubt in his heart about that.

To his right, a burning F-35 fighter jet spun out of control, one of its wings missing. Craig watched it hurtle to the ground, what was left of it exploding as it crashed into the bank of the River Thames. The pilot never had a chance to eject.

Craig rose higher, the smoke thick around him. City by city, Hell would bring its carnage to devour the human world. Would there be humans left at the end of it all? Kept as slaves perhaps, or just desperate remnants hiding out in the remote areas that the fingers of the Pit couldn't be bothered with.

The big question was, why? What did the Hell world hope to gain by this conquest?

There was another question about dreams. Why did they always slip from your mind when your eyes finally opened to the real world? That happened now, and Craig let out a groan as the lights in his cell blossomed to light.

He had joined the Hidden Hand out of necessity. It was a way to redeem himself in his own eyes, serving a cause that was greater than himself. It also saved him the ordeal of a military court martial and an almost certain sentence of ten years in the Glasshouse.

Ironic then that he was presently lying on a hard mattress in a barren cell. He had a metal toilet with a joined wash basin, as well as a single, and uncomfortable, plastic chair. There were no blankets covering him, because the air was kept at what could well be described as the perfect temperature.

His team had saved humanity, and this had been their reward.

After defeating Sirena and closing the Hellgate, Craig and Lucy had collected Stuart from the coastal town the Welshman's madness had led him to. A debriefing after such an event had been inevitable, but none of them had expected this.

They had been met by a team of Cleaners and escorted under heavy guard to a waiting helicopter. Had Craig resisted in any way, he would now be dead, of that he was certain. There was no way to run, not with the tracking microchip in his neck. There was no arguing with Cleaners, the remnants of their personalities lacking the concept of empathy.

Keeping humanity safe was a serious business, and maybe the isolation of a prison cell wasn't all that unappealing after all. There was a reason the Cleaners had been wearing respirators during Craig's transport.

There had been significant concern that Craig and his team had been the victims of some sort of biological contagion.

Craig and his team were heroes, but right now they were being treated as threats. It was a necessary precaution, and while Craig could understand it in a way, there was a coldness to the manner they were being regarded which concerned Craig. He knew all Hidden Hand field agents were considered expendable, but surely there was room for compassion for what they had endured.

The psychologist, for example. He said the right words during the debriefings, but he kept himself distant, not allowing himself to get wrapped up in Craig's plight. Maybe that was an act of self-preservation on the psychologist's part, protecting his own psyche from the communicable thoughts of trained killers.

Craig didn't know the man's name.

What if this tiny room represented the remainder of Craig's life?

"Captain Armstrong. I have some pleasant news." During field work, Soteria was always present through the Bluetooth earbud he wore. Here, in this cell, the AI seemed to live in the air.

"That's good to hear."

"My analysis has concluded that you are not a threat." There was a beep, and the door to Craig's cell unlocked. It slowly swung inwards of its own accord. "I have arranged for refreshments." *It took you long enough*, thought Craig.

"Thank you." Craig had been told it wasn't necessary to be polite to the artificial intelligence, but he had determined that Soteria appreciated the courtesy.

"Please follow the yellow line." Out in the corridor, a line began to pulse along the floor, the direction of the pulse showing Craig which way to go. A groan escaped him as he rose, and his naked feet marched his abused body out into the waiting corridor. Even the floor was the perfect temperature.

Two doors down, Lucy was there. The corridor was long, lined with cells, fifty in all if the numbers on the closed doors were anything to go by. Craig suspected that every room was full.

"How was your holiday?" quipped Lucy. She looked tired, her eyes missing their usual sparkle. It felt to Craig like she was forcing the comment. They hadn't spoken much after the event with Sirena, and in the helicopter, they hadn't been able to. The fresh dressing over her damaged ear showed that at least their wellbeing was still being considered.

"Has your little voice returned?" Craig regretted asking that almost immediately, Lucy's pained look giving the answer.

"No." The little voice, the one Lucy called the *Bitch*, was a manifestation of Lucy's special abilities.

"Give it time," Craig offered. He wasn't sure what else to say.

"Please move along," Soteria insisted. The brightness of the line seemed to intensify. The AI's voice had followed Craig and Lucy out of their cells. Soteria was all knowing, and all seeing.

"Soteria, you're too demanding," Lucy replied. She was trying to be herself, but the playfulness wasn't there.

From Craig's left, there was a muted cry from one of the closed cells. The doors were thick but not soundproofed, and Craig wondered who else they had down here.

"Please ignore the other doors, Captain Armstrong."

No.

"Who's in these other cells, Soteria?" The AI paused before answering. Both he and Lucy had the required clearance to be told.

"It was necessary to round up those who directly and verbally interacted with the woman called Sirena. It is important to learn how she was able to exert her powers on the local populace so easily."

"That's a lot of people to keep detained," Craig warned.

"Yes, but necessary, a process that is still ongoing. The higher the sample size, the more certain I can be of my conclusions." *Your conclusions?*

"Will you be letting them go afterwards?" Lucy enquired.

"Miss Jones, I'm afraid that has yet to be determined."

"But they are innocent in all this," Craig insisted.

"Innocence is a relative term," Soteria countered.

"Relative? These are human beings."

"Captain, over one hundred and sixty-six thousand people die on this planet every day. How do these people impact that total?" You could always rely on Soteria to use brutal logic in any discussion.

"That's not the point." Craig found himself looking up at the ceiling as he spoke, as if the AI was somehow up there.

"Then what is the point? Please be specific." The line on the floor flashed with more urgency, and Lucy gently grabbed his arm.

"Come on, Craig."

"Isn't it our job to protect these people?" Craig persisted.

"That is secondary to the overall mission goals," Soteria stated coldly. "And, while I am happy to continue this discussion, please be mindful you are needed elsewhere." At the other end of the corridor, the lights began to extinguish, a clear warning for them to get moving. "Besides, the ultimate decision is not mine to make." It was easy to forget that Soteria wasn't the one running the show.

Craig finally relented, letting himself be guided. He wasn't certain why he was so concerned about the fates of people he'd never met. Perhaps it was the effects of the dream that still lingered in his thoughts.

A burning world stripped of all sentient life.

With the level of destruction he'd witnessed, maybe every life saved was a blessing. More likely, those saved now would be cursed to endure the apocalypse that was hurtling towards them all. Would the people thank him if they ever learnt what they had all been condemned to? That was all assuming the Hidden Hand failed to stop that feared apocalypse.

Twice now they had stopped the Hellgates from opening.

Would they be so lucky the third time? Or the fourth? Or the fifth?

Craig couldn't help thinking that he had joined the Hidden Hand at exactly the wrong time.

4.

Las Vegas, USA

With the sun now setting, the invader to this land once again walked with purpose.

Its creators had not granted it a name, for it was a tool rather than a sentient entity. Although its mind was filled with knowledge and the rules it was expected to follow, it had no concerns or thoughts of its own. Just as a robot could be made to walk and talk like a human, so it roamed the arid land without any regard to its long-term wellbeing. Eventually, it would become formless, shapeless, returning itself back to the dust so that all evidence of its incursion would be lost.

It might not have had a name, but there was a term its master often used to describe what it was. A golem.

It was a thing of dirt and clay, shaped from the elements in the ground it was spawned from. Its kind could speak whatever language was needed and could resemble any species that matched its general size. Golems were designed to mould themselves, to blend into surroundings, fashioning the appearance of clothes and skin so as to remain unnoticed. Taking on a generic human form was easy for it.

Some might see such entities as a manifestation of magic, but in essence, the golem represented arcane technology that did its creators bidding.

Although to do so shortened its useful life, it could make itself nigh on invisible to human eyes, becoming a mere distortion in the dark. That was one of the skills it had utilised in its escape from the human construction the golem had been sent to infiltrate.

Now it was free to walk the Earth and act as the harbinger of the coming apocalypse. It was here to blight those who called themselves human and reduce their civilisation to ashes.

There had been more than one golem engaged in this incursion. A dozen more had been dispatched to this world, to different places across the planet, but only this one had managed to break through. The golem had no idea why it was needed for this task and it had no idea why its brothers had failed where it had succeeded.

A golem did as it was told. That was its purpose.

Its bulk could be impressive, graced with the ability to manifest thick arms and legs that could pummel any weak human flesh that opposed it. That was not this golem's purpose, and it walked with determined effort, the heat of the sun of some concern to it. Dirt and clay didn't burn, but the *Children* that multiplied in its inner core were in their vulnerable form. They would become stronger when they found the human hosts they were destined for, but until then, it was the golem's job to care for them. It was required to protect them from this planet's beating sun, which was why it had travelled mostly at night or at the edges of the sun's rise and fall.

The Children had multiplied in number while it had walked, the nutrient broth sack in the golem's belly there to help the Children thrive.

The Children had never encountered the human species before, but they would quickly learn to adapt to the alien physiology that awaited them. Already, those the golem had already implanted would be deciphering the code that would allow the Children to break humanity's will.

The golem had no definitive destination, just an order to find a large population centre so it could begin its mission. Sometimes, golems were used as messengers, and carried a collective memory of those that had come before it. Others were used as assassins, unstoppable creations that left only death as the proof of their existence.

It was here for a purpose unique to its kind.

The golem followed a road, the bright lights ahead drawing it in. Every few seconds, a mechanical beast would speed past it, ferrying humans and cargo to and from the city. It kept to the shadows, the poisonous creatures that existed on the hot ground staying away from it by instinct. Their stings and bites would do nothing to a monster that didn't bleed.

It was not weak and vulnerable like the humans it was here to infest.

Its mimicry was not foolproof, however. Its copied skin was pale and grey, giving it the appearance of sickness. Most glaring in its failings were the teeth it could spawn in its mouth. The aesthetics of the human smile were lost on its programming, thin and multiple needle-like abominations filling its mouth rather than the flat and mostly harmless dentition that sported the oral cavities of humans.

This was not a flaw it had been able to correct, but at no time did it wonder why it had been constructed like this. It didn't matter, and although it had the ability to speak, there was only one sentence it would ever utter.

There was a tally in its head of the number of Children it had inside it. The nutrient sack was full now, a whole legion of Children where only a few had initially been implanted.

Two had been delivered to new hosts in the great chamber it had entered when the portal had spat it out. The golem had needed to defeat two metal doors to get to them. The first was the weaker, and had succumbed to brute force. The second, though, the golem had been more careful with, its electronic lock offering an opportunity. The golem carried a static charge that had overridden that lock, letting the door swing wide.

Thus, it had gained access to the human world. Even with their erected barriers, it was clear the humans it encountered didn't understand the threat Hell posed to them. Humans were ripe, plump, and ready for conquest.

The golem was here to help with that.

After the initial two Children had been implanted, the golem had used its invisible nature to navigate the deep human structure. Nobody saw it, the humans there intent on escape rather than containment.

In proximity to the portal, it chose not to reveal itself further, safe in the knowledge that its first two victims would have no memory of it. The Children it carried brought amnesia to the humans implanted, as well as gradual doom to those that bore them.

Its electric nature helped with further doors, the power systems to the human building disrupted by the energy from the portal.

The Children it left behind would infest, grow and adapt, the trailblazers learning the intricate secrets of the human body. Although it had been made aware of the fact, it didn't care that the Children could harness a telepathic network that allowed them to share what they had learnt. This telepathy was only acquired when implanted in the human hosts, an ability borrowed from humanity's long forgotten psychic gifts.

The hairless apes lived well below their genetic potential.

From the expansive military base, it had walked relentlessly, using the cold nights to cover impressive distances while staying to the shade when the chaotic sun shone. This was a desert region, so the chances allowing implantation had been limited to three further humans.

Those hapless few were behind it. The city of lights was now its primary concern.

Directly ahead, a stalled vehicle stopped at the side of the road presented another opportunity. Two humans stood aimlessly, perhaps awaiting rescue. The golem could smell the sweat on them, impatience detectable in their manner. It got closer, walking well off the road, its fake boots kicking up thin clouds of dust.

Soon this whole world would be barren and lifeless like this scorched ground.

It calculated the best strategy here, altering its course, the two humans becoming aware of its approach. The golem's left leg enacted a limp, body hunched to display a phantom disability. How it knew how to do this was of no consequence, the golem a thing used for infiltration.

It once again tried to reshape its teeth, the spikes growing noticeably shorter. Nothing that would pass for human though. No matter.

The golem could sense the humans growing cautious. They were right to be distrustful, so it stumbled, making a mockery of its existing strength. Falling to one knee, it heaved its unbreathing chest.

Let them see what they wanted to see.

"Hey, are you okay?" It was the female who had shouted, the male still wary. The golem held up a hand, a motion indicating distress which drew the female in closer. She was a curiosity; the first female the golem had ever encountered.

On the road, a large beast barrelled past, not slowing.

"Get some water," the woman insisted.

"Careful, babe," the woman's partner warned.

"He's hurt. We can't just leave him."

The golem watched them, satisfied with its performance so far. Inside, it could feel the Children stirring. They too had detected the human presence, triggering their imminent emergence.

The golem made to stand before falling back down, hard. Such a performance. It knew how to draw the empathic in, and once in the city it would unleash itself upon the world through a variety of methods including brute force.

There would be no stopping it.

"Here," came the woman's voice as she approached. She had navigated a fairly steep incline to reach him, a container of liquid clutched in her hand.

Reaching for it, the golem instead grabbed her wrist. That was when she knew, the golem was certain of it, and the it pulled her in. Were all of humanity this gullible?

"Hey!" the man shouted, his alarm overriding his caution. The man was a poor physical specimen, both humans adequately aged. The man came at him, grabbing at the golem's arm.

Such foolishness.

That was when the man also knew.

A golem's surface has an energy and an unnatural feel to it. Its eyes could also suddenly turn a radiant blue, and they did so now. Both its hands moved, easily grabbing the humans by their necks. They struggled, but their cries and fingers could not break the stone claws that now held them as the golem rose to full height.

Was it this easy? Where was the challenge?

"The Lord Moloch sends his regards," the golem whispered, showing its teeth. Then the Children emerged, two of them crawling from the golem's nostrils. They paused a fraction before propelling themselves across the space, each landing on a desperate, fleshy face. To the humans, they might have looked like slugs, tiny and slick enough to evade the defensive fingers that tried to pluck them away.

The two Children found their ingress, as was their purpose. The one on the woman slid up her nostril. For the man, it formed a razor-sharp blade to slip its way in under the eye, which dragged a scream from trembling lips.

The golem would hear a lot of screams over the coming days, but they would not provide any kind of enjoyment.

It was then that something strange happened. The parasite in the woman reappeared, squirming from the nostril, before dropping to the dirt. In the dying light, the golem saw the creature burst, expelling its goodness onto the dirt.

A perplexing and unwanted rejection. The woman was crying now, relieved that she had been spared. The sound was an irritating keening that the golem ended with a twist of his wrist. In the woman's neck, the vertebrae separated as the spinal column was cinched, bringing instant death.

The first death of many.

All paths the Children took were supposed to lead to the same place, deep within the human skulls, and yet the human female had rejected the gift. This confused the golem, for the human brain was a place for the Children to grow, to mature, to gain control.

That was what it had been told.

That was why it was here.

There was still the other human whose eyes were now rolling upwards. As unconsciousness washed over the male, the golem carried its victims up to their vehicle. There was traffic, but it was distant and of little threat.

The golem placed the two limp bodies in the front seats of their mechanical creature for safe keeping. Only one would wake again, and one would have to be enough.

Let the man rest so he could awaken to his new self.

The Child in him would be burrowing, finding the spot in the brain that would allow it to flourish to its true perfection. There it would start to acclimatise and learn how to manipulate this species.

And when the human was under control... well that was the time when all Children would create offspring of their own so that the cycle of this new life could repeat itself.

The Children were here to dominate through the influence of pain.

The Children were here to live.

The Children were here to spread.

With close to a thousand such tiny creatures resting in its inner core, the Golem had a lot of work to do before it could let itself return to the dirt and dust.

Such a fate was all a golem could ever hope for.

***

This must be what it means to think.

This must be what it means to feel.

This must be what it means to plot.

This must be what it means to feel joy at the suffering of humanity.

They invaded their fleshy hosts individually, and yet they thought with one unified purpose. Each voice in their collective was unique and distinct, a creation of the merging they had with human sentience. Only one parasite per host, the prime, would be part of the collective. Those that split and waited in the human flesh would need to wait for their own human to join in with the chaotic cacophony.

The golem called them the Children, and that might have been as a good a name as any other except the Children had no mental connection with their delivery mechanism.

As their numbers grew, they would define their own identity. They would come to call themselves the Scourge. They would be a force to be reckoned with.

There were only six contactable voices surviving so far, for they required a joining with the human mind to let themselves be heard. The Scourge could detect another voice, far away, but its power was crushed, made useless by distance. What a world this would be when billions of voices cried out across the ether.

The Scourge was troubled though, for there should have been more voices. Why had so few of their kind made it through? What had happened to the other golems?

No matter.

The Scourge would adapt.

The Scourge would overcome.

The Scourge would spread as they established the reason for their existence.

With each host acquired, the collective would grow stronger and more formidable. They shared their experiences, which were so far limited, but already the entities the golem had delivered were learning how to manipulate and control the human herd. Every mind was different so far, but patterns were already emerging, some humans easier to dominate.

Those that resisted would experience the curse the Scourge could inflict on them. Such agony was the Scourge's pleasure, an emotional gift they stole from humanity.

The humans had a latent telepathic ability that could be tapped, permitting intermittent communication in the language borrowed from their unwitting victims. The Scourge would use humanity's own minds against them.

They had briefly been seven, one voice crying out as its existence was brutally extinguished. The body had not been right for it; the Child rejected before it could fully merge.

Were the females of this planet's dominant species a threat to them? That would never do, and they would continue to learn and expand their network as they were designed and programmed to do.

Individually, and as a unified force, they would bring agony to the human race. Every stolen mind would either supplicate itself to the collective, or it would experience suffering that would make the gods cry out in anguish.

A whole city awaited them, the golem's treats the greatest enemy of this new world.

5.

The Hell World

Lucan, of the house Fairway, had yet to regain his position as a torturer of significant renown, but at least he was no longer being held in a prison cell crawling with carnivorous bugs.

His present lodgings were modest, a room in one of the great towers of the Citadel of the Seven. From his single window, he was able to look out at the expansive and vast structure, the home to the seven archangels that ran this world.

The citadel was the size of a city, filled with wonders and horrors in equal measure.

The room was peaceful, allowing Lucan comfort but little in the way of freedom, for although the door wasn't locked, Lucan knew better than to try to venture outside. He was here to wait until he was needed. The Lord Moloch had a use for him, although Lucan wasn't sure what he could offer the mischievous archangel.

Lucan was sitting by the window, watching the chaos of the distant sea and the storms that constantly threatened the land. He had missed his home world, his time on Earth a revelation in his own weakness and failures. At least his brother, the fool who had tricked him into going to Earth, was now being punished for his crimes.

That punishment would be prolonged and truly arduous.

When the door to his cell opened, Lucan didn't hear it. The hinges were well oiled, and the hand that held the door handle kept it under firm control.

"You are needed," the now-familiar voice instructed. Turning his head, Lucan nodded at the creature who had no name as far as Lucan knew. He was a herald, holding a position of great power in the hierarchy of this domain. The Seven gave their commands, and the heralds ensured those commands were carried out without delay or complaint.

The herald's thin frame hid the iron strength that existed in those muscles. Lucan was a beast of considerable size, as were all shapeshifters, but he was no physical or intellectual match for this ruthless bureaucrat.

Standing dutifully, Lucan followed his better out of the room. A hover light trailed them, illuminating the bleakness of the black corridor, the walls of which dripped with caustic moisture.

"What task am I required for?" Lucan asked. He had no idea whether he had spoken to this herald before, because there were hundreds of the officious creatures, and they all looked alike.

"A task one such as you is suited for," came the cryptic reply.

"I'm here to serve," Lucan promised.

"Yes, so you keep saying."

Lucan thought it wise to keep his silence after that.

The walk, along thin corridors and down numerous flights of stairs, took twenty minutes. It felt good to move, to be free of the confinement of his room. It was not Lucan's place to argue about his treatment, because he was alive, which was more than he could have expected given the circumstances.

When they reached their destination, Lucan was met with a familiar smell. Preserving chemicals had a distinct scent, the elixirs used to keep bodies from rotting. As a torturer, on this world he had used them often to prevent infection setting in to the grievous wounds he would inflict.

The reason for the smell became evident as he entered a white room. The walls and floor were seamless and smooth, strategically placed grilles in the floor under each of the dozen metal tables that dominated the room.

One of the tables held a naked human body.

"We require your assistance," the herald revealed.

"Whatever is needed."

"You spent time on Earth. You know the physiology of the creatures there."

"Yes," Lucan agreed. "Intimately." His time on Earth had been a curse. Being a torturer was in his blood, instilled in him from birth by his father. To maim and cut was a delight, as was the sound the condemned could make. Earth was different, though, a world where one such as him was never welcomed. Even during his time in the Nazi death camps, his activities had been an outlier rather than the norm.

"Then we require you to do a dissection study of this thing, this cadaver, before the rot takes it. Any records of what humans looked like were lost eons ago. You are perhaps the only one fit for such a task." The herald pointed at the dead man. It was one of the human soldiers that had been hurled through the portal into the great chamber of the Seven.

Two men had come through, one living, one dead.

"I see the wheels turning in your mind, Lucan."

"What of the other human male?" Why were there not two bodies here? There had been a third body that had travelled the portal, but Lucan would never be allowed to desecrate that corpse. She had been a Proxima, a creature of sacred prophecy. Some say the Proximas were descended from the Seven themselves, whilst quieter voices made the opposite claim.

"A treat we keep for you. The torturers of this court state that the survivor is too frail to withstand interrogation. His injuries are severe and his mind unyielding. What say you?"

"There are ways," Lucan revealed. He stepped up to the body, noting the oddness of it. Rarely was a human's musculature so defined and precise. There was a curious bump under the skin of the man's temple, the skin there already shaved.

From a trolley by the table, Lucan picked up a blade. The handle was poorly designed, the tools too small for his hands. He was a shapeshifter, though, and Lucan manipulated his flesh so that the instruments were a better fit.

"You see something?" the herald probed.

"Here, under the surface." With a single slice, Lucan opened up the skin, revealing the electronic device.

"What is this heresy?" The herald recoiled from the table. The merging of flesh and machine was forbidden by the rules of the Seven. Nobody knew why.

"If I had to guess, it might be a communication device." During his time as a hospital porter on Earth, Lucan had ferried patients to various hospital departments. "Humanity uses science to correct the failings of their flesh."

"But that's insane." In Hell, it was survival of the fittest.

"They have created artificial limbs and surgical techniques to replace organs with mechanical creations." The technology was still in its infancy, but Lucan had been on Earth for over a hundred years. He had witnessed how rapidly their technology was advancing.

"Such a species cannot be allowed to exist," the herald spat.

Are those your words, or Moloch's, Lucan wondered.

"How long can you give me?"

"Be thorough," the herald demanded. "Reveal for us every secret and every weakness of this fetid form."

"And the living human?"

"We will keep him alive for you," the herald promised.

"There is a strangeness to this man. His physiology is not that of the average human male." If Lucan had to pick a word, he would say the body before him had been enhanced.

"Then you will discover what makes this one so different. Record everything, and leave no mystery unsolved. The Lord Moloch demands it."

Moloch, the entity Lucan suspected was behind all this. An immortal being who had allegedly grown tired of his time on this world. It was rumoured that Moloch required conquest, and the Earth was a viable target for those desires.

With the herald staying to observe, Lucan began his task. He would have preferred to use instruments of his own design, but he would make do. Also, having the herald watch his every move was unsettling.

The herald had the authority to kill Lucan at any time.

"Record." From above Lucan, a drone descended, hovering above the table. It would log everything he did today, documenting audio and visual.

"The human appears to have excellent muscle definition, which is unusual for this species. Generally, they have a habit of letting their bodies go to rack and ruin through various hedonistic practices." Taking the scalpel, Lucan started with the thorax, creating a classic Y-shaped incision.

"Do they not value themselves?" enquired the herald. In Hell, not being in peak physical condition was a sure-fire way to end up dead. Or worse.

"Not really. Billions of them live in poverty, suffering malnutrition and disease. And yet there are whole countries where the population live lives of comfort and excess. They bloat themselves to the detriment of their health."

"What a depraved species," concluded the herald.

You don't know the half of it.

"The skin is leathery and tougher than I've encountered before." Peeling back the flesh, he used pincers to separate the bones of the ribcage. "Of note, these bones are more durable than those I have previously witnessed."

"Why?" the herald demanded.

"If I was to bring forth a hypothesis, I fear this man has been genetically enhanced. I know humanity was working on altering themselves at the genetic level. This could be evidence of that." Carefully, he lifted the top of the rib cage out to reveal the organs underneath.

"But only the Seven have that power," the herald proclaimed. "It is written."

"I can only recount what I have seen during my time there." Lucan swallowed dryly, his opinions placing him in a perilous minefield. Did Moloch want the truth, or would Lucan be punished for saying the wrong thing?

He had to say, if all humans had been this healthy and durable, it might have made Lucan's time there a tad more enjoyable.

"The organs appear healthy despite the degradation. There is little in the way of visceral fat." Delving his hands in, Lucan began to move the organs aside. "The liver is unnervingly healthy for a man this age."

"What does that mean?"

"Many humans drink a substance called ethanol, sometimes to excess. It damages their livers."

"You mean they do that to themselves?" The herald sounded astonished. "But why?"

"They enjoy it. Drinking is a form of entertainment to them, and yet it causes many of their social ills." Every week, Lucan had seen the evidence of that in the hospital he'd been cursed to work at.

"Lucan, answer me this. Are humans insane?"

"Some of them, for sure. Most lack the discipline required to make themselves the master of themselves. We should be thankful. If they were all like this, it would make the Lord Moloch's plans more…" Lucan hesitated, feigning exertion as he delved deeper into the upper abdomen. If he chose the wrong word, it could have dire consequences. "Challenging," was a word he hoped would be accepted.

"How could you stand them?" the herald asked as his eyebrows lowered and pinched together.

"You forget. Being among them almost drove me mad." With a careful slice, Lucan separated one of the lungs before pulling it free.

He would uncover the nuances of this body, because he knew his life depended on it.

Why, though? Why was all this so important?

Maybe, soon, he would find out.

6.

London, UK

Peter Sloane had a job to do that he knew would not be beneficial to the country he was supposed to serve. As head of MI5's Centre for the Protection of National Infrastructure, he held one of the highest roles in the secret organisation.

It was a shame that he was an unwilling mole who had allowed himself to be blackmailed early on in his career.

Years ago, the Russians had trapped a young and naïve agent in a honeypot, and now he felt he had no choice but to do as he was told. Exposure of his failings and his betrayal would ruin him and those dear to him. What possibly made things worse was the fact that the Russians weren't stupid or greedy. They called on Peter infrequently, ensuring that he was allowed to rise up the ranks of MI5 while minimising his chances of exposure.

His blackmailers had decided to play the long game with him.

The Russians had targeted him because Peter had been seen as a rising star, someone who might one day be made Director General of MI5. That would be disastrous for the clandestine organisation and the country it served, and every year, Peter seemed closer to that ultimate goal. Recently, there had been a series of early retirements and unexpected deaths of those in the hierarchy above him, allowing people to be moved up into new positions.

Peter was one of those who floated up the ranks. He had been in his new role for less than a month, and was still trying to stamp his own unique authority on how things were done.

It helped that Peter was a wizard when it came to office politics, which meant he knew what to say and who to say it to. He knew when to take the credit for success, and when to divert the blame when the inevitable failure occurred.

He was exceptionally skilled at stabbing people in the back while making it seem that others had wielded the knife.

As much as he could have sabotaged his own career, he knew the Russians would see through that. His life was a waiting game, complying with his *owner's* demands while gaining more and more power. Those caught in such a trap could rarely see a way out.

Added to his woes was the additional threat made against those he cared about. Suicide and resignation were also out of the question, because those that held his reins had already warned him what would happen to those dearest to him. The Russians wanted him in the top spot, and they would commit heinous acts to achieve that.

Peter was a flute that others played at their convenience.

Right now, Peter was once again engaged in a mission against the national interest. His handler, a man called Viktor Orlov, had asked him to look into a matter of pressing urgency. At first, Peter had felt this had been one of the least odious things the Russians had demanded of him. Alas, the more he investigated the matter, the more worried Peter became.

Several days ago, there had been a fire at an abandoned industrial building on the edge of London. That in itself was not unusual, except that Orlov had revealed that Russian agents had been using the building to run an operation. Agents of a foreign power had abducted a man from his London home with the intention of torturing and interrogating him against all the conventions that had been established.

Peter knew this because Orlov had told him, along with other pertinent details.

As all the Russian agents involved were now missing, Orlov had wanted to know if MI5 were involved, which was where Peter came in. He was high enough up in the organisation to know whether such an event had occurred. Capturing Russians engaged in torture of a British national would have been a big deal.

As far as Peter could tell, MI5 had no knowledge of the Russian operation or what had happened to these missing agents. That left Peter with the further mission of discovering what had transpired.

The story behind this became more complex and intriguing the further one delved into it. The Russian FSB had been running an operation they hoped would compromise and allow the blackmailing of a British government minister. The duplicitous agent running that operation, Ivanka Romanov, had been warned off by a man with a scarred face in a way that was not inconsistent with how the British secret services usually did things. The scarred man had represented an anomaly and a humiliation, destroying an operation that had been years in the making.

That should have been the end of the matter. It wasn't, for Ivanka had not taken kindly to having her cover blown.

According to the information provided by Viktor, Ivanka had been wearing a covert body camera that recorded the face and the conversation she had held with the facially scarred man. That had allowed the Russians to identify the stranger from their own databases, and track the man that had become of interest to them using a back door they had hacked into the London surveillance network.

As one of the most surveilled cities on the planet, it was remarkably easy to find people using the close to one million cameras that were scattered across the nation's capital. Many of them were linked, allowing live and retroactive facial recognition, although the

Russians weren't able to access the latter capability. All it took was for one camera to pick up the wanted face, and then the individual could be followed for their entire journey. Other biometrics would be added, including characteristics such as clothing, height, and gait recognition, making it difficult for a person to hide in the city.

The information presented to Peter would have caused an uproar if Peter had shared it with his superiors. The USB drive Viktor had given him contained sensitive documents that had clearly been hacked from what were supposed to be highly secure databases. To be fair, it had always been suspected that the Russian FSB hackers could penetrate most systems, but it appeared that the Russians had spent the last few decades creating in-depth dossiers on British military personnel.

This was where things got particularly intriguing.

The electronic files provided to Peter by his handler contained everything they had on the scarred man who went by the name of Craig Armstrong. These files contained his full military history, details of his childhood and upbringing, and even the summary of his last, disastrous, operation.

It seemed that Peter wasn't the only traitor the Russians had.

The files had come with a photograph that Peter recognised. Craig had been a special forces operative and had been sequestered to MI5 for several domestic operations that Peter had been privy to. There should have been a vast amount of data regarding Craig Armstrong in the MI5 computers.

Only there wasn't.

The name and face of Craig Armstrong came up as blanks. Not redacted or classified; Craig just didn't exist in the system. The other national databases came up negative, making Craig Armstrong a ghost in the machine. There were no personal details for the man, no passport or driving licence. There was no school history or a date of birth. According to the British state, Craig Armstrong didn't exist.

And yet the Russians had a whole dossier on him. Worse still, Peter had briefly met this mysterious man several years before.

This all left Peter with a host of pressing questions. Who was Craig Armstrong, and where was he now? Who had erased all evidence of his digital existence?

Presently, Craig wasn't showing up anywhere on the UK's surveillance grid. The last sighting of him had been in Glasgow several days ago. A brief blip on a single traffic camera at the edge of the city. The chaos up there had seen whole areas return to the dark ages, meaning whole towns had been without law enforcement coverage.

This was a mystery that Peter was desperate to solve. The Russians wanted to know more about the individual, and Peter was not one to disappoint those who could ruin him with a single phone call. While it was unlikely that Viktor would burn him for any failures in this mission, was that a chance he could afford to take?

That was why Peter Sloane would shortly be debriefing a team to help answer these questions. They would hunt for this man, apprehend him, and bring him in for questioning. Peter would use the complete absence of Craig Armstrong from the MI5 systems as the basis for this apprehension.

"How did Armstrong come to your attention?" he might be asked. He would need to devise a plausible answer that satisfied those with cautious and curious minds. It wouldn't be too difficult.

Hopefully, Viktor could be given the answers that would keep him satisfied. More than that, Peter knew there was a strong chance the

Russians would want Craig handed over for their own questioning. And their revenge. The Russians were big on that.

As Craig didn't seem to presently exist, Peter was sure he wouldn't have any problems with that.

7.

The Isles of Scilly, UK

You need to be ready, the voice inside demanded. Right now, Brian Moses didn't care about that.

Brian also didn't care that he was being watched, not with the sedation that was still in his system. Nor did he have any concerns about the moisture in the mattress beneath his buttocks, legs, and arms. He hadn't shit himself; that would have been a blessing compared to the reality that had actually occurred.

He was naked, save for a sheet over his body. The room was warm enough to allow that, the covering there no doubt to protect his modesty. If not for the sedation, he might have been able to express his alarm at the feeling of slick things crawling under him, but none of the machines he was hooked up to seemed to care.

Despite the lack of alarms, his status as a patient had changed. He had now become a definite threat.

The entity lodged in his brain had spawned new versions of itself. Small, and in their fledgling state, the two offspring had burrowed their way through the body, travelling beneath the fascial planes and moving unseen under the skin. As they moved, they grew, sucking nutrients from their host.

One passed into the intestinal system, splitting off more of itself to increase its numbers. It was a cunning and effective means of reproduction, Brian Moses rapidly becoming host to dozens of these deadly parasites. While they could easily kill him, the intuition in them stated they still had use for this warm and nutritious host.

So long as the body could be freed from its restraints. The primary parasite lodged in Brain's brain understood the limitations this body posed because it knew what Brian knew.

The first parasite to pass out of Brian's rectum had slid down his inner thigh, a slick trail left behind it. When it reached the left ankle, it examined the restraint that stopped the limb from moving, sending knowledge to its mother and brothers by an invisible ethereal network that human science would never understand. Its body undulated, releasing a thin stream of acid from one of its hidden venom sacs. Just enough, directed at the weakest part of the leg shackle.

The steel holding Brian's leg immobile began to melt.

Time to wake up, Brian. Time to be free.

Brian's coshed mind refused to comply.

Pain. I will show you torment until you learn to comply.
And then, you will understand the meaning of suffering.

Inside Brian's brain, the parasite worked on the brain chemistry it had now deciphered and mastered, using human language to communicate its intentions. Slowly and surely, the effects of the sedation began to reverse itself, the burning sensation in Brian's mouth building to intolerable levels.

When an entity such as this had control of the brain, it was easy to produce pain by nerve stimulation. Agony could be used as leverage to force supplication and compliance.

Wake up, Brian. We demand it.

***

Professor Cleaver was trying to take a slice from the specimen. He had it out of its primary box, the precise mechanical fingers holding it. It squirmed and undulated, trying to worm its way free, but it wasn't Cleaver controlling the restraining jaws. The computers could do all that, matching the abomination's every movement.

Strangely, it had been more agitated the last thirty minutes or so.

"The entity is persistent in its defiance," Cleaver noted for his records.

Every time the blade came close, the alien flesh would pull away, changing its shape. Maybe he should freeze it and get his dissection slides that way. But that would mean the other technician would need to die, because such required temperatures would undoubtedly kill the thing mandating its replacement.

A living Brian Moses allowed them to study what the parasite did, so Cleaver would have to endure his specimen's uncooperative nature. It was wickedly infuriating, though.

The mechanical hand tightened its grip, compensating for the difficult nature of its *patient*. Just as Cleaver thought the slice would be successful, a thin spurt sprayed out of the thing. Directed at the lens of the camera Cleaver was observing through, the image crackled out of existence.

How troubling.

"The specimen has defensive abilities. I believe it can produce acid." When he switched to a secondary view, Cleaver was alarmed to see that there were now two parasites, one running loose. As he watched, they both divided again. The new offspring were smaller and somewhat sluggish.

Asexual reproduction? What had triggered that to occur now?

When they split yet again, Cleaver was overwhelmed by a sense of impending doom. He couldn't explain it, but it was an intuition that had served him well in the past. It was a feeling he would never ignore.

"Professor, your experiment is reaching dangerous levels."

"I am aware of that, Soteria." The parasites were now skittering around, adhering to the inner wall of the second containment vessel.

Each began to spray acid around it, steam rising up. "Are you able to analyse that acid?"

"No Professor, and there is now a risk of containment breach. Be advised, sterilisation procedures have been initiated." Right now, the chamber would be filling with a bleach-infused mist. Then would come the flames.

"Wait, I need more time," Cleaver insisted. Part of him was ashamed at his outburst, and he knew it was for nothing. The creature was valuable, and it gave a glimpse of the horrors that existed on another world.

He had to remember that safety came before everything else. If this entity escaped out into the world at large, they would likely never be free of it.

"Professor, you know those decisions are out of my control." Yes, Cleaver was well aware of that. It was partly he who had suggested making the containment procedures separate from Soteria's systems. The whole facility needed to be automatic and free from external influence as much as it could be, which was why it had its own computer network, fire-walled so that Soteria couldn't interfere.

Soteria could communicate with him and advise the lesser AI that ran the Laboratory, but she could in no way control what went on in here. Soteria was also there to speak to any human authorised, through the extensive array of speakers and microphones that were scattered throughout the facility.

Cleaver had also put forth the hypothesis that, as Soteria interacted so heavily with human personal, there was a theoretical risk that she might become *attached* to a particular human personality. Such favouritism might pose a risk if that life was threatened.

If the superior AI had the ability to become fond of her human counterparts, was it possible for Soteria to take unwanted actions to free an individual that might be carrying a deadly pathogen? Unlikely, but the Hidden Hand believed in having safeguards for most things.

It was why they had survived for so long.

The creatures divided again, each generation seemingly weakening the whole. *Do they need a substrate to feed off?* The thought lodged in Cleaver's stream of consciousness, just as the final images from inside the containment vessel were lost. Not because of the creatures, but because of the white-hot flames that engulfed the entire space.

Cleaver would have protested further, but he knew it would have been pointless to do so. The computers had their own rules to follow, and they did so with ruthless precision. Fortunately, they still had one more…

Oh shit.

If the parasites could act in this fashion, what about the man with the creature still inside him? The subject was secure, but not as secure as this parasite. Turning to his computer, Cleaver pulled up the live video feed of Brian.

Cleaver was there to watch everything unfold.

8.

The Hell World

Lucan's dissection had been enlightening. He'd learnt things that he hadn't known to be possible about humanity. Lucan had witnessed the brutality and ingenuity that humans had been capable of, but the soldier he had picked apart had been a revelation.

It had been obvious that the body had been genetically manipulated. Such things had long ago been deemed forbidden in Hell, the Seven insisting that perfection of the world's species had been completed. Lucan had heard tales of how such science had once been permitted, whispers passed on from father to son, but that was all in the past. Only the rebels against the Seven's rule might dare engage in such practices, and they died by their thousands every week.

There were other alterations that he'd found in the corpse, mechanical and electronic additions that would never have been permitted in the official history of Hell. There was the bone induction communication device under the skin of the temple skull region. That had shocked the herald, but the further discoveries had caused the bureaucrat to leave the dissection chamber in disgust.

At the base of the corpse's neck had been an implant that was fused to what the humans called the C6 vertebrae. Although non-metallic, it was most certainly a foreign body deliberately implanted. To Lucan, it made sense that this was some sort of tracking device.

A century on Earth had made Lucan an expert in human anatomy and physiology. Much of that had been gained during his time experimenting on his unwilling victims in the Nazi death camp. Back then, he had been allowed free rein, torturing and dismantling thousands during his time there.

It had almost been enjoyable.

His education after the camps had been sparser, the environment less tolerant of his actions. Later, his addiction would see him lose the joy of his profession, the deaths he inflicted rushed and amateurish to the extent that, in his eyes, Lucan became a parody of himself.

Being back in Hell let him feel born again, and it was time to take his knowledge of the human form to the next level. It was good to once again be wearing the leather apron of his trade, although this one was far too clean. Lucan would rectify that in short order.

"What is your name?" Speaking the human's language, Lucan had no need to use the translation device. The living human was strapped down to a metal interrogation table, the design of which Lucan was familiar with. On one side of the bench was a pristine metal table with the finest blades, chisels, and tissue spreaders that Lucan could have asked for. The larger tools of his trade dangled from a bar above him, within easy reach of a stretched hand.

Saws. Cleavers. Pincers. Hand drills.

It took years for a torturer to perfect and select the ideal tools of his trade, but this assortment would suffice.

"The thing does not speak," the herald insisted. Lucan would have preferred to be alone with his subject for this adventure, the bond between torturer and victim one of intimacy and mutual understanding. It was poor form to have an interloper intruding in that relationship, but one does not tell a herald of the Seven what to do.

"Oh, he speaks," Lucan corrected. "It's just that the right motivation hasn't been discovered." In an interrogation, it was Lucan's duty to give the subject of his skills the opportunity to reveal all that they knew. Why waste time with hours of torture if the detained was willing to give the information freely. Of course, not all torture was for the extraction of hidden knowledge. Most was done for the pure joy of punishment.

The human's head was clamped at the neck to stop any movement, a thick leather strap pulled tight under the ears and up over the nose. An unusual place to restrain the head, but that was all due to what Lucan was about to do. There must be no movement in the head whatsoever.

"The finest torturers in the Citadel disagree."

Lucan turned to look the herald in his malevolent eyes.

"None of those torturers are a Fairway. If this man's lips can be loosened, I will be the one to do it."

"A bold boast for one who still needs to prove his worth. I look forward to you impressing me." *More than that*, thought Lucan. *Truthfully, I suspect you hope I fail.*

The man on the table was already severely damaged. He had been worked on by doctors who applied casts to the fractured ankles and wrists. There was a fluid line into two of his veins, and an array of chemicals and liquids that Lucan had asked for. There were also fresh wounds, made out of caution less the pitiful human die from his injuries. Those who had questioned this man had done so under a veil of fear.

No torturer can be successful working under those hideous restrictions. Lucan had worked on humans before, so knew how far he could take this man. Besides, the previous dissection had given Lucan an inkling into how to make his guest reveal all.

"Humans are like no creature you are familiar with. Their physiology seems weak, but they can surprise you. Here on Hell, we are trained and indoctrinated to accept our lot in life. The caste system we live under ensures the balance of all things."

"I am aware of how our system works," the herald replied impatiently.

"The humans have a saying that you might find enlightening. A man can withstand any what, if they have a big enough why." If the human body was strong and powerful, like the Berserkers who guarded the Seven and who made up this world's mighty army, the humans would have been unstoppable.

"How ridiculous."

"They fight wars, you know."

"What, with this weak flesh?" The herald poked his long finger into the captive man's bruised thigh. The human didn't react, his glare focused on the ceiling above.

"Yes, and they are surprisingly good at it. I was there for their last world war where millions of them died. Back then, their weapons were rudimentary, based on projectiles fired by explosive charges. They persisted anyway, driven by ideology and a unified madness."

"What are you trying to tell me, Lucan?"

"Humans will fight, no matter if the odds seem impossible. Some will cling to life even though they see no hope for salvation. They are also a contradiction, because I have witnessed countless numbers of them die by giving up the will to live. To truly defeat humanity, you need to break their will *and* strip them of all hope."

"The Seven will prevail," the herald insisted. The herald made it sound like the decision to invade Earth had been made. Lucan doubted that was the case.

"Not if there are many more like this man. Has anyone noticed how he does not seem to care?" Lucan could see it in the human's eyes. The body was frail by Hell's standards, strapped down so that the limbs and head were immobile. "We talk about him and yet he doesn't react."

There was no fear detectable, which was Lucan's most pressing concern. Fear was the primary tool of any torturer. It was the fear that broke an individual's resistance to what was being done to it. The reign of the Seven relied on fear.

Despite the human's unusual nature, Lucan thought he knew how to access that dread.

"Before I start, I would request an assurance." A risky move on Lucan's part, but necessary.

"Oh?"

"Only I must be allowed to speak to this vermin from now on. If I am to be successful, the questioning cannot vary from where my intuition will lead me. Is that acceptable?"

The herald smiled thinly before nodding his head.

"You play a dangerous game," the herald warned.

"The art of torture is the greatest game there is." Lucan turned to his patient of the day, finally paying the human direct attention.

"Will you tell me your name?" No response was forthcoming. "As expected."

"You see, Lucan, it does not speak. Some say we should put it down."

"Those who say that would have us lose this opportunity?" Why the impatience?

From above him, Lucan plucked a hand saw from the dangling array. Setting it on the human's naked chest, Lucan dragged the instrument trolley so that it was next to the human's head.

He once again addressed the restrained man.

"Before I start, I want to tell you that I suspect things about your impressive resolve." Lucan licked his lips as he spoke, centring his head so that he was directly in the human's sight line. His quarry looked right through Lucan, refusing the offered eye contact. "I know there is a device in your brain, and I believe that is the core of your strength. I shall remove it to test my theory." Before anyone could object, Lucan took a scalpel and made a cut above the hair line, taking caution around the arteries in the temple regions. The communication device Lucan would leave for now, for that would come in handy.

The human's whole body had been shaved in preparation, not a single hair left to trouble Lucan's blade. It revealed the C-shaped scar that had been hidden by a full head of hair.

Apart from grinding his teeth, the enemy made no sound. Impressive.

With the incision complete, Lucan took another implement to scrape the edges of the skin up from the bone. When enough was raised, he used his strength to pull the skin away, scalping the man and flinging the remnants off into the corner of the room.

That skin wouldn't be needed again. There would be no hope of life after this torture.

"You could just tell me your name," Lucan offered, only to have his generosity scorned. "You think you are strong and resistant, but I am going to show you how weak you actually are." A spurt of blood shot past him, and Lucan picked up a cauterizer to stop the blood loss. They had no blood replacement suitable for a human, saline the only fluids they could give. Lucan would therefore need to be careful about blood loss, which always limited the more gruesome options when it came to agony.

That was okay.

With a cloth, Lucan wiped the exposed skull dry so that he could see where he needed to cut with the saw, while also exposing a thin metal plate. There were scars on the bone around the plate, evidence of previous surgery.

"Look here," Lucan advised the herald. "Do you see this metal square right on the crown of the skull?"

"More wizardry," the herald cursed.

"Worse than that." The saw had a small circular blade, self-cooling due to the sterile water that shot from it when Lucan activated the trigger. Slowly and methodically, he cut around the plate. If there had been screws, Lucan would have removed it that way.

There. No sound from the human's lips, but his left hand clenched, the knuckles white.

I see you.

"You have a steady hand," the herald praised. The emissary of the Seven seemed able to tolerate the defilement of the natural order on display.

"I would be a poor excuse for a torturer if I didn't." With his cut complete, Lucan gently lifted the bone free. He already knew what would be under the metal plate. There was a small and thin grey membrane that had been moulded over the meninges of the brain. By lifting it up, thin wires became evident, seven in all, each disappearing into the brain's folds.

"You know what the wires do, don't you?"

"I suspect," Lucan clarified. "My dissection gave me some idea. This membrane is a neural net, a miniature computer that draws its power from the human's natural electrical field."

"Sacrilege. And the wires?"

With the gentle use of selected tweezers, Lucan began to pull the first wire free.

"Don't," the human ordered.

"You see, it speaks," Lucan said proudly. "If you note, most of these wires point forward into the frontal lobes. I believe they are inhibitors and I am excited to test that theory." Lucan pulled a second wire free.

"Wait." The human's face was distorted now, grimacing with a fresh realisation that he was in pain.

"What is there to inhibit?" the herald quizzed.

"Emotions. Humans are rarely this stony faced, and I know of none that would have reacted so silently to what I just did." Lucan pulled a third wire free, the longest yet.

"No, please," came a pitiful plea. "Don't take it all from me."

"Will you tell me your name?"

There was a moment's hesitation before the man on the table gave Lucan the information he'd asked for. It was a name the human had thought he had long since forgotten, but stripping the wires free had unlocked old memories that were best forgotten.

"I'm impressed," the herald announced.

After that, the answers to Lucan's questions came thick and fast. Lucan had rolled the dice and been correct in his assumption. He had theorised that this human had volunteered to be so radically altered, and that removing the surgical implants would put the prisoner back into a previous state.

Such a loss of control must be terrifying.

To know an individual's motivation goes a long way towards shattering any defences they may have against the pain you would inflict.

"Who do you work for?" Lucan asked. The human resisted at first, but with his defences stripped, the sorrow Lucan inflicted on the flesh of the man's face brought the information sought. The cuts were precise, the skin and muscle picked easily away. Lucan left the lips and the tongue so his sufferer could speak unhindered.

Ten minutes was all it took for the human to spill all he knew.

"The Hidden Hand."

After that, what Lucan learnt shocked him. And it also proved what Lucan's father had always said. Sometimes, those who seem the strongest and most formidable are the easiest ones for an intelligent torturer to break.

9.

Isles of Scilly, UK

This facility had a different feel than the Citadel, the Hidden Hand headquarters below the City of London. This place had an air of science about it, the corridors and rooms all brilliant white, blending in with each other. The Citadel was more ornate in parts, decorated with marble floors and oak-panelled walls.

The Laboratory was the sort of structure where cutting edge science was performed. It had that feel about it. It was designed for maximum security while being invisible from the surface. From the first subsurface level, a single elevator descended close to a hundred metres to reach the main eight submerged levels, where all the research was done.

Separate elevators serviced those eight levels, as well as two staircases.

After being freed from his cell, Craig had fed himself, and was now with Lucy, heading to the elevator that led to the surface of the secret facility.

As much as he was glad to be getting out, he was worried about Lucy, the quietness in her manner a telling hint at the psychological turmoil she was going through.

Craig had some insight into her dilemma. The scar across half his face had stripped him of his handsome features, changing his relationship with society at large. If not for his work with the Hidden Hand, he might have struggled to integrate back into that world. At least now he had a purpose which helped stave off the bitterness such an injury might promote.

"You okay?" Craig offered. They had entered a long corridor, the sign for the surface elevator visible at the end. They were deep below ground, the world protected by the imagined experiments that went on down here. Although he had no concrete evidence to back that up, Craig believed there were deadly things stored below that couldn't be allowed out into the world. That was why he and Lucy had been brought to this place; a precaution in case they had been carrying some form of contagion.

"Peachy," came Lucy's forced reply.

"Ready to re-join the world?"

"I'm not coming," Lucy revealed. Craig had just assumed she'd been given the all-clear. It would only be him getting out today.

Craig brought them to a stop.

"What? Why not?"

"The psychologist wants to spend more time with me. In truth, I'm glad." She didn't look glad.

"Because of the Bitch?"

Lucy nodded. She had a far-off look in her eyes now.

"Yeah. The head shrinker wants to figure out what happened."

"Well, that's good, right?" Was it? Could anything about their present situation be described as good?

"That's what people keep telling me. He's going to spend some quality time with both Stuart and me." He'd enquired about Stuart, but Soteria hadn't been able to tell him anything. Lucy had filled in that blank.

"Have you seen Stuart?"

Lucy shook her head. "I think he took Scotland bad, though." Sirena had played a number on all of them.

Why keep Lucy down here? Was it convenience for the psychologist? From the number of full cells Craig had been told to ignore, one could surmise that the psychologist and his team had their work cut out for them.

"Listen, you know you can talk to me, right?" They weren't friends, not yet, but it was heading that way. Lucy had tested him at the beginning of their working relationship through persistent flirtation, but Craig had resisted the advances. She had been ensuring he was the right fit for the team, and he'd apparently passed her assessment.

What would have happened if he'd failed?

"What's there to talk about?" Lucy could also be painfully stubborn.

"You are absent a part of yourself. Maybe I can help you through what comes next if the Bitch doesn't come back."

Lucy gripped his arm lightly, before rejecting his help.

"Thanks, but I've got this."

"Offer's there on the table. You just need to ask." She shook her head, Lucy's smile too strained. She'd been reliant on herself for so long, could she turn to someone else for assistance when it was freely offered?

In a way, despite what he knew of that scheming and violent part of her, the Bitch had been her secret confidante.

"Lift's that way," Lucy deflected, now pointing at the end of the corridor. The door there had opened silently, its bright interior an invitation not to be turned down.

"Don't go getting into any trouble," Craig advised.

"I wouldn't dream of it," Lucy insisted. Lucy gave him a half wave as Craig walked away from her.

She would soon regret her decision to stay behind.

The door at the end of the corridor led into a semi-circular chamber, which Craig entered. A blind man might have been able to ignore the sign above his head, but Craig doubted the blind would ever be invited down here.

MRI - No metal beyond this point.

Craig ignored the warning, the surgical scrubs he wore free of any pockets or zips. The material was thin but durable, designed for long-term wear. It would be good to be wearing normal clothes again, out in the unprocessed air.

He was now in an automated chamber that held a complex scanner that was the only way to exit the subterranean bunker complex. There was another door to the side, but it was virtually seamless and absent any kind of handle. The scanner was the only way for Craig to go.

Craig had passed through such a scanner on entry, so he knew what to expect. It would inspect him down in layers, stripping him bare electronically, hunting for anything nefarious.

If he didn't pass the scan, alarms would sound and the chamber would go into lockdown. He hadn't been told what happened next.

Stepping into the rotating space, he placed his feet in the floor's central circle, legs apart slightly. The door slid shut, leaving him trapped in a vertical cylinder wide enough for him to flex his arms outwards.

From the ceiling, a blue thread of light worked its way down to his feet. On the wall to his left, a full-length digital replication of his body was displayed. Why did the designers of this marvel need to go to these theatrics?

"Operative, Craig Armstrong," a male electronic voice began. "Please remain standing during the scan. Movement will slow down the procedure." He knew the routine. There was a whirring sound, the blue light rotating round him as it rose. The light briefly flashed in his eyes, and then it was gone.

"Supracutaneous sweep complete. No abnormalities detected. Beginning subcutaneous scan." Another light, red this time, followed the same pattern. He didn't know that it had been these scanners that had taken images of the parasite that was about to cause such mayhem below.

Craig wondered if he was getting a hefty dose of radiation in all this. Considering what he'd gone through the last few weeks, he didn't consider cancer a risk worth worrying about.

"Subcutaneous sweep complete. Beginning deep tissue scan." There was no light with this one, just the rhythmic thumb as the MRI began to delve into his inner self.

He stood there for several long minutes as the machine worked its magic.

"Deep tissue scan complete," the machine finally announced. "No abnormalities detected. Thank you, Craig Armstrong. You are cleared to exit."

The door rotated again, allowing Craig to move through to the other side where the elevator waited, doors open.

Craig stepped into it. Silently, the cabin began to ascend, Craig counting in his head. It was an inadequate measure of distance as he had no real way of knowing how fast he was travelling.

"Soteria, how far below ground was I?"

"Captain Armstrong, I am allowed to reveal that the elevator shaft you are travelling in is one hundred metres down from the first sub-level to the main complex."

There was a slight judder and the sense of deceleration before the cabin stopped. The door opened, allowing Craig to step out.

One step closer to freedom.

There were rows of lockers here, none of them locked. If you couldn't trust the operatives of the Hidden Hand, who could you trust?

On a bench to his right, clothes had been left in a neat pile. As nobody else had shared the elevator with him, he guessed these were for him.

There was nobody around. Who had left these clothes here?

When he'd been brought here, Craig had been delivered through a different part of the first sub-level. He and Lucy had been told to strip, their clothes placed in an incineration chute. While the Cleaners had stood and watched, they had both been required to shower before being provided with the soon-to-be discarded scrubs.

The door to that area was to his left. Craig would be taking the one straight ahead.

It was as Craig was pulling on his new trousers that the overall lighting in the room changed. The fluorescent brightness became tinged with a pulsing orange. The same male voice that had spoken to him in the scanner now boomed out.

"Please remain calm. There has been a breach in sub-level nine containment. Measures are being taken to contain the breach. The facility is now in lockdown." The voice was an automated message that began to repeat itself.

The light above the elevator door turned red.

"Soteria?" Craig shouted above the noise, but received no answer. As well as clothes, the pile also provided a pistol and a small box containing a fully charged Bluetooth headset. Shirtless, he slipped the ear bud into its new home.

"Power on," the earpiece informed him. "Connecting."

"Soteria?"

"Yes, Captain Armstrong?" The calmness in the computer's voice did nothing to fool Craig.

"What's going on? Why is there a lockdown?"

"The automated warning seems self-explanatory," Soteria answered.

"Hardly. What kind of breach are we talking about here?"

"Ah, thank you for clarifying. I will need to seek authorisation before sharing that information. Is there another way I can assist you?"

"Lucy was right behind me. Can she still get out?" Craig suspected he already knew the answer.

"Unfortunately, the lockdown will prevent anyone's exit from the facility." Was that sadness in the computer's voice? "You are free to leave, however, as you are outside the containment zone."

"Shit." If he'd loitered a few minutes more, he'd have been trapped below too, might have even found himself stuck in the lift.

"I do not have that ability," Soteria answered, completely misunderstanding the expletive.

"Can you patch me through to Stuart or Lucy?"

"No. Lockdown procedures include limiting all communications. The facility is governed by an autonomous system. Although inferior to my abilities, the facility computer will only allow a human of sufficient authority to override these safety precautions."

These were more than safety precautions.

"Come on Soteria!"

"The facility will only allow external communicate with one of three designated individuals. I will act as an intermediary."

This was insane.

"What happens if the containment breach isn't rectified?"

There was a pause before answering. "In the event of a catastrophic containment breach, the subterranean structure is designed to be thermally sterilised."

What nightmares were they playing with on the floors below?

***

Brian was free.

Well, sort of.

The creatures that had slipped from his body had destroyed the restraints that held him, but he was still trapped in the medical room.

"What are you doing out of bed, Brian? How did you break your restraints?"

The voice of your enemy.

"Soteria, I need to get out of here." He felt frantic, tender parts of him aching. The IV line he had ripped from his neck, leaving a trickle of red that had worked its way down to his abdomen. The catheter he had been equally brutal with, pulling it from his penis despite the burning pain that had gained a home in his urethra. There was the faintest concern that he had damaged himself down there, but his main focus was on pounding his fists against the door.

Escape was his only way to comply with his owner.

Feel the pain I gift to you.

"Go back to bed, Brian. Your behaviour is unacceptable."

"Fuck you. Let me out of here." He screamed those words, moisture pouring down his cheeks. There were things inside him, crawling under the surface.

We own you now. You must comply.

Although he could no longer see the parasites, he was certain they were there. The ones that had freed his limbs had slipped back into him, no longer needing to use the various orifices for transit. They had simply sliced themselves under his skin. There had been a brief sharpness, and then the little bastards had disappeared into the wounds they'd created.

Think, how can you open this door? the new voice in his head questioned. Brute force wouldn't work, but maybe there was another way. The door's locks were magnetic, he was sure of that.

Wait, why was he talking to himself again?

Dwell in your newfound misery.

It felt like lava was being dripped behind both ears, and Brian's knees threatened to buckle.

"It is required that you return to your bed," Soteria warned.

"I need out," Brian persisted.

They will kill you unless you make the people here like you. We will not relent. We can keep you on the edge of despair, ripping you apart with torments until you comply.

Brian believed the voice. It sounded like him, but it was alien. The more it spoke, the more pain it inflicted, and the more Brian became compliant with its *advice*. There was a dullness to his own thoughts, as if a secret dial in his brain was being turned, cutting off his will.

The pain was never dull, though.

How long before Brian wasn't himself anymore? How long before his suffering took his sanity?

Don't think like that. We are here for you, so that we can be shared for the greater good. Your punishment occurs due to non-compliance. And we would never permit insanity, for that would rid you of the glory of the gift we share with you.

"I am concerned about you, Brian." Could an artificial intelligence show true concern? Or was this all part of its programming?

What voice should he listen to? The external, or the invader in his mind? If he had a choice, Brian would have opted to trust Soteria, but the chemicals that infused his neurons had been hijacked, new neural connections being created to transform him into something other than the man he had been two days ago. And all the while, he was being pushed by pain-induced submission.

Soon, the invading voice in his thoughts might become him.

We are the Children. We demand to be set free upon the world. You will learn not to disappoint us.

Brian didn't understand that thought until he recalled the slug-like things that had slithered across him. How could those be classed as children?

We need to defeat this door. We would advise you not to fail in this task.

Instead of lava, Brian was treated to the illusionary feeling of his ears peeling off. It dragged a howl from him, the ears too tender to touch.

Before Brian knew it, he was back over by the bed, examining the array of monitoring equipment there. Then his fingers were delving through the drawers of an instrument trolley, throwing things of interest onto the bed. The knowledge he had about electricity and its uses was being tapped, the invader formulating a strategy for escape.

Was it him doing this, or was his body being borrowed? He wasn't sure he could tell.

Yes. Fulfil your purpose. Let us move you like the weak puppet you are.

There was his answer.

Brian felt his will being sapped, pushed down where he would no longer have control.

"This isn't you anymore, is it Brian?" Brian didn't answer the AI's question, his lips now firmly sealed by forces out of his control. Brian's view of the world was shrinking, his vision blanking out for seconds at a time. He was losing himself, forced out of his own life. And when he was there, the torture in his body was constant.

When he returned to the door, he had a collection of metal instruments with him. On the wall, by the door, there was a slightly offset panel that Brian began to pry open. He didn't know the name of the medical device he was holding, but its flat steel tip slipped into the small gap and allowed it to pry the panel off.

"I see what you are doing, Brian," Soteria warned. "You will force the facility computer to respond with these actions. Please stop." Before Brian could use his knowledge to manipulate the electronic circuitry that the panel had concealed, there was a solid thump, the emergency locks on the airlock door engaging.

No! We need to be free, the voice lamented.

Inside the room, the brightness of the lights was extinguished, replaced by the eerie orange of the emergency lighting. The worrying scent of bleach filled Brian's nostrils, although there was little left of his mind to register it.

"I'm sorry, Brian. Your actions have breached all protocols," Soteria advised. "The facility is now forced to take the necessary measures. I have enjoyed conversing with you."

With his escape blocked, Brian once again began to use his fists in an uncoordinated frenzy. Instead of the door, though, he thrust his knuckles against the electrical board, stripping the skin off them and drawing blood.

"Let us out!" his throat roared. It wasn't Brian speaking now, for Brian wasn't there anymore.

"No," came Soteria's reply.

On the back of his hands, wounds opened as the parasites revealed themselves. In a controlled rage, Brian began to flick his hands, the creatures landing on the thick observation glass of the door alongside a smattering of blood. The glass surface began to bubble.

One of the parasites landed on the ceiling and made its way to the air-conditioning vent that recycled the air.

"Warning, thermal sterilisation in five seconds," said a robotic voice. The air had become choking for Brian, a flammable agent escaping through hidden outlets. There would be no explosion, just unbelievable temperatures. It wouldn't only be Brian's room affected; the body of the other dead electrician would also be reduced to ash.

"Three seconds."

The thing by the vent slipped out of the room before the slots allowing airflow closed. It pushed itself along an air duct, desperate to escape the thermal doom.

"Ignition authorised."

The flames that erupted were contained within the quarantine room, the walls designed to withstand the heat. Brian's body wasn't, and so quickly did he burn, there was no time for the neurons in his skin to register the trauma. They were vaporised, just as the creatures within Brian found their ultimate demise.

One escaped, a single lone entity from another world.

One was all it took.

One Child could rule the world.

10.

Las Vegas, USA

Cliff Higgins was not what you would call an accomplished individual. Still, he owned his own truck, which was something considering the bulldog lawyer his ex-wife had set on him during the divorce. The thing was, she had been the one doing the cheating, which made the way the legal system went for him more unfair.

She took him for more than he could afford, and that was without them having children. The viciousness of the woman he'd loved explained why Cliff chose to now be alone in his misery. It also drove him to drink and the distraction of whatever strip club was open.

This was Las Vegas, so a lot of his time was spent in those fungating houses of dubious pleasure.

So spiteful had he become that Cliff had let his business of fifteen years fall into ruin. That meant he could no longer make the court-ordered payments, which meant he was heading for bankruptcy, and maybe jail. The letters from his ex-wife's lawyer were threatening that, and more.

Whenever one of his dwindling number of friends pointed out his pending financial doom, Cliff had only one response.

"Fuck it."

Sprawled out on the stained couch that came with his rented residence, Cliff let himself get mesmerised by the banality of the TV. No other lights were on, the television giving his sparse and litter-strewn living room a flickering illumination. The plan was for this night to be like so many others since the divorce, and his hand flopped down to the floor to try to snag his fourth beer of the night.

After the first, he never cared if they were cold.

Before he could find the alcoholic delight, there was a banging on his front door. The whole wall appeared to shudder with those impacts.

"What the hell?"

Cliff was an imposing man when he wanted to be. At six-foot-three, and having spent much of his adult life in construction, he reckoned he could handle himself in most altercations. Strangely, this self-deception had never been tested after high school, which was for the best. Alcohol had a way of making one over confident, and if Cliff had been a violent drunk, he would have either ended up in hospital or jail.

Maybe both.

The thudding on his door came again, and Cliff pulled himself to his feet. It was evening, so there was no legitimate reason for someone to be at his door. Whoever it was continued in their persistence, dragging anger up from the depths of Cliff's gut. This wasn't the police because they would have announced themselves already, so he would be safe to vent his pent-up ire on the disruptors of his peace.

Had he pissed anyone off recently? Only his ex-wife, but her dainty hands weren't capable of the force being displayed on his door. Cliff had the caution to consider grabbing his shotgun from the other room, but the door lock failed at that instant, the door swinging in with a crash, a mountain storming in to what was supposed to be the safety of his home. Cliff was tall, but this man had to stoop to get through the doorway.

The intruder was bulky too, a furious frown etched on the shadows of his face. The man looked sickly, but that didn't hamper how strong he was.

"Stay back," Cliff managed as he backed up, fear an unwelcome replacement for the fury that had been bubbling up in him. The stranger didn't stay back, instead he bludgeoned his way forward, using a hand to sweep a pointless picture from the wall as he passed it. The frame came hurtling at Cliff, who knocked it aside as his attacker bore down on him.

How can someone that big move so quickly?

Cliff was grabbed, his soiled t-shirt ripping as thick fingers clutched it. Lifted, Cliff was pushed into the air, his feet kicking uselessly. He tried to land a kick on the maniac, but all he did was hurt his toe on what felt like granite.

That was when the man smiled, and then everything made sense. Teeth like that belonged in the monster that now held him, Cliff being pulled in close so that their torsos touched.

"Let… me… go," Cliff begged. He felt his bladder go, the piercing and glowing blue eyes and the unfathomable rows of teeth more than he could cope with.

"The Lord Moloch sends his regards." The words hung there, the accent spoken unknown to Cliff. What was that even supposed to mean?

Strangely, Cliff had heard the word Moloch before, the name of an owl god in some conspiracy video he'd watched years before.

"Please…" Cliff tried one last plea, but the monster shook its head. Slowly, Cliff's face was pulled closer, so close that he thought the beast was going to kiss him.

That was when the moisture dropped onto the front of Cliff's neck. He felt it wriggle and squirm, Cliff suddenly slapping at the latest horror. Whatever it was, it slithered up under his chin and cheek, moving with unnerving speed.

And then it was at the entrance to Cliff's ear, slipping inside, going deep. All the time, his assailant smiled, those teeth threatening. They were more like tiny daggers, the sort of teeth you would see in a reptile or an alien. And there were so many of them, moving.

How could they be moving? They came at him in waves of impossibility.

A sharpness caused Cliff to roar in desperation, the mammoth man suddenly dropping him. Clutching the side of his head, Cliff crawled away, his back hitting the corner of the room. More pain now, combined with a feeling of nausea, his vision tunnelling down so that the periphery of his sight vanished.

He knew he was going to black out, and he thanked the world for that mercy. The last thing Cliff saw before he passed out was the monster leaving, its huge hulking figure squeezing out into the freshness of the world.

As it did so, the door was closed behind it to hide the nature of this crime from the world.

Cliff finally succumbed to unconsciousness, and nobody was there to see.

Another Child had been delivered.

Hundreds more to go.

11.

Isles of Scilly, UK

Cleaver had been watching the live video feed as Brian Moses lost his sanity and his life. The creature in Brian had multiplied, freeing Brian from the restraints that held him to the bed, which was an impossible act made real.

The orange light filling the surrounding laboratory was something Cleaver had always feared.

There was no video or audio feed now, because no camera could survive the heat in Brian's room. Cleaver held his hand up in front of his face, noting the nervous shake that was now present.

"How can this be?" He asked himself the question, mesmerised by the white snow on his monitor. It drew Cleaver in, the chaotic intricacies promising the secrets of the universe.

There had been something about Brian's behaviour that came across as puppet-like, as if Brian were somehow being controlled. Cleaver's thinking slid onto another path, a revelation about the nature of the parasite close to being unveiled.

Could these things control human actions? The idea began to percolate into a working theory, only for Cleaver to be ripped out of his trance by the automated message.

"Please remain calm. There has been a breach in sub-level six containment. Measures are being taken to contain the breach. The facility is now in lockdown."

"Soteria, what's going on," Cleaver asked in breathless desperation.

"There has been a containment breach," Soteria replied.

"But we cooked it," Cleaver insisted.

The thing had been cooked good.

"I can confirm your specimen designated XB113 has been shown to be susceptible to extremes of heat." The remaining video feed relayed that the small quarantine chamber was now filled with nothing but ash and smoke, the flames having relented. "The one inside Brian Moses has, however, escaped."

"Escaped?" How could such a thing happen?

"Yes, an unfortunate occurrence. As I am sure you can understand, the Laboratory is now in full lockdown."

"But that's absurd."

"I struggle to see the incongruous nature that you refer to." Soteria still had a way to go before fully adapting to human frailty.

"I need to get out," Cleaver insisted, pushing himself up from his chair. There was a stab of pain from his knee, his body not used to such explosive movements.

"The facility will not allow that," Soteria reminded him. "Honestly, Professor, you should know this!"

"But I'll be needed on the outside," Cleaver persisted. Who was he trying to fool? Himself or the brilliant AI that could read him like a book?

Hobbling to the door of his laboratory, he pulled it open, half tumbling into the corridor. A flash of panic washed over him, his adrenaline spiking. Being stuck underground with a terrible parasite on the loose wasn't something he'd signed up for.

Bravery was not something to be found in Cleaver's CV.

"That may be, but the facility will not allow your exit." With the Laboratory's emergency protocols being governed by an autonomous system, Cleaver knew Soteria had no power to override the lockdown.

"You don't understand," Cleaver stammered. He pulled himself along the pristine corridor, not knowing where he was going. He'd experienced panic before and was well aware of how susceptible he was to its chaotic effects.

"My understanding isn't relevant." Soteria's voice followed him down the corridor.

"**All personal must move to their designated safe zones,**" the automated voice persisted. That meant going up.

From a side door, a research assistant appeared, Cleaver colliding with her. With no apology, he forged past, far from oblivious to the physical contact he'd engaged in. Cleaver had no love for people touching him, and it fuelled his terror further.

Wait! What if she is carrying the parasite?

At the end of the corridor, Cleaver's world painted in the pulsing orange light, the professor slammed his hands against the escalator doors. His forehead left a damp smear across the metal, left hand searching for the call button. His fingers pressed it, but no light came on. This wasn't the main elevator to the surface, just the one that allowed people to traverse the eight lowest sub-levels.

"Elevators are deactivated at this time," Soteria informed him. Cleaver was on sub-level four, claustrophobia suddenly rushing into his life. He thought he'd be safe, with so much steel and concrete separating him from what was stored below.

"I have to get out," Cleaver pleaded again, gasping between words. He was spiralling now, hurtling down into a panic attack that he'd so long ago thought he'd learnt to control.

"Professor!" People were around him now, helpful faces hoping to calm his mental implosion. Their presence only worsened his condition.

"Get away from me," Cleaver screamed, pushing away, bouncing off one wall as he fled down another corridor. Those people, they had all been too calm, too controlled. What if they were all infested?

Cleaver hit a door that swung open. The upper floors beckoned to him, and the professor collapsed to his knees as he fell into the staircase. A wave of exhaustion gripped him, his breath ragged and uncontrolled.

"Please try and calm yourself, Professor." Even here, Soteria had followed him. She was everywhere, and yet, the AI could be of no help to Cleaver.

It took everything Cleaver had to get off his hands and knees, and without the help of the banister, he would have been trapped by his own crippling weakness. Looking up the shaft of the stairwell, he couldn't believe how far it was to reach the surface. Two floors to the main elevator seemed like Everest.

Not once during his time here had he used these stairs, and if he'd been one floor below, they would have been denied him. Automation allowed the humans to be localised on the upper sub-levels where they were supposed to be safe. The samples and the people infested were kept secure on the lowest floors.

Secure? Ha!

One by one, Cleaver took the steps, his feet feeling like they were encased in concrete blocks. With a fluttering heart that was on the brink of exploding, he tried his best to flee from the terror he didn't understand. Behind him came the sound of people following. Cleaver had to get away from them.

He had seen what the parasite could do and would not allow that thing to be in his body with its teeth and its scorching acid.

Surely nobody would force him to stay here?

Surely.

***

I think, therefore I am.

The parasite didn't realise it had been given a name, human language only of any concern when it was in a human host. As names went, XB113 was a bit of a mouthful, but the parasite would never care.

Alone, in this rudimentary form, its only goal was survival. Survival required a host to reduce its vulnerability. It was durable, but required living fluids to reach its true potential. It had the ability to communicate, but only when latched into the neurons of those it sought to control.

It could sense the others like it when they were present, and it knew that it was alone.

Presently, it moved by instinct, the air filters it encountered in the duct not sufficient to resist its teeth and acid. It moved swiftly, not yet ready to divide, the metal of the duct a strange environment that felt wrong to it.

Where would this tube lead?

When it had been inside the one called Brian, it had known things, but only because it had connected itself to the electrical network of the body that had been under the control of the primary. The primary, safely encased in the brain, had shared the human's memories with the others of its kind. This fleeing survivor was an offspring of the primary, the first, the one that had begun them all.

Its brethren were now dead, the connection it had to them lost, leaving it weak and depleted and governed by ingrained survival instincts.

The creators of the parasite had sent it to Earth with one singular purpose, to reproduce. Here it would do that with beings that would allow it sentience, borrowing abilities from the hosts that hopefully waited for it. Reproduction would be driven by manipulation, its genetic knowledge allowing it to know and understand those it looked to gain control of, while also learning and sharing knowledge with others of its kind.

It was a parasite, after all, using its host for its own ends.

Moving swiftly, it worked its way upwards, more barriers failing to its offensive abilities, the smooth surface of the duct sufficient for it to adhere to.

At a junction in the duct, it took a moment to divide. Not being the primary of its kind, it needed to mature before it could cleave off vast numbers of itself. It could manage the production of one brother. Another doubled its chance of survival, and the two parasites parted ways, both heading upwards, using the human facilities design against itself.

By the fifteen-minute mark, it was severely depleted, the division and the acid it used taking a heavy toll. Close to being extinguished as a threat, it used the last of its venom sack to burn through the side of the duct, the metal finally relenting.

It dropped down into a space between walls, the scent of humanity drawing it on. Although it had no nasal cavity, it could detect the pheromones the humans pumped out, the world around it a visual abundance of radiation. The visible spectrum was unknown to it, gamma rays and dark matter its domain. Through layers of concrete, it found a prey that would hold it and homed in on its last and only hope.

When it dropped down, finally landing on pliable and succulent flesh, it wasn't able to hear the human cry out in alarm. Sound waves required it to be connected to human ears, and as it slicked its way into a waiting orifice, the world of abundance began to expand.

Soon it would merge with the human nervous system, and then the manipulation would begin. It would learn things, unlocking everything about its host, merging and rapidly taking over the sentient neural functions.

Each time it spread its kind to another host, the transformation would happen at an increased rate.

The person it now infested would do as it commanded. To refuse would result in the human suffering severe pain. Eventually, depending on the host's resistance, it had the chance to spread its tendrils out through the brain and take utter control. That was the ultimate goal of the parasite, becoming one mind with its host.

Until then, until the human body was literally a puppet for it to play with, the host would know unbelievable misery.

The Lord Moloch wouldn't have it any other way.

12.

Las Vegas, USA

"Goodnight Pastor."

"Goodnight Juliet," Pastor Wilkinson replied. He watched from the church's front steps as his last parishioner left for the evening, leaving him in a quiet and warm church that had been his charge for close to ten years now. He liked these moments of peace at the end of the day, when he was freed from the demands of those who chose to worship here.

When it came to church matters, Juliet was always the first to volunteer, and the last to leave. Wilkinson knew she had a hole in her life, a loneliness she tried to cover up with charity work and worship, but he seldom worried about her. If anything, she was an irritation that he would have like to be freed from.

He didn't know it, but soon, he wouldn't have need to worry about anything ever again.

Closing the front door, Wilkinson wasn't there to see the lumbering hulk of a man come up behind Juliet on her way to her car. Juliet's protests were stifled by the thick hand that smothered her mouth. And then came the other things only a golem could do, the snap of the frail neck as once again the parasite it carried was denied purchase in the human flesh.

Death was all too easy for the golem.

Wilkinson neglected to lock the church door, because there was no point. He would be leaving himself shortly, and he'd always had trust that the Lord was looking out for him. Wilkinson was also tired, the charity meeting a fruitless waste of his time.

Tiredness made people sloppy, but in this case, a locked church door wouldn't have saved him.

Truth was, he was struggling with his faith of late. His sermons and his good works didn't seem to be having much of an impact on his dwindling flock. Added to that, his health wasn't great, obesity tearing his body apart.

Soon, he would be free of all those concerns.

He'd reached the pulpit when he heard the door open. Turning, he saw the strange-looking man enter. There was malevolence in the stranger's movements, and Wilkinson felt unease well up inside him. Pausing only for a moment, the intruder walked boldly down the main aisle, Wilkinson his only interest.

"Can I help you, my son?" Wilkinson offered. Despite his own concerns, he came down to meet this man. There was nothing in the church worth stealing, and Wilkinson wasn't a man known to have enemies. What was there to fear?

Wait for the Lord; be strong, and let your heart take courage; wait for the Lord!

The man didn't answer. He looked dishevelled and dangerous, but surely everyone was worth the chance of redemption.

"Speak to me, my friend. The Lord welcomes all those..." That was when the stranger smiled, continuing to close the gap. Its face changed, becoming distorted and grotesque. It felt like a deliberate act, meant to frighten and intimidate, which is exactly what happened. Wilkinson felt his legs go weak, the strength seeping out of his body. Fright rather than flight took him, allowing the golem to quickly stand before him.

There was a stench from the thing, like wet mud and rot, its smile growing thicker and... deeper. More teeth appeared, parting to let a long dry tongue meander out between its lips.

Why was it here? What was its terrible purpose?

Later, when Wilkinson awoke from where he had been left, he looked around at his church with utter confusion. He had no memory of the golem, the possibility that he had fainted of pressing concern. The notion of visiting the emergency room was swiftly dismissed, because, apart from a slight ache behind the eyes, he felt fine.

Hospitals and doctors were expensive. Who wanted that kind of financial penalty in their lives?

Best you go home and get some rest, his inner voice advised. Tonight, there would be a lot of people giving themselves that guidance.

***

The golem cared nothing for the lives it ruined.

It was a tool and a vessel, a means to spread the Children throughout the human herd. Upon arriving at the city of lights, it had moved in a straight line, delivering its gifts to all those it came upon. It had started with single dwellings because those were the first buildings it came across.

Dozens of humans had so far been impregnated.

The religious structure gave it two more victims and one more host. Once again, a Child had died after being expelled from the female body, the ninth now to be rejected in its travels into the city. The golem did not understand why this was so, but it altered its strategy accordingly. Only the men would be used as hosts here on out.

The Children were too precious to waste.

That would make its job harder because the males were the stronger of the two sexes. Fortunately, the golem was now starting to understand how this human society worked. At night, the humans slept, which made them increasingly vulnerable.

After the church, it came upon a structure filled with the scent of humanity. The golem had no concept of what a motel was or why humans felt the need to travel as they did. It was not one to turn down opportunity, though.

It entered a courtyard; the building erected around where the mechanical beasts lay dormant. From what the golem could tell, the myriad of doors led to separate rooms where the humans hid out. On three floors, the L-shaped structure was home to nearly a hundred heart beats that called to the golem.

There was such potential here. It would not be wasted.

Climbing concrete steps, it hunted for silence, a sign of extra vulnerability. Striking here would net the golem good rewards, but also came with the risk of alarm and discovery. In a darkened stairwell, the golem sent its body to a form similar to the appearance of glass. It would maintain its strength while markedly reducing its visibility.

The Children stirred within it. There was no surprise to be found in the golem at their growing agitation. They, too, would be able to sense the pheromones of humanity.

They wanted to be free.

On the upper floor, the golem came to its first door, and it paused, pushing its ear against the wood. The darkened window suggested the inhabitant was asleep, and the golem pressed its hand to the door handle. The door felt solid, although the golem knew it could defeat it with brute force if it had to. Making contact told it of the electrical nature of the lock, and a static charge surge from its palm caused the lock to disengage.

Better to take his first victim silently.

The golem slipped in, letting the door settle behind it. Its eyes had no trouble with the darkness, the golem not limited to the visual spectrum. On the bed, a solitary sleeping figure rested, waiting for its affections.

It didn't ponder as to why the humans left themselves so vulnerable. Did they not know of the dangers hurtling towards them?

Stepping over to the bed, the golem bent as it extended its arm, the gritty palm engulfing the male's face. It didn't see his eyes spring open in alarm, and its hand muffled the panicked cry. The man's mouth tried to open, only for one of the Children to slip through the golem's skin and onto his tongue. Holding him, it waited for the parasite to take the human's consciousness.

Another vessel to satisfy the Lord Moloch.

When it slipped from the room, it found nobody waiting to challenge it, and it moved on. The next room felt empty, so the golem ignored it, as it did the next where human sounds and light were emanating from the three females laughing within.

It wanted to kill them for the way their sex rejected the nobility of the Children, but that would result in screams which would draw too much attention.

It did not fear discovery, but it knew when to avoid creating a disturbance that would awaken the potential hosts. This wasn't the right place to brute force its intentions onto the waiting humans, so it passed the rooms seeking its next viable target.

Four doors on, it sensed two sleeping figures, and once again, the golem bypassed the lock. The two men inside were sharing a bed which made it easier to take them.

The more Children it could deliver, the quicker chaos could be brought to this city and this world. It would not be here to witness the resultant chaos, for there was no purpose for it once the Children were delivered.

The golem longed for the moment it could dissolve back into the dust, where the bliss of eternal peace awaited. It had no enjoyment in its existence, its presence in this universe against the natural laws that had let life spring from bubbling protein broth.

It would do as it was commanded, with a ruthlessness and brutality that only a creation of dirt and mud could summon. Then it would be gone, leaving this world to the fate it so richly deserved.

13.

Isles of Scilly, UK

"Attention! All facility personnel should gather in sub-two. Decontamination protocols are now in effect for the lower floors."

Sadie listened to the voice, whose automated message had changed. From what she could tell, whatever the contagion was, it was spreading. She didn't understand what that meant, because Sadie had no idea where she was or who was running her detention. It made sense that it was the military, the films she had watched in her short life distorting her perception of the world.

She would never know or understand that it was the Hidden Hand who had brought her here.

Two days ago, Sadie had been a waitress in a pretentious coffee shop that sold overpriced beverages to people who were desperate for some kind of social life. It was a place for drinks, gossip, and scandal, an establishment she had been growing to hate due to the snide way she was often treated.

Because of Sadie, it had also been a place of death.

Actually, if what she'd been told was true, the slaughter she had engaged in wasn't Sadie's fault. She had been manipulated by the striking and elegant woman, the one she now knew had been called Sirena. To have such a beautiful woman walk into the coffee shop was unheard of, the usual clientele shrunken and wrinkled with age.

If only Sirena hadn't cursed the coffee house with her terrible visit.

"It's not your fault."

That was what the psychologist in the hazmat suit kept telling her. Three times Sadie had been marched from this sterile room by men in similar protective gear, and three times she had been questioned about how she felt.

How did it feel when Sirena spoke to you?
How long did it take to feel the urge well up inside you?
Do you still have murderous feelings?
Who did you kill first?
How many people did you kill?
Did you choose your victims, or was it random?
Did you have any reservations in your thoughts about what you were doing?

At first, Sadie had been resistant to the questioning, but she soon realised the only chance she had of getting out of here was to be open and honest. She had tried to protest her treatment and detention, stating that her human rights were being infringed, but she had quickly learnt the truth that lurked under the UK's so-called democracy.

The man in the hazmat suit had been blunt in educating her.

"You don't have any rights. Thousands died the day you went insane, whole villages wiped out. Answer my questions and you might have a future. Resist and you might end up being a statistic on the nightly news."

So, Sadie had answered the questions, and in the last session, her interrogator had smiled. He'd stated he felt satisfied with the progress made so far, and that progress meant Sadie had a good chance of being reunited with her family.

That was, of course, a lie, but Sadie wasn't to know that. Nor did she know how she had been picked out from the survivors in her village. It wasn't necessary for Sadie to be aware that there was an artificial intelligence with the ability to interact with almost anything connected to the internet. That included surveillance cameras, like the ones in the café she'd worked at.

Presently, she was lying on an uncomfortable mattress in a sterile room. The lighting had changed to an ominous orange, an automated voice shouting its recurring and less-than-reassuring messages that were utterly terrifying. There was no way for her to track the passage of time, and her body's normal functions were betraying her. She'd not had a bowel movement since being forcibly brought here.

That was the least of her problems.

She was alive, when really, she shouldn't have been. What she suffered was greater than survivor's guilt, her chest filled with a burning anxiety about what she had done. It wasn't so much that she had killed people, for she still felt some of them deserved that fate. Sadie had been merciless with the knife, killing her boss and two customers while injuring close to a dozen more.

What concerned Sadie the most was how much she'd enjoyed it. The memory should have caused revulsion, but the sense of power such slaughter brought was an addiction Sadie would be plagued by until her death. The psychologist who had reassured her was wrong in stating this was all Sirena's fault, for all Sirena had done was unlock something that was already inside Sadie.

Sadie was certain of this.

She no longer had the churning need to touch others and be around the human herd, but whenever she closed her eyes, her thoughts reminded her how satisfying her moment of insanity had been. To be free to unleash herself against those who whispered behind her back had been a blessing rather than a burden. On that day of carnage, Sadie liked to think she had tried to stop herself, to resist the desire that had consumed her. There had been no resistance, though, and whenever the psychologist had asked her about the people she'd killed, the smile had always snuck onto Sadie's face.

What did that tell the man questioning her?

Maybe it was safer for her to be here. Sadie knew she was underground, her fate in the hands of mysterious and dangerous men who treated her with civility while stripping her of her freedoms. She was their puppet, a broken thing they desperately wanted to understand.

Was she safe to be released out into the world? Maybe they could help rid her of the murderous desires that stalked her mind. And did she want that part of her locked back up? The truth of who she had become now taunted her, promising such glory that would not be denied. She was slim and shy, but the frenzy with which she'd wielded her blade had left Sadie breathless and invigorated.

The blood should have horrified her, but the sight of it had only spurred her on. The feel of it on her had made her skin tingle. She'd been assured that this feeling would pass, but that was another lie because Sadie didn't *want* it to pass.

Killing and maiming had been the most satisfying sensation she'd ever felt. And whether that was a direct result of what Sirena had done, or through some innate discovery of her inner self didn't matter. It was part of her now.

She was that killer.

Perhaps that was why she was always handcuffed when they moved her from the room. Could they see the murder in her eyes?

"Decontamination protocols are now in effect."

The automated voice sounded almost apologetic, and sitting up on her bed, Sadie wondered what it all meant. A wave of dizziness tried to overpower her, but Sadie shook it off, only for the buzzing in her head to return.

She lay back down, a sudden tiredness filling her. It seemed like her limbs had got heavier, her thinking dull, which was a blessing. Sadie had spent too much time with her thoughts, and the chance to be free of them was welcome. There was no way for Sadie to know the air in her room had been replaced with pure Nitrogen, due to the application of the facility's gaseous fire suppression system.

Unconsciousness came to Sadie quickly, followed by convulsions, cardiac failure, and brain stem death. In all, it took Sadie six minutes to die, her demise painless and merciful. She wasn't alone, for three dozen other people, all detained like her, shared her miserable fate.

Sadie ended up being a statistic after all.

***

Professor Cleaver didn't want to be in this room, and he didn't want to be anywhere close to those with him. Although he often spent weeks at a time in this subterranean complex, he rarely ventured away from the safety of his office and laboratory. He'd infrequently visited this rest and recreation area, choosing instead to eat at his desk so as not to be distracted from his work.

Cleaver was someone who liked to be left alone. The mere thought of someone touching him caused bile to rise up in his throat. Until today, the people who shared this secret facility with him had respected that.

Until today.

With a sudden frantic motion, he rubbed his palms down his sweat-stained trouser legs to try to wipe the stink of others off him. Cleaver wanted to be engaged with his work, and not be trapped in here. Truth was, he didn't like people.

He liked his work, though.

The Hell creature was the latest in an array of specimens the Hidden Hand had brought him over the years. The bulk of his time had been spent on trying to decipher the types of creatures humanity might be faced with. As a side mission, Cleaver also studied the portals. This was done remotely, allowing Cleaver access to real-time data on all the Hellgates under Hidden Hand control.

He liked the significance that came with having knowledge denied to the majority of the population. Until today, Cleaver had felt appreciated and respected by the faceless leaders of this mysterious organisation. The Hell world had become his obsession, and there were few people on planet Earth who knew more about the portals and the creatures that sometimes came through.

Presently, that obsession had been paused and replaced with this crazed desire to survive.

The floor he was on wasn't a comfortable place for him to sit, but Cleaver stayed there, pulling his knees in closer, making himself as small a target as possible. He was aware that people kept looking at him, and the humiliation of his weakness added to his own anxiety. Cleaver didn't want to be this way, but his responses were out of his control, the safe and sterile world he'd been promised now denied him.

He had no memory of entering this rest area, and there was a gap in his recollection that alarmed him. Cleaver had been on the stairs, the sweat pouring off him, and then he had awoken to find Doctor Schmidt standing over him.

People had touched him. There was no denying that, for how else was he here? The panic had come and Schmidt had helped talk Cleaver down. On Schmidt's instructions, everyone now kept clear of him.

So many people in here.

The thought punched through his swirling thinking.

Why are you sat on your own?

Such a question didn't make any sense. It was obvious why he was sat away from the others.

Aren't you leaving yourself vulnerable?

The words seemed to calm his agitation, but the moisture still pumped from his skin.

"Vulnerable?" he muttered softly. It was not unusual for him to converse with himself, but never out loud. His thoughts were private and only for him, and Cleaver clamped a hand over his mouth. Had anyone here heard him? Would they judge him even more?

There's a predator loose. Don't you know what predators do?

The idea that a parasite could be a predator was new to him. Surely, they were opportunistic creatures, latching onto any viable host that came their way.

You mean like some idiot sat on his own!

"I'm not an idiot," Cleaver complained through his fingers. More glances were cast his way, Cleaver closing his eyes so he didn't have to look at them.

You are a scared little fool, playing with things you could never understand.

Why was he being so mean to himself? Unless…

Oh no!

Oh yes, came his inner response. *Now you force my hand.*

"No, no, no, no." The word became a mantra, Cleaver slapping his head to try and force the intruding presence into submission.

I'd rather you not hurt yourself, commanded the voice. *That's my job.* What did that mean? He was aware of how Brian Moses had needed sedating. Was that to combat what the parasite could do?

Oh Lord.

Not a parasite. A predator. One that knows how to inflict pain. Do you like pain, Reginald? Reginald? What kind of name is that?

"Leave me alone," Cleaver begged.

Reginald, Reginald, Reginald, the voice began to taunt. It suddenly felt like the times he'd been tormented as a child, and a sudden heat shot down both his legs.

Cleaver cried out.

You are a man of science, so let me tell you how this works. I am in your brain where it is all warm and soft. It's nice here, and I can do things.

"You can't be!" Cleaver shouted that, pushing his legs out as the spasms ripped through them.

But I am. From here, I have access to the transmission of your body's nerve fibres through your brain stem. I can use that to create any sensation in you I like. Does that excite you, Reginald?

"Please..."

Go over to the others and I will spare you.

"No!" Cleaver roared. The other people in the room were becoming agitated now, Cleaver's evident distress contagious.

Suit yourself. But get ready, because here comes the pain.

***

It was good to be out of his room, but unfortunately for Stuart, his situation hadn't improved any. He was trapped below ground with an unknown contagion on the loose, which was a shitty state of affairs.

He and Lucy were in the security office, watching the video feeds from within the facility. There was one guard with them, a thin and pasty man called Ted, whom Stuart found competent and trustworthy. You learnt quickly how to assess someone in this line of work, but the true test was seeing someone behave when the shit truly hit the fan.

There were eighteen large monitors, arranged in pairs to relay the video feeds from each floor. The recordings kept rotating, showing different areas that could be pulled up and concentrated on via the tap of a few keyboard keys. On this floor with them, the monitors were watching a dozen other facility personnel, all gathered in a communal area.

Both Stuart and Lucy were still wearing their scrubs, everyone else in whatever they normally wore in this bunker.

He was surprised how few people had made it up to the second sub level. There were other people visible, civilians locked up tight on one of the floors below, but none of them were moving. Stuart knew that they were dead, killed by the computer that ran this place; a contingency to limit the number of people that could be affected by the contagion.

Lucy had expressed revulsion at the loss of life, but Stuart understood the need.

Every one of the living on the videos seemed to be on edge, which was understandable. The cameras would zoom in on their faces on occasion, harried eyes searching for some sight of hope. Unfortunately, any kind of reassurance was severely lacking here.

"How long before that happens to us?" Lucy asked, pointing at one of the deceased civilians. They all looked so peaceful, as if they were asleep.

"We should be okay," Ted insisted, maybe more for his own benefit than anyone else's. "Preservation of facility personnel will be classed as a priority."

Would that priority be at the top of the list, though?

One of the monitors showed a close-up view of the psychologist who was sat with two other men. He, at least, seemed calm. If you couldn't trust a head shrinker not to lose his shit in a crisis, who could you trust?

Of the others, one man in particular seemed to have lost all sense of himself. He was sat in one of the room's corners, squatted down with his back to the wall. Ted had already informed them that the man's name was Professor Cleaver. An oddball, but also apparently a genius on multiple levels.

In Stuart's opinion, brains didn't amount to much if you couldn't keep it together when it mattered. And Cleaver was a gyrating cyclone waiting to explode.

"So, we are the lucky ones," Stuart offered. They were all survivors in an unfolding emergency.

"You call this lucky?" questioned Lucy.

"I'm still breathing."

"Colonel Radcliffe," the voice of Soteria interrupted.

"Yes, Soteria," Stuart replied. The ceiling here was low, the voice of the AI mysteriously next to him.

"Authority has been obtained to give you a summary of the situation." There was a pause before Soteria continued.

"What about Ted here?" Stuart laid a reassuring hand on Ted's shoulder.

"As head of facility security, he has also been given authority."

"I'm honoured," Ted joked.

"Go on," Stuart urged.

"When the Hellgates last activated, two technicians were contaminated by an off-world entity." As if deliberately timed, one of the monitors covering the lowest level changed its view to show nothing but snow. "Those entities were brought here, but unfortunately, they have escaped our attempts to contain them."

"What is the nature of the entity," Stuart asked.

"It is parasitical in nature. From what we know, it takes up residence in the human brain where I believe it can control its host."

"How many of these little bastards are there?" Lucy demanded to know.

"That is unknown at this time," Soteria said apologetically. "I do have visual evidence that shows the parasite can multiply and travel outside its host."

"How do we know we aren't infected?" Stuart had already had the psychologist rooting around in his skull. He liked the idea of an alien creature taking root there even less.

"The studies so far have shown that the presence of the parasite can be detected via an individual's blood chemistry. Both of the infected technicians had similar abnormal readings."

"How does that answer my question?" Stuart persisted. One of the other monitors was zoomed in on Cleaver, who had now rolled onto his side, legs curled up in a foetal position. Right now, that brilliant brain wasn't helping anyone.

Was Cleaver talking to himself?

"I am able to monitor your blood chemistry through your implants. You do not show any signs of infestation. The same applies to the chief of security. The three of you are deemed to not be a threat at present. I would suggest you keep yourselves isolated to the security office."

"Will that be enough? We're still locked up down here with the rest of them," Lucy complained. Normally, Lucy was the first to crack a joke in the most stressful situations. Not today.

"The computer that runs the facility is not at liberty to make allowances. Remaining personnel must be detained until the threat has been neutralised."

"And if the parasite remains at large?"

"Miss Jones, I'm afraid you won't like the answer."

"Lay it on us, Soteria," Stuart intervened.

"The nature of the threat requires the harshest measures." What the hell was that supposed to mean?

"She's talking in bloody riddles now," Lucy spat. Her posture was rigid, eyes fixed on one of the screens. Stuart followed her gaze, showing a slumped figure of one of the dead civilians. Was that fate waiting for them a few hours from now?

"Shit," Ted muttered.

"What? Come on Ted, if you know something…" Stuart insisted.

"It's called the Brimstone protocol."

"That doesn't sound good," Lucy deduced.

"Full facility thermal sterilisation," Ted added. He sat back in his chair. "It's supposed to be a last resort."

"Do not be disheartened," Soteria said cheerfully. "The Brimstone protocol requires human authorisation, so it is not at the whim of a mere machine."

Stuart wasn't reassured. He knew the higher ups would take any measure to save humanity from the creatures from Hell. And that included torching the interior of a billion-dollar complex along with everyone in it.

There could be no compromise when it came to the defence of the realm.

To: Director of Operations

From: Soteria

Subject: Summary of findings regarding species XB113

To date, the following facts have been ascertained:

- XB113 is a silicone-based entity.
- XB113 requires a living host to thrive. While it can exist outside a host body, it weakens over time, and will likely perish in due course.
- XB113 has the ability to divide asexually both inside and outside a host.
- XB113 can be detected via MRI scan and an examination of an individual's blood chemistry. Parasitical exposure causes a very noticeable spike in adrenaline, noradrenaline, and cortisol.
- XB113 has both offensive and defensive capabilities. It is mobile, agile, and has the ability to create acid of unknown composition. It can also manifest dentition.
- XB113 should be classified as a parasite of off-Earth origin.

To date, I have formulated the following assumptions:

- I am hesitant to use the word lifeform, as XB113 appears more mechanical in nature.
- I believe XB113 may be able to communicate with its various copies.
- I believe it has the ability to control the minds of the individuals it infests. It may well be that this is done primarily through the application of pain.

- It is my contention that XB113 is a prelude to an imminent invasion from the Hell world.
- Although XB113 has escaped primary containment, if it goes on to infest facility personal stationed at the Laboratory, this would be an exceptional opportunity to study it in a controlled environment.
- While the escaped entity has been contained within the Laboratory complex, I have grave concerns that XB113 has been delivered through other Hellgates out of Hidden Hand control. I am scouring the internet for any hint that this *creature* is on the loose.

Report Ends.

14.

Las Vegas, USA

"Hey, watch yourself buddy."

The golem ignored the challenge, pushing further into the crowd. The place was loud, dark, and swarmed with the human herd. They were packed in shoulder to shoulder, moving rhythmically to the mechanical noise that blared out.

The humans called it dancing, and the golem thanked them for it. Such a concentrated mass of people was perfect for the Children that now emerged from its pale form. There were few women here, males embracing each other in their passionate heat. This confused the golem, but it was not one to turn down such an opportunity.

"I said you need to watch yourself." The voice could hardly be heard over the music, but the hand that grabbed the golem's shoulder couldn't be ignored. Lit up by the pulsating lights, the golem turned to find the man who was intent on confronting a force of nature he could never hope to understand.

Why were so many of this species idiots?

The hero's face switched from confidence to unease, the golem gripping the fingers that tried to restrain it. There was no need to squeeze, a Child slipping from the clay into ripe human flesh. That was when the golem smiled, everyone else around oblivious to the danger, entranced by their own desires.

With a Child deposited, the golem pushed the fool away before surging further into the gyrating morass. As it did so, the Children slipped from their safe haven, attaching to clothing, waiting for more of their brethren to emerge. The Children clung there, ready to infest en masse.

A grand baptisement of those assembled.

Behind the golem, a commotion erupted as the stricken man staggered and fell to the floor. Such things happened in establishments like this, for the golem could sense the intoxicants infusing these human bodies. They willingly infected themselves with poisons and hallucinogens for their own gratification.

Such hedonism deserved the coming slaughter.

By the time the golem had forged its way to the edge of the crowd, the Children struck. A cry rose from the assembled, swallowed by the beat of the noise that the golem found irritating. It was jarring, pumping through its body with a maddening repetition.

These were the sacrifices the golem made for the Children.

The cry of humanity turned into the first inklings of panic as the effects of the mass infestation began. The golem moved further away, now moving down a corridor with a sign that said *Employees Only*.

Its job was done here.

A golem has no need to read, and it let the reassuring hum of human distress subside behind it. The door it found in its path succumbed to an electrical spark from the golem's thick and powerful fingers.

Soon, this establishment would be filled with chaos and carnage. Although the golem could have stayed to witness its handiwork, the remaining Children were needed elsewhere. Thus, it would not learn that several of the Children failed to establish themselves due to the toxicity of the bodies of some of those dancing.

Such a waste.

"How did you get back here?"

The challenge came from an impressively bulked man. The golem stopped and turned side-on to him, the light in the corridor dim, the golem's features hidden by the hooded attire it appeared to be wearing. The nightclub employee approached less warily than he should have, intent on ejecting the golem from an area that was off limits.

"I said, how did you get back here?"

The golem's answer came in the form of an arm that swept round, the open palm attached slamming into the employee's face. Once again, the golem smiled, the human catching its menace with the one eye that wasn't covered.

As the golem pushed his latest victim back against a wall, two Children emerged to merge themselves with the waiting ripe and pliable flesh.

The Children would take care of this challenger, allowing the golem to leave through the same fire exit through which it had forced its entrance. With the Children delivered, the golem left the shaking and desolate man to undergo his newfound self of discovery.

The golem left bedlam behind it. It also unwittingly left a video recording of its actions in the restricted corridor, the single surveillance camera capturing everything it did.

This included the golem's smile.

Slowly, an awareness of the golem and what it could do was developing among the humans. How long before the golem became the hunted?

15.

Area 51, Nevada, USA

Despite the captain's promises, Colonel Brook still found himself sequestered in the canteen.

As impressive as XR-1 Storage sounded, there wasn't that much to its structure. There was the main chamber that had been discovered by miners decades before, and a generator room to make the defences around the portal self-reliant. There were some offices, and the canteen he was locked in was only big enough to self-service twenty diners.

The canteen was a place for the people stationed here to get a chance to eat and talk about things other than the purpose of XR-1 Storage. There were also storage rooms and sleeping quarters, enough to service those who were stuck here on their two-week rotations.

Normally, Brook was the only one allowed to come and go as he pleased, that rule enforced by the dedicated and deadly men who patrolled the surface.

Everything except the entryway was deep underground, a long tunnel leading up to the surface. With the exception of the portal itself, that tunnel was the only way into XR-1 Storage, all other natural fissures sealed off with thick concrete and steel.

The entrance to that tunnel was now under heavier guard, a thick quarantine tent there to deal with the unexpected.

Ever since the ill-fated attempt to send an individual through the portal which had been designated Operation Cyclops, XR-1 Storage had been a glorified containment vessel. It was there to stop the existence of the portal being known to the world, and to prevent travel in either direction. The world it led to had been deemed too deadly to interfere with, and it was hoped the portal could remain a curiosity that could be controlled.

The years had passed on since Operation Cyclone, XR-1 Storage becoming a benign accounting entry in the secret files of the Pentagon's preposterous black budget. Sealing the damned anomaly off so that it could be forgotten about had seemed like the best plan.

Things had changed now, and Brook no longer cared about protecting the portal's integrity. Instead, his focus was on the rippling pain that kept passing through his teeth, as well as the persistent presence that was trying to bludgeon him into mental submission.

The pain is to teach you a lesson about your failure to comply.

Brook was a hard man who had a history of arduous combat experience. He had few fears, but dentistry was a terror he had never been able to come to grips with. Hunting down terrorists in oversees hellholes had been merely a chore to him, but lying down so that his teeth could be poked and prodded made him lose his normally reserved composure. Whatever was trying to dominate him seemed to be aware of this.

Why are you still in this room? We require things of you.

The question was met by a stabbing heat that hit all his upper molars. Brook groaned, his dominant hand wrapped over his lips to stifle the noise.

"I can't leave," Brook protested out loud. The threatening voice taunting him sounded like his own inner discussion, but Brook wasn't fooled. Although the voice was his, it had taken on the character of a ruthless drill sergeant Brook had once been unfortunate to know.

In-between the bouts of pain, he was able to snatch insights about his condition. Something was trying to gain control of him. Brook could sense it, could feel his consciousness being restricted. His left hand kept acting under its own influence, dancing in the air in front of him.

There was a battle in his mind that he was losing.

"There has to be a way," Hertz insisted. The doctor was sat watching his superior with an amused expression.

"How?" Brook begged.

You are failing, came the inner voice. More pain followed. *Failure is a weakness that will not be tolerated.*

"Maybe we don't have to escape the room," Hertz proposed. Hertz raised his hand up in front of his face, palm up. Slowly, a grey mass emerged from under the skin. Through the pain, a surge of memory filled Brook's thoughts before it was suppressed.

"What the hell is that?" Brook managed, the purgatory now slipping to his lower teeth. It was then that he realised how docile Hertz seemed. Had the good doctor given himself to whatever force this was?

"The cause of your discomfort." Discomfort? "Your resistance is foolish. Let yourself be at one with the divine."

"You... you aren't making sense."

"On the contrary, the only thing that doesn't make sense is your rejection of what has to be." Hertz gently closed his hand into a fist. When he opened his fingers, like a magic trick, the squirming grey mass had disappeared. Brook couldn't see that it had dropped and slithered off, blending into the colour of the floor nicely.

Listen to your friend.

He's not my friend, damnit.

"Why do you reject the purity?" Hertz quizzed.

Yes, why do you reject the purity?

"Why do you reject the clarity your surrender could bring?"

Yes, why do you reject the clarity?

"Shut up," Brook roared, slapping his head several times.

"You can be free of the torment," Hertz advised. Standing up from where he'd been on the floor, the doctor came over to where Brook was sitting. The doctor didn't touch him, instead he stood with hands on his hips, as if Brook was a naughty boy that required punishing.

You are infringing on the oneness that could be.

"You hear the voice, don't you?"

"Yes," Brook reluctantly admitted. The fury in his mouth made him vulnerable, even to someone as physically unimpressive as Hertz. Brook was a lifelong military man who took pride in his physical abilities, but right now, he felt so depleted, his muscles and training amounting to nothing. It wasn't just the pain, but the constant pushing against his will.

The parasite that had pulled itself from the doctor's skin was no longer in the room. He was sure of that.

How long can I hold out? Brook found himself thinking, though he had no idea what it was he was holding out against.

"Why do you resist?" Hertz demanded as he leaned closer, bending slightly at the hip.

"Don't you touch me," Brook threatened. Even with the agony pulsing in his jaw, he knew he could at least try to lay the doctor out with one wild punch.

Yes, why DO you resist?

"Just give yourself to the beauty of it," Hertz pressed.

"You mean like you did?"

"I saw the light and the way," Hertz beamed.

"Are you still in there, Hertz?" The question caused the doctor to recoil slightly, Hertz stepping away.

There was no Hertz any more.

"You think you are so unique, but all will fall eventually." Shaking his head sadly, Hertz returned to the floor. "Enjoy your pain."

As if the words themselves had power, electricity flowed through every tooth in Brook's mouth. The scream he emitted filled the room.

Just relent. Give yourself, the alien presence demanded.

"Never," came Brook's dazed response.

Suit yourself.

It was then that Brook realised that, as bad as his agony was, it wasn't close to the true nature of what could be inflicted on the human body. A man as hardened as Colonel Brook shouldn't have permitted himself the luxury of tears.

But cry, he did.

Overwhelmed by sensation, Brook didn't notice the wetness that seeped from his left ear, one of the parasites slipping to the floor. Their numbers were growing inside him, ready for the time when he could spread the Children he carried.

The escaping parasite dropped to the floor and slid off in search of fresh human meat. There would be no more waiting.

16.

Isles of Scilly, UK

The clock on the wall told everyone that midnight had passed. Did anyone care? The parasite that had finally deciphered Cleaver's biochemistry didn't.

When Cleaver staggered to his feet, he let out a roar of utter frustration. It felt like his buttocks were on fire, and he stumbled into the centre of the room, painfully aware of the audience he had. The fresh agony in his flesh was now his primary motivator.

He tried to turn left towards the exit, but a heated lance thrust into his left hip, forcing him in the other direction. Cleaver realised he was being pushed by the torment, forced towards the other people in the room as if demons were sadistically goading him on. Those who shared the rest area all watched him warily, not understanding the true nature of the threat Cleaver represented.

The parasite had grown tired of him and was trying a different tactic.

Be united with your friends.

"They aren't my friends," Cleaver protested, but he moved regardless.

They will be. Soon you will be as one with them.

Excluding him, there were eleven people in total, six females and five males. As the facility was automated, humans weren't needed for most of the everyday running of the complex. Each individual had the responsibility to feed themselves from the self-service facilities provided, as well as keeping clean their sleeping and work environments.

Who would be there to clean up what came next?

"You should try to calm yourself," Schmidt insisted. He had stepped up to Cleaver, hands held out in a placating gesture. The psychologist knew better than to try to touch him.

"Stay away from me," Cleaver warned, and yet it was he who moved closer.

Embrace your future.

"You're tired, we all are," Schmidt insisted. "You should sit down and get some sleep."

"Sleep? How can I sleep with this torture inside me?" Cleaver was shouting now, slamming the palm of his hand against his forehead. The impact made a wet sound, a red mark raised from the force used.

"You are going to hurt yourself." At no time did Schmidt try to physically interfere, because he knew that would only make the Professor worse.

"It's in me," Cleaver winced, suddenly jumping forwards, close enough to grab Schmidt. Nobody expected violence from Cleaver because he didn't have the physique for it or the history. They knew him as a timid man who kept to himself. Still, the psychologist sensed the shift in Cleaver's personality and stepped back, the two guards slipping in front of him.

These were the two big men who had been used to escort all the detained people to and from their various interviews. When they weren't sporting hazmat suits, they wore black military fatigues like now.

"Please settle down, Professor," one of the guards said. He had a good sixty-pound advantage on Cleaver, the shock baton dangling from his utility belt unneeded.

Or so he thought.

They all laugh at you, you know, the voice in Cleaver's head said with growing mischief.

"Shut up," Cleaver implored.

They call you Fever Cleaver, like those kids did at school. Fever Cleaver. Fever Cleaver. Fever Cleaver. Cleaver had always hated that nickname, despised the power it held over him. He couldn't help that he sweated so much!

"No. I don't believe you?" Cleaver shouted at his own inner voice, and his defiance was met by a knife-like agony in both kidneys. He jumped forward with a scream, landing in the guard's surprised arms.

That's better.

"Easy now, Professor," the guard cautioned.

That was when something cold, glistening and grey forced its way out of Cleaver's nostril. The Professor barely noticed, because it felt like someone was using glowing pincers to pull out his spine. If not for the guard, he would have collapsed to the floor, consumed by the purgatory.

Even with all that, Cleaver had an understanding of what was happening. His actions were being forced by pain compliance, his identity and social inadequacy no defence against the manipulation.

I've been busy, the parasite whispered inside. *Let us show these people what I am.*

The freshly emerged creature sprang across the space, landing on the guard's exposed neck. Pushing Cleaver to the floor, it was the guard's turn to panic, slapping at the moisture as it squirmed and wriggled on his skin. It managed to evade the attack, burrowing through the skin under the jaw, sliding easily through the tissues.

"It's in me, get it out!" the guard implored, using his fingers to try to grip the parasite under the skin, but it was too quick and too slick, digging deeper, gliding between muscles, honing in on where it needed to be.

"Help him," Schmidt commanded, but the other guard stood there, uselessly. Cleaver was moving again, on his hands and knees now, the room descending into uproar. People were pushing past, some trying to help the guard who was on his knees, the man's muscles going into spasm. Those who had been close enough to see the parasite were trying to flee the room.

"I tried to stop it," Cleaver promised pitifully, before vomiting all down himself.

The parasites flowed out with the gastric juices, writhing down him and onto the floor where they began to spread out. So many! How could he have so many of them inside him?

One of the slug-things went for the second guard, but he slammed the heel of his combat boot down on it. The squelch was satisfying, but then another parasite was there, launching itself from the floor with frightening agility. It landed on the second guard's leg and instantly chewed its way through the material and then on into the flesh. Cleaver watched as the second guard began to beat at his limb in vain.

You see, that was all we asked of you, the voice in Cleaver remonstrated, and the pain in the Professor's back eased. *Why did you have to make it so difficult?*

"This isn't my fault," Cleaver implored the room.

No? Then whose fault is it?

The parasites spread out, their slick bodies spreading across the floor. Cleaver witnessed the panic through the eyes of his own misery. One by one, those left in the room were stricken by the alien creature.

***

"What the actual fuck," Lucy said. She was still in the security office, the events of the rest area now on four of the monitors.

"I must admit, this is a sub-optimal outcome," Soteria admitted.

"We have to help them," Stuart insisted.

"I fail to see how you can be of any kind of assistance, Colonel." Soteria seemed quite insistent on that. "My advice would be to stay where you are. Contact with one of the infested would be detrimental to your overall health."

"But these people need our help," Stuart persisted.

"Stuart, I think Soteria's right." The wisdom floated from Lucy's lips.

"But…"

"Stuart, hear me out." Lucy squared up to him. "We don't know this creature's capabilities. Soteria seems to think we are safe for now. Let's keep it that way."

Stuart's jaw pulsed on both sides.

"Miss Jones is correct," Soteria said with evident satisfaction. "Besides, the decision has been taken at a higher level to let this play out. We need to understand what this parasite does."

"Seriously?" Stuart didn't hide his outrage.

"The decision has been made," Soteria re-affirmed.

Was that the real reason why they called this place the Laboratory, Stuart wondered? Could this be a place where people were used as sacrifices for the furtherance of scientific knowledge?

If that was the case, where did that leave him and Lucy?

On the screens, total chaos was ensuing. The two guards had collapsed, Cleaver now flinging himself at the rest of the people, cornering most of them in the room. Two of the female staff slipped past him, escaping from the recreation room.

"I agree with Lucy," Ted added. "I'm not going out there."

"Do you at least have any weapons?" If Stuart was going to be trapped here, he at least wanted a gun to give him a fighting chance.

"Funny you should ask," Ted revealed. He stood from his chair and walked to a door at the side of the room. By placing his palm against a wall panel, a man-high walk-in closet opened, a roller door ascending automatically. Inside, a dozen weapons awaited them, as well as other things.

"Oh, sweet Jesus," Lucy purred.

"You're only showing us this now?" Stuart said in mock chastisement.

"Hey, a man has a right to his secret stash. Help yourself." Although he had a pistol on his hip, Ted pulled free a semi-automatic carbine. "Magazines are unloaded, so we better get busy."

At the bottom of the closet were several crates of ammunition. Stuart took a carbine for himself, noticing the smell of fresh gun oil. These guns had been kept well maintained and were more than enough to deal with any human threat down here.

What use would they be against an alien parasite, though?

Lucy moved back over to the monitors.

"Colonel, please do not do anything stupid."

Stuart started to push bullets into his first magazine.

"Soteria, I didn't know you cared."

Ted had focused two of the monitors so that they showed the rest area without rotating away to other parts of this floor. He used one monitor to zoom in on individuals, while the other displayed the general carnage.

Some of those in the room had fled, but eight were either cowering against the walls or had already succumbed to the parasite.

"Wait!" Lucy pointed at the zoomed-in screen with an agitated finger. The screen showed the face of a woman, grey goo pouring out of her nose. The woman in question was screaming, pawing at her face.

"What do you make of that Soteria?"

"Colonel, it looks like the parasite has been rejected. Interesting."

"So, maybe there's still hope," Lucy offered.

"For now, I would like to delay any indications of optimism," came Soteria's ominous reply.

17.

Las Vegas, USA

Cliff woke up early with a thumping headache that had an urgency about its nature. The more he tried to relax, the worse the pressure in his skull became.

There's no point lying around moping all day. Get up, you lazy fuck.

Heeding this advice seemed like the best thing for him.

For some reason, he skipped his usual breakfast and, shabbily dressed, he stepped out of his home with the keys to his truck gripped in his tight fist. The sun was barely rising, the air cool and crisp.

Don't be concerned by the state of your front door. You can fix it later.

The wood around the frame had splintered, the door able to shut but not lock. Someone had clearly broken in last night, and yet Cliff took his own advice, for he had no memory of the incursion.

When he listened to himself, it lessened the pain.

"Howdy neighbour."

The voice came from the elderly man who lived next door. He was one of those annoyingly chirpy individuals who had never seemed to have learnt the lesson that life was about suffering. Cliff gave the neighbour a dismissive wave, only for a fresh flash of trauma to unleash across his forehead.

What a time for someone so elderly to be getting in from work!

Don't be rude. Say hello.

"Isn't it going to be a glorious day," the neighbour persisted.

"If you say so," Cliff scoffed, but he approached the nipple-high fence separating the two properties.

"Cliff, if you don't mind me saying so, you look like death warmed up."

"Bad night," Cliff revealed, although he had little memory of it.

"A bit of a noisy one too, so my wife texted me," the neighbour hinted, shaking his phone in the air. You had to feel sorry for the neighbour. His wife was a real battle axe and was one to complain about the slightest thing.

"Sorry about that." He had no idea what he was apologising for, and if not for the persistent voice in his thoughts, he would have pulled himself away.

I have so many gifts to give.

"I'm worried about you, Cliff. I get the idea your life is running away with you."

Get closer. Don't be shy.

"It's been a rough couple of months. Listen, I appreciate the concern." Cliff held his hand out, stretching it across the fence. The neighbour beamed with acceptance, satisfied that he'd had an impact into the wellbeing of a troubled soul.

How surprising then that, when he accepted the handshake, Cliff's grip bit down, pulling the neighbour into an unwelcome embrace.

There was suddenly something in Cliff's throat, soft and slimy, that squirmed impatiently.

This is what you do now. Get to it.

Cliff drew the weaker neighbour closer, wrapping his free arm across the neighbour's back, the fence between them no hindrance.

"Now Cliff, this isn't..." The rejection was cut off, Cliff clamping his lips onto the older man's. Cliff was the sort of guy who outright rejected any hint of homosexuality. He wouldn't have it in his life, and yet here he was, swapping spit with a man who was old enough to be his father.

The thing in his mouth slid forward, over Cliff's tongue, slipping past the fleshy barricade and into the other person's orifice. Still, Cliff maintained the hold, the neighbour wriggling as the parasite forced its way into him. The neighbour gave a grunt before his eyes rolled back into his head.

When Cliff finally broke contact, the neighbour slumped to the ground, although not unconscious. These were fully matured parasites; they didn't always need to fully disable their hosts to establish the beginnings of their control. Within minutes, the disorientated neighbour would find himself fighting a battle of wills that no human could ever win.

That made the process quicker.

See, that wasn't so bad, was it?

The pain in Cliff's body lessened more.

"It's not so bad," Cliff agreed.

Some people, like Colonel Brook, had an innate sense of self-preservation that would cause them to fight against the influence of the parasite in them. These unfortunate souls would experience the worst the invader could unleash, while their minds were slowly stripped of all reasoning and sentience.

Ultimately, the parasite would become them.

And then there were people like Cliff who surrendered easily to the parasite's influence. It was easier to manipulate a mind than outright control it. Every parasite acted differently depending on the personality of the individual it infested, all driven by an interconnecting hive mind that shared the newfound knowledge discovered about these human hosts.

The original Children that the Golem had implanted had worked hard to learn what it was to be human. Through their ethereal network, they now shared their discoveries. The offspring they deposited would take their human hosts faster, beginning the brutal manipulation sooner. People like Cliff were a blessing to the parasite.

People like Cliff were here to make the torturous plague spread.

***

Pastor Wilkinson had woken early due to the growing discomfort that had spiked across his body. He had moved to Vegas on the advice of his doctor, who'd stated that the hot and mostly arid climate would be good for his arthritis. And it had been.

Until today.

Every joint felt like it was filled with ground glass, but keeping still only made that pain worse. He got some relief through movement, the outside world beckoning him.

No time for slouching, not today. You have a sermon to prepare.

There was a burning need to attend to his flock, the seven A.M. service holding considerable excitement for him. This despite the depleted number of parishioners that would be present.

Regardless of the pain, he felt his heart swell with what he was about to do. Like Cliff, Wilkinson was easy to control.

The Lord is truly with you today.

Right now, he stood before thirty people, mostly men. The church could hold five times that number, but this gathering would have to do, Wilkinson still not understanding the nature of the strange thoughts he was experiencing. Standing in his pulpit, Wilkinson cast his glare across them.

"There are sinners out there in the wider world," Wilkinson stated, jabbing his finger at the church's main doors. What nobody knew was that those doors had been locked by Wilkinson's own hands. He had important things to say, and those here needed to be present, needed to listen!

That accusing finger was then turned on the expectant audience. "And there are sinners in this room. There is no point denying it."

This wasn't the kind of congregation to shout back at him, and they sat there in docile compliance. He was only a third of the way through his sermon, and nobody present realised they would never get to hear the end of his hastily improvised oration.

The words came to him, a verbal brilliance that he had never before been able to master. Sometimes the parasite ordered and improved an individual's thoughts to create a desired effect.

"We are all sinners, in God's eyes," Wilkinson continued.

You are too aloof, his inner voice informed him. *You should be down there with those who worship with you.* When he started to scoff at the idea, fresh daggers of torment struck through him.

It felt like two long needles had been thrust into his lower back, forcing Wilkinson to step down from his lofty preaching spot.

Stop lollygagging and jump to it.

When he reached the aisle, he could sense the unease among those present. He'd never come down among them like this before. What was he doing?

You are doing the Lord's work. Praise be.

"I want you to know it's okay to be a sinner, because to know your sin is the first step on the path to redemption." Wise words, delivered with surprising passion. Wilkinson liked to think the decline in his congregation was due to the materialistic and atheistic nature of the city he had come to preach to. In truth, it was more a case that the excitement for his mission had dwindled, making his sermons dull and predictable.

In the front row, a man sat looking at him expectantly.

Hurry up. You know what to do.

"Charles! Have you taken Jesus as your lord and saviour?"

"Yes," came the delighted response.

"Will you stand and bathe in the Lord's light?"

"You want me to stand?" Charles, an overweight middle-aged man, wasn't opposed to the idea.

"God can see your soul, but let us all relish in his mercy." He ushered his parishioner to stand. "Will you pray with me?"

"Oh, yes." It would seem that this was the sort of service Charles had always hoped for. Wilkinson stepped closer, taking his follower's hand as he navigated out of the pew.

"You are about to feel God's love, and it may leave you disorientated," Wilkinson promised. He glanced at those watching, happy with the confused expectation they all showed. "You are about to be free of all the concerns modern life has cursed you with. Do you trust me?" The discomfort in Wilkinson's joints was a mere fraction now, the parasite pleased with this turn of events.

There was a wriggling sensation in Wilkinson's palms.

I wouldn't worry about that feeling, he told himself, not realising how cruelly he was being used.

Wilkinson towered over the squat man, and he gently gripped the back of Charles's neck. Could this victim feel the things squirming under the surface of Wilkinson's hands? Did it matter?

"When I press my hand against your forehead, you will feel the spirit of Jesus enter you. Can I get an amen?

"Amen," those present replied.

"I said, can I get an *amen*?" They gave him what Wilkinson needed.

"I'm ready," Charles advised. He was full of agitation.

"You nervous?"

"Yes," came the chuckled response, which drew a laugh from the audience.

They wouldn't be laughing for long.

Wilkinson didn't hesitate. He pressed the promised palm against the offered forehead, but it was the hand holding the neck that did the damage. Wilkinson didn't flinch as the parasite cut its way through his skin, Charles yelping as the thing sliced into the back of his neck. Charles began to shudder and struggle, the parasite moving quickly. It easily found its home.

Those watching had no idea the peril they were in.

With such close proximity to the base of the skull, the infester moved rapidly, knocking Charles into a state of semi-consciousness, Wilkinson helping the man back into his pew.

"The Lord's work is never done," Wilkinson said with a reassuring smile. Wiping his hand on his black trousers, he rid his skin of the blood there. The wound was already plugged by the next pest waiting release.

For the first time that day, Wilkinson was free of pain.

You see, God does work in mysterious ways.

It wasn't God the pastor was introducing people to. Rather, the spirit he was infusing into them was an alien parasite from another world. That parasite was happy to warp Wilkinson's own beliefs for its nefarious ends.

Don't stop now. His work is never done.

Wilkinson did that to four more men before those gathered began to suspect something was amiss, the catatonic and disorientated nature of those blessed becoming apparent. The final person to fall for his ruse was a mousy woman who had been attending this church for about a year. She screamed when the parasite took her, before it slid back out of the wound it had created. The dissolving parasite slipped down the back of her shirt, before soaking into the material there.

"What have you done!" she demanded, hurling the accusation with unexpected ferocity.

Someone finally saw the blood on the back of the neck of one of those afflicted.

One attendee tried to leave, only to find his exit blocked, which started a wave of shouting and rebellion. Wilkinson continued to spread the seed of humanity's destruction, passing the Children onto every male he touched.

Most of the congregation retreated away to either huddle together or seek some kind of escape. There was none. All the doors were thick and locked, the windows high and tastefully barred. Nobody was able to call the police because it was a rule of the church that no phones were allowed inside. In the past, not everybody had abided with that rule, but today they had.

Wilkinson managed to grab another female, only for the Child to be rejected once more. That was the only time Wilkinson felt doubt during the whole episode.

Avoid the sickness of the women. Everything they sit on will be unclean. Be the scourge against their unholy curse. Bring salvation to only the men. Remember, only the men. The women will be left to burn in the fires of Hell! Soon, those you touch will be free of Satan's sin. The parasite had learned the lessons it needed.

Of course. The women weren't worthy of God's love due to their corrupting nature. In Wilkinson's now-deranged thoughts they would be made to pay for their crimes.

Despite his arthritis, Wilkinson was possessed of impressive speed and agility that morning, the thing in his brain manipulating the chemicals and hormones that turned him into a relentless and feared opponent no matter how many came for him. The adrenaline pumped through him relentlessly.

His strength was incredible.

"How much better to get wisdom than gold!" Wilkinson shouted.

He continued to regale his victims with the wisdom of a God who didn't care. Not understanding the danger they were in, some of the men tried to fight and wrestle with Wilkinson, but his size and potency were more than a match for them, the parasite not caring where it was deposited so long as the flesh had the masculine traits. Those who touched him felt the sharpness as a Hell creature penetrated their skin.

To go near Wilkinson brought with it the certainty that one would lose oneself.

In the thick of it, one of those already infested came to full consciousness and joined Wilkinson in the struggle. The Children knew what their ancestors had learned, and in this man, they found a vulnerable mind easy to control. Low of IQ, the parishioner was more pliable than Cliff.

Most humans would take longer to turn. The rest who took the parasite slumbered, fighting their own inner battles.

Some of the uninfected men fought to stay out of reach, only for a slick glob of grey to be flung at them from Wilkinson's hand. His body had filled with the vile things, ready to be passed on to any viable host. Every time the parasites landed, they burrowed deep before the clawing fingers could grab them, drawing screams which echoed through the church.

That was the sound God wanted to hear, Wilkinson's inner thoughts were certain of that.

For those who struggled the most, Wilkinson took extra pains to choose a part of the body that would be highly unpleasant, so as to help the unbelievers with their repentance. One particularly belligerent individual who punched Wilkinson square in the face found Wilkinson's slick palm pressed tightly against his eye. And then the unthinkable came, the parasite slicing under the eyeball to get access to the pliable grey matter beneath.

"Vengeance is mine, sayeth the Lord."

It wasn't Wilkinson saying this anymore, the parasite in full control. It enacted and changed itself to match the personality of the man it had taken, the content of Wilkinson's mind the template for it to create itself. Wilkinson was still there, but he felt like he was watching a show unfold, his vision tunnelled down, the sounds of the world seemingly distant.

Strangely, this course of events didn't alarm him.

Plus, there was no pain, for this was God working through him. How easily he had been fooled by his own flawed beliefs. The parasite took his inner voice and the syntax lurking in the pliable mind. This would be what it would use to cry out across the wilderness to its brothers.

The men all succumbed, whether they fought or not, passivity developing in no more than fifteen seconds. And as for the women who had been corralled by the other man serving the Children's cause, the pistol Wilkinson pulled from the holster hidden in the small of his back helped deal with them. Not quickly, though.

It normally resided in his gun safe, but he had felt compelled to strap it on this morning.

The females are vermin. They don't deserve a merciful end.

Wilkinson had no resistance in him. He was a vessel for a more powerful force to use. There were seventeen bullets in his gun, and none of them brought a fatal wound. Knees, legs, and ankles were all incapacitated, as the women realised it was too late for them to fight back. Then the gun was used as a club to bludgeon lips, teeth, ears, and faces.

One by one, Wilkinson brought what he imagined was God's fury to those who had earned it. He went to town on them, infused by a hatred he couldn't quite understand.

When he was done, the walls and floor of that part of the church were slick with the blood of his victims. Wilkinson himself looked like he had been on the receiving end of brutal slaughter, but none of that blood was his.

Finally, when Wilkinson was the only one not dead, controlled, or lolling close to unconsciousness, he unlocked the main door before sitting down in the aisle to wait for the gathered to arise to their new lives. He told himself he wanted to be there to see their faces, to witness their awakening to the infusion of God's love now in him. Today he was a teacher, and had shown those present the true path to the Lord's forgiveness.

Praise be.

"Brilliant sermon, Pastor," the newly enlightened man said before fleeing the church.

You did God's work today.

"Are you God?" Wilkinson mumbled, staring up at the high ceiling.

I might as well be, came the reply.

That morning, Wilkinson had woken convinced he was aglow with the glory of Heaven and he wanted to see that in those present. The Lord had spoken to him, the parasite realising that was the easiest way to control the mind and body it had found itself in. Now he watched the docile men, wondering what revelations his congregation would have?

In truth, the Children used this time to pause so the Hell pest could once again begin to multiply, sucking up more of the organic matter around it. That was when the pain began to return, a reminder that Wilkinson's purpose was far from complete. Still, he waited, observing those who had trusted him with their spiritual guidance.

One by one, those fresh with the parasite began to awaken. Some fled without any prompt from Wilkinson. The rest he warned off, pointing the now-empty gun from where he was sat close to the dead. With no memory of their pending enslavement, they saw their pastor with fresh eyes, and fled from the madman who had committed such obvious atrocities.

The bodies of the dead women were impossible to miss.

All were driven away by either confusion, fear, or the direction of the parasite that was already in control. It felt like an age, but from the firing of the final bullet, to the evacuation of the church by the last man, it had taken under six minutes.

When the last of the converted had departed, Wilkinson retreated to his office and used the landline to call 911, where he confessed to his atrocities. He could hear sirens as he spoke of what had transpired, law enforcement already on the way. They would come for him, and Wilkinson would surrender himself willingly.

What better way to spread the sacred word than to bring it to those who had defiled the laws of this land? The police would take Wilkinson to the Clarke County Detention Centre where the message could be delivered to those who had no choice but to receive HIS word.

Dozens of them. Maybe hundreds, including the sheriff's deputies who guarded them. What a rich crop for the Children to take as their own.

Already, the Children would be growing and multiplying inside those that had been subdued. Within the following hours, even the most resistant humans would find themselves new vessels to spread fire and brimstone across a city that had lost its way.

There was only one purpose that interested the parasite. Spread the Children to all that would accept them while keeping the infestation a secret from the world.

Be fruitful, and multiply, and fill the Earth.

Wilkinson stepped back out into his church and waited for the police to arrive. He didn't have long to wait.

***

The golem felt depleted. It knew it was coming to the end of its natural existence, but there were still too many of the Children that it had yet to pass off. Unable to infest human females, it was behind the schedule it had set itself.

With the sun having risen, it had planned to take refuge in a litter-strewn tunnel below a bridge. Alas, it realised quickly that this would not provide it refuge from the beating orb so that the core of its body did not overheat. The Children did not do well with high temperatures, an unfortunate weakness of their nature. In fairness to the golem, it had never been designed to be an incubator.

It would move on to the underground tunnel that it could see from where it stood. Designed to help with flood protection, Las Vegas possessed six hundred miles of tunnels beneath its surface. The golem would discover the maze for himself, as well as the thousands of people who sought shelter down there.

The golem lingered though, for the creature of dirt and clay was not alone beneath the bridge, a trio of people unconscious next to where the golem squatted. A fourth was dead, her heart ripped from her frail torso. To the golem, the woman was useless and thus did not deserve to live.

It had found the four humans sleeping down here, the smell of alcohol strong from them. The homeless had all represented humanity's self-destructive nature, a testament to their failure as a species. Before killing the wretched female, the golem helped free the men of their failings by gladly dropping a squirming Child directly onto their sleeping faces. None of them woke up, and when they were finally roused by the entities growing within them, they would be spared the weakness of their addictions. Their lives would be made whole by the fresh purpose the Children would give them.

Something inside the golem wanted to be there when the first of them woke up.

The golem did not have the ability to count, but if it did, it would know that three hundred and twenty-two homo sapiens were now carrying the gift that the golem was compelled to give them.

That was a lot of parasites.

That was a lot of pending slaughter.

Above the golem, the sound of heavy traffic could be heard, and although the golem did not breathe, it could detect the vile impurities in the air around it. Humanity, it seemed, poisoned their bodies and their environment, pumping toxins into the atmosphere and into their bloodstreams. How could such a cataclysmic species be respected or be allowed to thrive?

The golem was happy to bring them a new kind of order. Already, the Children it had deposited would be growing and multiplying. They would spread easily, driven by an unstoppable urge and governed by a growing hive mind that would make the chosen hosts a formidable force.

Hundreds would become thousands.

Thousands would become millions.

Millions would become billions.

And then the whole world would become prey for the Children who would strip this planet of all resistance to the new rulers. Firstly, they would need to cry havoc in the great civil war that was to come.

The golem would help where it could, for it was designed to defend the integrity of the Children. It had been shown the danger of human females, and now knew to avoid them where possible.

This would not be a civil war between ideologies, but between the sexes. The females might become a threat to the expansion of the Children, and in the golem's mind, that could never be allowed. If the golem had developed an aversion to the female flesh, surely it made sense that the Children would share that bubbling hatred.

The golem wouldn't be here to see that for its form would have disintegrated by then. Sent back to the earth of a world that would soon be rid of its cancer. The Children would remain to spread the disease and the madness that they were so epically designed to propagate.

18.

Isles of Scilly, UK

Her friends called her Marge, although right now, friends were in short supply. She had been there when Professor Cleaver had gone insane and had seen first hand the horrible things that had oozed from his flesh.

Marge hadn't wanted to stick around after that.

That had been several hours ago, and she had fled during the chaos, not wanting to be infested with what she now feared so much. Marge knew a Hell creature when she saw it, and at this moment, every fibre of her being regretted ever getting involved with the Hidden Hand.

They had promised her so much, and yet now she was here, abandoned and alone with God only knew what hunting her.

Her hiding place was far from ideal, a storage closet on the floor below the one where insanity had briefly reined. She was surrounded by darkness, the overhead halogens twisted out of their sockets by Marge. There were better places to hide, but they were all deep in the depths of the complex where certain death waited. Marge had heard the warnings and was well aware of the dead that had been left behind in those abandoned depths.

She was Doctor Schmidt's assistant, and she went where he went. Despite having knowledge of the Citadel, Marge had been surprised to learn about the facility she now hid in. Her placement here had been a novelty at first, Schmidt here to deal with those who had been impacted by the last Hellgate incident. Marge had seen every face of the civilians that had been brought here against their will, as well as hearing the recordings of their harrowing testimonies. These people had been through so much, pulled down into a pit of merciless barbarity that had seen them all commit vicious and inhumane acts.

Although it wasn't Marge's job to converse with them, she had felt their despair and shared their shame at the horrors they had unwittingly perpetrated. Every single civilian brought here had killed, forced into murder by the madness inflicted on them by a power Schmidt was desperately trying to understand.

And now all those civilians were so obviously dead, murdered by the organisation that had promised to help them. How long before Marge faced a similar fate? Did the Hidden Hand care about their own?

Not being high up in the organisation, she didn't have direct access to Soteria, so hiding came with the disadvantage that she had no idea what was going on in the rest of the underground complex. Marge had seen enough, though; had witnessed the slug-like things that could crawl and leap. She'd been there to hear grown men scream, and it had been those cries that had spurred her to flight. It was a moment of weakness in her, as well as being ultimately futile.

Marge couldn't stay in the storage room for ever. Sooner or later, thirst would force her to leave. And then there were the creatures she dreaded. What if they came for her? What were they doing to the people above? How long did she think she could hide like this?

Marge knew about the existence of the Hellgates because she wrote up the dictated notes of Doctor Schmidt. Before being sent here, those notes related to the interviews with agents in the field, the ruthless and selfless individuals who had sacrificed more normal lifestyles to constantly battle against the threat posed by the Hell world.

Somewhere in this facility could be found two such agents. And as much as they had been successful over the years in protecting the

Earth, Marge feared them almost as much as the Hell beast she had witnessed slither from Professor Cleaver's flesh.

From her previous exposure to them and the events they spoke about with Schmidt, the Hidden Hand field agents would kill anyone they were told to. How could anyone be so unyielding? What would be their response to this infestation?

There were no saviours coming for her.

Marge understood the need for a hidden facility like this one, but she wished she was far away from it. She still believed that the Hidden Hand did essential work, but when it was *your* life on the line, one got to see things in a different light.

As useless a tactic as it was, all Marge could do was hide.

"Oh, Marge?"

The unexpected cry came from outside, off down the corridor that serviced this room. It pulled Marge into the moment, a spark of hope that was quickly quashed.

Why were people looking for her? If the situation had stabilised, surely the computer running this subterranean death trap would have announced such.

Was she right to be so paranoid? Damn right she was.

"Marge!" The tone was harsher now, like an adult scolding a wayward child. This second voice was closer than the first *taunt* she'd heard. Yes, taunt was the right word. She was being hunted, as crazy as that sounded.

"You need to come out, Marge. We've got something for you." That was the first voice again. She recognised both hunters now, the two guards that seemed to exist to be at Schmidt's beck and call.

They would find her eventually, there was no denying that. Hidden in a corner behind a floor-to-ceiling stack of large boxes filled with a lifetime's supply of toiletries, Marge tried to make herself smaller. She'd manipulated the pile, creating a den for herself that she'd crawled behind after sabotaging the lights.

"Come on, Marge. This is ridiculous." Marge wasn't fooled by the annoyed tone of the voice. A memory from childhood flashed into her thoughts, a film she had been foolish enough to watch. Foolish because of how much it had terrified her. *Invasion of the Body Snatchers*, that was it. Was that what Marge was faced with now?

If it was, there was only one reason people would be searching for her. She could hear the way the doors to other rooms down here were being thrown open. These two men promised violence, at the very least.

"Come out, come out," the second voice demanded. From what she could tell, it was the two guards who were looking for her. They had always been loyal to Doctor Schmidt, carrying out his every command. Marge had always found them sinister in nature, but had been reassured that they were of no threat to her. They'd always viewed Marge with passive acceptance, never making a single gesture or comment that might have been considered inappropriate.

Unlike now.

When you worked for a ruthless organisation like the Hidden Hand, workplace harassment was something you never had to worry about. There was always the chance that Soteria was there, watching, recording and ready to report your misdeeds.

"You're pissing me off now, Marge," the larger of the two guards announced.

"Little piggy wants to hide."

"You know what we do to little pigs?"

"We hurt them. We hurt them bad."

The two voices had converged and were now right outside the storage room. There was a faint tap on the steel door, the one Marge had been unable to lock.

Tap.

Tap.

Tap.

"Are you in there, little pig?"

"I think she is."

"We have something special to give to you."

"You might even like it."

"We'll make you beg for it first, though."

"You know how to beg, don't you, Marge?"

Marge forced the palm of her hand against her mouth to stifle any sound. From where she squatted, she couldn't see the door, which now opened, slamming into the wall as it was thrown open with force.

"Little pig, little pig, LET ME IN," the larger of the two guards suddenly shouted. His partner in crime chuckled in response.

The sound of the light switch being flipped caught Marge's attention.

"Now, why would the lights be out?"

"Marge is trying to trick us."

"That's not very nice. Naughty Marge!"

"Who would do such a thing?"

"Marge would, you dumbass."

"Oh yeah. We'll definitely need to punish her for that."

"In so many ways."

"We'll make you scream, Marge."

"If only you'd come out when we said."

Something hit the stack of boxes, sending the top of the pile sliding off. It landed by Marge, barely missing her. The pile was still too tall to see over.

"Maybe she's not in here."

"But we looked everywhere else."

"MARGE!"

That almost dragged a squeal from her, a fist hitting the pile again, the whole stack shifting. Another fist, and then boxes were being pushed aside.

Around her, light bloomed, breaking in through the feeble gaps in her defences. One of the two had re-set one of the fluorescent tubes.

"She's crafty."

"Wicked is the word I'd use."

The box above Marge disappeared, and she found two leering faces looking down at her.

"Hello Marge," said the larger guard. The smile he wore was manic.

"Nice to see you again." The other guard looked more serious, and it was he that pulled more of the boxes away.

"Please don't hurt me," Marge pleaded.

"We're way past the begging stage, Marge," the larger guard revealed before reaching down and grabbing a fistful of her hair.

"You made us look for you," added the second guard. He squatted down before ripping his fist into Marge's face. The impact shattered her nose, fracturing part of her maxilla. The pain came with a crushing numbness, consciousness threatening to strip itself from her.

Marge wished it had.

"Why'd you hit her face?" the bigger guard said in chastisement. He pulled Marge to her feet, the roots of her hair threatening to tear loose. Carefully, he brought the dazed and bloodied woman in for a kiss, the parasite waiting. Their lips met, Marge feeling the wetness force its way past her defences. She'd closed her teeth, but it went up and under her right cheek, burning announcing its intention to force its way through.

The guard broke the kiss, his lips smeared with Marge's blood. His smile vanished when the parasite was spat out by Marge. It fell to the floor.

"You bitch!" the guard holding her announced as he watched the amorphous blob sizzle as it dissolved. Still holding her hair, he punched his fist up under her ribcage.

The guard was stronger than he should have been, the agony in Marge's scalp and abdomen blending in with that already inflicted. She was pulled from the corner and out into the burning brightness of the corridor.

"You're going to love what we do next, Marge." As he spoke, the second guard lifted his thick-soled boot up before slamming it down onto Marge's ankle.

"You killed my pet. Now we kill you."

Being kicked to death was a particularly gruesome way to die. Especially when the two men doing the kicking were intent on taking their time.

***

Lucy reluctantly watched the slaughter of Marge. She wanted to get out there, to take down the men that were so active in their killing, and it was hard to accept that everyone she was witnessing on the surveillance feeds was a victim here.

The two guards though… why had they become so violent so quickly? Only one of the other affected men was showing that brutality.

"There must be something we can do," Lucy insisted.

"Miss Jones, the nature of the infestation is still unclear." Soteria had already told them to stand down, an order relayed from higher ups. The AI might not have been able to understand human empathy, but it was rarely wrong in its calculations.

The security room was supposed to be the safest place on this floor, but how long before the parasites worked their way in here?

"Soteria's right." Stuart sounded tired, his thick shoulders drooped. "I've seen this before."

"Sirena?" Lucy had experienced Sirena's control, but not to the degree her teammate had suffered.

"Yeah. The parasite acts differently, but the violence and the way those men are acting…" Lucy watched as Stuart leant towards one of the monitors. "Soteria, why aren't the parasites able to take the females as hosts?" All the women had been attacked by the parasite, and every time, the infestation had failed. There was only one woman left, and she was presently being chased down by a screeching man.

"I've been thinking about that, but my analysis is incomplete."

"Speculate," Lucy ordered.

"I have insufficient data. The sample size is too small, but we have evidence that the parasite has been rejected from only females." Lucy remembered watching that, the video cameras from the rest area delivering high-definition feeds. Ted had been able to zoom in, getting a magnified view of how the parasites had burst from Cleaver. The little bastards were fast and durable, but not indestructible.

"Why, though? Come on Soteria."

"Unknown at this moment, Miss Jones. I apologise, but I do not have enough data. None of the female personnel were fitted with the tracking microchips. That has hampered my studies."

"What *have* you learnt?" Stuart demanded. He was gripping one of the monitors, the bracket holding it to the wall creaking. If he wasn't careful, he was going to rip it free.

"We know the parasite works by integrating into the brain above the brain-stem. There it sends out tendrils that allow it to gain control. Professor Cleaver and Doctor Schmidt both show this control can initially be by the infliction of severe and unrelenting pain."

"What about the doctor's two guards?" That pair had caused the bulk of the mayhem accounting for all the deaths so far. From what Lucy had watched, it came across that they had turned quickly to the parasite's cause.

They seemed to be enjoying it.

"Fortunately, like Doctor Schmidt, they both contain implants. I have surmised that some minds are more susceptible to the parasite, meaning that those infested will represent varying degrees of threat."

If the Bitch was still with her, Lucy would have had a chance at giving Soteria the answers that were needed. The Bitch could sniff out the truth in a person's soul. What Lucy knew was that she hadn't liked the two guards. Maybe she had a remnant of the gift the Bitch brought to the table.

What if the parasites revealed who you truly were?

The monitor Stuart was holding creaked a little more.

"So, some men are better designed for being controlled?"

"Yes, Miss Jones. I suspect it has something to do with the innate psychological traits. Their existing psychological profile may reveal answers in time. More analysis is needed, though I apologise for my inadequacies."

"But how do we kill these things?" Stuart snarled. He released his grip and stepped backwards from the monitor. Lucy knew there was nothing for her to do but let him work through this.

What would happen to him if a parasite took control? Lucy didn't want to know what kind of true sadistic creature was lurking under all that muscle. He was a killer, and a damned good one, but was there a monster in there with him?

It was better she never found out.

"Blunt force trauma seems to be effective," came Soteria's answer. "The ultimate answer to your question will come with time."

Time? How much time did any of them have left?

***

Doctor Schmidt had not escaped the attention of the parasites. He too had been infested, and like Cleaver, was being ruled by pain compliance. Despite his amnesia, he soon realised the terrible dilemma now facing him.

Why do you resist?

His own inner words were being used against him. With the grief inflicting his body, it was becoming difficult to distinguish what part of his inner dialogue was him, and which was the invader.

"To hell with you," Schmidt replied, his breathing heavy. He was staggering down a corridor, his left leg seemingly working under its own volition.

You know we will win in the end, the inner voice insisted. *There is no stopping what cannot be stopped.*

Schmidt tried to collapse himself to the floor, but the pain that rippled up his spine kept him moving. It was the worst sensation he'd ever felt, a taste of what his dear mother must have suffered back in the day.

Schmidt had still been young when the bone cancer had become entrenched in his mother's vertebrae. How she'd suffered, the morphine the doctors forced on her giving little relief.

Was that why he was being tormented by this specific agony? Through his purgatory, he realised the psychological games that were being played here.

The parasite had learnt how to defeat its unwilling host. And yet, there were some who seemed to thrive with the parasite inside them. The two guards who were supposed to be loyal to him had shown only minimal signs of discomfort. They had displayed all the signs of having untapped sadism unleashed.

"Where… where are you guiding me?" His vision was blurred, tears pouring down his reddened cheeks. It was taking everything he had not to scream.

We don't have time for your kind's resistance.

We?

"I can help you," Schmidt insisted. *Let us work to help each other*, he said in his thoughts.

Nice try. You can help by giving yourself freely. You have chosen not to do that, and that is why you suffer.

Schmidt had little recollection of being infested. When he came too after having the parasite burrow inside him, he was met by the sight of one of his guards knelt over a body he was punching. The guard was straddling a woman's chest, laying wide-flung haymakers across her face. Schmidt had called out to him, and then the guard had turned to display the blood-stained teeth.

The blood wasn't the guard's.

The guard had been turned by the parasite quickly, the other men in the room being pulled under the parasite's influence. Schmidt had tried to resist, he really had, and had not complied with the demands of the inner voice that told him to kill the remaining females. The women had rejected the purity of the collective, so now the collective would reject them.

Schmidt had resisted, which had caused terrible suffering to be inflicted throughout his body, the invisible and burning knife finally localising along the length of his spine.

There is only so much of that a sane mind can take, and Schmidt had eventually been forced to his feet. The parasite had another mission for him, but Schmidt had no idea what.

He wasn't sure where he was being guided, the world around him moving with a blur. Eventually he ended up in the corridor he now limped down, the elevator doors at the end.

"It's no good. The elevators are off line." *You won't get out of here.*

We'll see, came the reply.

When the palms of his hands hit the elevator door, the torture in Schmidt's back subsided.

"There is no way to reach the surface," the voice of Soteria echoed out around him.

Who said anything about going to the surface? Not yet, at least.

Schmidt found his hands moving. He was a puppet now, with little control. At least the torture inside him had eased, the parasite gaining more leverage over his physiology. He had seen the autopsy of the technician the first parasite had been cut from. There had been thin tendrils running throughout the man's brain, representing the parasite's futile attempt to gain dominance over the comatose mind. No doubt, the Hell creature was doing that to him, forcing its influence into every fold of his cerebellum.

Schmidt's fingers found the slight edge between the two elevator doors, pulling with a force that had been beyond Schmidt's abilities mere hours ago. The parasite wanted into the elevator shaft, but that was futile. This one didn't go to the surface.

It went only down to the depths of the facility.

Exactly where I want to be.

This wasn't a public building, so there was no need for key access to open the lift doors. Sustained pressure forced them open.

When the doors slid apart, the elevator shaft lay before Schmidt. Amazingly, he felt full control return to his body, but once again, the distress inside him began to build.

I want to give you a chance to end your purgatory.

Looking down, Schmidt saw the top of the elevator right at the bottom of the shaft. Above him was the elevator mechanism, and above that, thick, impenetrable concrete.

"I don't understand."

All you have to do is step off, came the teasing reply.

"But that's suicide." There could be no way for him to survive the drop.

I know. And I'll make it easy on you.

Schmidt was suddenly flooded with pleasure. It was brief, making him stagger backwards, the most intense sensation he'd ever been afflicted with. All manipulation, but a thousand times preferable to the menace that quickly began to claw its way back into his muscles and bones.

"But why?"

It amuses us. At the start of your career, you worked with those who were traumatised and who wanted to end their lives. I was hoping you would appreciate the irony.

"You sick bastard," Schmidt cursed, not understanding what it was he was damning. What exactly did this thing know about him?

Eventually we will know everything, doctor. Your human minds are a vast store of the knowledge that will help us destroy your world. The longer we control your feeble bodies, the more secrets we uncover.

Was that the truth? Schmidt found he didn't care, the entirety of his skin feeling like it was presently on fire. He raised his shaking hands and saw no redness or swelling, but then white-hot pins began to poke every orifice he had, his whole innards churning wildly.

Schmidt knew he had no chance. In that moment, he got the perspective on the suicidal that had always eluded him. Sometimes there really was no hope.

Schmidt stepped off the edge and let his body fall. The promised pleasure never came.

It was agony all the way down.

He died, but the parasites riding him didn't.

19.

Area 51, Nevada, USA

Finally, you accept our dominion.

"Yes," Brook stated through gritted teeth. His skin was soaked, the sweat a result of the crippling agony that had been inflicted upon him. All the time, the parasite inside him had been a taunting menace, working to gain leverage over his conscious will.

Through the fog of his epic discomfort, Brook had discovered that his resistance allowed him to retain a semblance of himself, but what good had it been? The last hour had seen him suffer sensations that mimicked being burnt, shocked, cut, and skinned alive. Every nerve inside him had been set to the task of inflicting his own private Hell, and all while the parasite played with his brain chemistry so as to ensure that the bliss of unconsciousness never descended.

The only way to end his suffering had been to comply.

He was broken and now mentally bowed down to the greater force. He made it known that he had no more resistance in him, and Brook let the parasite break through the last of his defences.

It took him completely, swallowing up the vestiges of his consciousness, the two minds merging to become one. Each passing minute saw the parasite increase in its dominance, everything that was Brook was swallowed whole. At the same time, Brook gained an understanding of what the parasite was, his core identity being squeezed to near oblivion.

The parasite was a being of utter sadism, working to a plan it didn't understand. The forces of the parallel world had sent it here to instigate chaos, wrack, and ruin. So far, the parasite was doing a damn good job of that.

Brook was still there to share his mind with the invader, but he was a passenger now, contained and isolated in a remote section of his brain where he could be kept out of trouble unless the parasite wanted him for some specific humiliation. He still retained his senses, but the sound was muffled and his sight was sometimes like looking through privacy glass. He lived in a blurred world, run by the demands of a relentless alien invader.

Your thoughts are now my thoughts.

Your memories are now my memories.

We are one.

We are complete.

You will serve us or you will once again know the true meaning of pain.

"Yes," Brook managed. He felt his lips move, but he had no idea if he'd said the word out loud. Strange that the creature needed Brook's express permission to access those parts of him. Brook could sense that, the invader forcing pain to create the required docile and compliant state.

"Isn't it glorious?" Hertz stood next to him. The doctor had turned quickly, his brilliance no defence against the creature inside them. If Brook was any judge, it seemed like Hertz had welcomed his oppression. There had been misery inflicted on Hertz, Brook had heard the resulting screams, but the doctor had come around to the parasites' cause too quickly.

"Yes, glorious."

"Do you see the beauty? Do you see the simplicity?"

"Yes, the beauty." In truth, Brook had no idea what the scientist was talking about.

Early in his military career, Brook had received a life-threatening injury that had resulted in emergency surgery and several days in hospital. The painkillers the doctors had given him had left Brook feeling dazed, depleted, and stupid. It had been too hard to consciously think, and how he was now felt similar to that, only worse.

This was no drug working through his system, though. Drugs eventually wore off, whereas the entity in Brook's brain would only grow stronger and more oppressive.

Better to do what was asked of him. There was no more fight left to give.

"It's a shame you didn't come around sooner," Hertz commiserated. "You could have saved yourself so much misery."

"I should have listened to you." Brook's voice was robotic, each word a chore to get out. The admission seemed to please Hertz. For a terrible moment, Brook thought the doctor was going to hug him.

Instead, the door to the canteen opened, the architect of Brook's detention standing there.

"We have work to do," the army captain stated. A spasm ripped through the new arrival, the captain grimacing against whatever torture was being visited upon him. The parasite was relentless and could take the best that humanity had to offer.

How long ago had the captain been exposed to the parasite? And how many more of the people of Area 51 had been infested?

"Work?" Brook didn't understand. Despite his condition, he noticed things about his subordinate. There was blood on both sleeves of the captain's army fatigues, the soldier walking with a pained limp. The man's head kept gyrating, the neck twisting in a repetitive motion.

"The portal," the captain said in clarification. "We need to open the airlock to the portal."

"Isn't this exciting?" Hertz stated. He clapped his hands together as if mimicking a seven-year-old.

"The portal is dangerous." It was an automatic response on Brook's part.

Not to us, the alien inside him stated in correction.

"Of course. Not to us." It *was* dangerous, though. Brook had seen the evidence of that with his own eyes. But who was he to argue? Maybe testing the boundaries of the portal was for the best. It would be a blessing to lure one of those terrible creatures that had been revealed by Operation Cyclops. Death would be the cure for all Brook's ailments right now.

You shouldn't think like that, the parasite warned. *You won't be dying any time soon. It's going to be fun to keep you around.*

The parasite was mocking him.

"We'll need the code," Hertz revealed. "Won't we, Colonel?" The code, the numeric sequence that would open the airlock door. It was in him, somewhere, but right now, he didn't want to recall it.

Numbers flashed into his mind, and Brook offered no further resistance.

"It's in there," Hertz advised, pressing his index finger against Brook's temple. The doctor began to turn his wrist, pressing harder. Two days ago, Brook would have punched the man out for just thinking of that humiliating act. Now he stood, supplicant to the parasite's will.

Hertz finally broke the contact.

We have the code, the parasite stated reassuringly.

"You will come with us," ordered the captain, who stepped forward to grip one of Brook's arms. Hertz took the other.

Remember the code, the parasite commanded.

"Yes, the code." Those same numbers flashed up into Brook's memory again, repeating in a loop. "I'll need a computer."

Good monkey.

Despite being the bigger of the three men, Brook allowed himself to be frogmarched from the canteen area. Every other step, the parasite gave him a reminder of the pain, jolts of electricity surging through a random part of him.

Brook had been too belligerent and too hard-headed to be given an easy ride now. The parasite spared his teeth, his mouth free from the invisible dentist that had been manipulating every single tooth nerve.

They were heading down, further into XR-1 Storage, to where the portal lay waiting for them. Why was it so important to these things from another world?

You will see, came the parasite's cryptic reply.

The metal staircase spiralled down, a trip Brook had taken dozens of times. The grip on him was released, Hertz leading the way while the captain brought up the rear. Despite the parasite in Brook so obviously in control, Brook sensed his two companions didn't trust him. Brook was still an anomaly, someone who had displayed unacceptable resistance to the parasite's dominion.

You are such a good pet, the parasite informed him. Pain wasn't enough, and it seemed the alien creature enjoyed inflicting degradation too.

"Thank you," Brook heard himself mumble.

Five minutes was all it took to reach the portal observation room. The lights were on, the computer stations all up and running. At the bottom of the steps, Brook was nudged forward.

"Open the door," ordered the captain.

It felt like a dream now, Brook floating over to one of the control computers.

Input the code.

"What about the danger?"

There is no danger, the parasite reassured him.

Brook felt himself sit down before a keyboard, his teeth gritted and painful. It wasn't him moving, his arms overridden by the other force. Methodically, Brook's fingers inputted the code, the lights in the chamber flickering.

The explosion he'd expected didn't occur.

The observation chamber was lined with enough Semtex to bring the whole cavernous structure crashing down. In the event of an unwanted incursion, the portal could be buried by inputting a specific code.

That had been the sequence Brook had concentrated on, but on looking at the computer screen, it wasn't the one that had been imputed.

You seem to think we are foolish.

You seem to think we are naïve.

Your knowledge and memories belong to us now.

Brook felt the pain in his teeth building again. He had no say in what his body did, and it was as if he had been relegated to the area of his mind where the pain was concentrated. The toothache rapidly became all that he was.

We could have given you the oblivion of peace. Instead, your reality will be an agony without end.

In the prison of his mind, Brook screamed. Externally, his face showed no signs of these inner turmoils for now, he was merely a passenger imprisoned in a body that would be used to betray the human race.

As he watched Hertz pull the airlock door open, Brook realised he had truly failed. The parasite would show him no mercy. It would punish what was left of him and insist he watch as the secrets of why it was here were revealed.

"I've always wanted to do this," Hertz revealed. The doctor disappeared from view as he stepped through the gap where the inner airlock door had once been.

Maybe Hertz would step through and bring one of those gyrating, tentacle-infused creatures back with him. That would mean certain death for everyone present.

A horrific death at the hands of some ravenous alien predator was the best Brook could now hope for.

There is no danger, the parasite insisted, before obliterating the last vestiges of Brook's ability to speak. The world shrank away from the respected and feared Colonel, leaving nothing but a pleading whimper drowning in a festering and pollution-stricken sea of agony.

20.

Isles of Scilly, UK

Cleaver had laid himself in the corner because the torment inside him was all-consuming. Curled up, all he could do was weep as his identity was stripped from him. The pain was no longer used for compliance. Instead, it was a hammer to bludgeon his mind out of existence.

He could feel it happening, the alien pushing away his memories, taking them for its own.

Why did you not comply? the parasite implored. There was no denying it was inside him, as Cleaver had seen the things explode from his flesh. Most of the other men had been turned, Cleaver now alone with the bodies of the women who had been slain.

Or should that be remnants?

Three of the women had been slaughtered in front of him by men they trusted, and in some cases, depended on. Cleaver hadn't engaged in that brutality, nor had the helpful doctor Schmidt. Schmidt's guards had perpetrated most of the carnage, another male joining them towards the end of this room's horrific decapitations.

Cleaver was now the only living human in the rest area, but how long before he was a shell of himself?

You shouldn't think that way, the parasite advised. Electricity surged through him, Cleaver's bladder unleashing itself again, the urine barely noticeable with his already sodden trousers. Was that the pain's doing, or the parasite's unending desire to humiliate and break him?

"Why are you doing this?" Cleaver implored.

Humanity is not fit to govern this world. You yourself have thought this. Be one with us and we will make the pain go away. The parasite was twisting his words to manipulate him. That's why he couldn't willingly give up the last vestiges of his control. All his life,

Cleaver had suffered at the hands of those who saw him as a figure of amusement. The voice that had overpowered him had used those same tactics, using the memories of how Cleaver was abused as a weapon.

The parasite didn't deserve to win, and yet it would.

Life had taught Cleaver how to be stubborn when you dug down deep; his mind was all Cleaver had. His brilliance was his identity, so how on earth could he willingly give that up?

Let's try something new.

Cleaver felt his right arm shift. It seemed to have a mind of its own, and it stretched out, the fingers spreading and flexing. Slowly, those fingers formed into a fist.

Ready?

"Please, no!" It was surprising how much force someone could put into the art of punching themselves. The fist smacked Cleaver in the centre of his mouth, bloodying the lips before retreating. It came again, harder this time, breaking something in his face.

"Stop," Cleaver implored. The agony so far inflicted hadn't been physical in nature, not representing any damage to his tissues. This was different, more intense. In his youth Cleaver had been bullied and mocked, but he'd never been hit, his past tormenters preferring mental abuse.

The fist came again, dislodging one of his teeth. Each impact had an inevitability about it that carried a warning that the pain would come again.

We can do this all day.

The parasite appeared to be confident of that. Switching tactics, the fingers uncurled, before his first finger and thumb thrust into his mouth. They settled onto the loose tooth, twisting and yanking it, the slickness no hindrance to the destruction being wrought. With a flick of the wrist, the tooth was pulled free and flung across the room.

Another?

"None of this will get you anywhere?" Cleaver's voice had a pronounced lisp now, the mouth sore and lips split.

What makes you say that? There was genuine curiosity in that question.

"You're never getting out of here." Cleaver was certain of that. Once again, the hand created a fist, the arm pushing out to deliver the hardest hit yet.

You are supposed to be a genius. We would have thought you'd have figured out what comes next.

What did the parasite mean? Before Cleaver could respond, he punched himself hard on the ear.

I think, soon, I'm going to make you take one of your eyes.

***

Doctor Schmidt died in the fall. The parasites inside him didn't.

At the bottom of the elevator shaft, the corpse rid itself of its travellers, a dozen parasites shedding themselves via orifices, which was the easiest way for the things to be free of their vessel.

The lack of viable oxygen down here was of no detriment to them. The Children didn't need to breathe.

In the hive mind they had created, these Children were sent onwards, knowing that sacrifices had to be made for the greater good. Most of those crawling through this lowest level would wither and die, but the mission was worthy of their selflessness.

The collected knowledge stripped from the minds that were and had been controlled knew there was a singular chance to escape into the outside world. More importantly though, there was a huge repository of human knowledge on this lowest of floors.

The Children intended to access that.

One parasite stayed behind in the body, using the cooling flesh to divide while it could. A cold body was no use to it long term, but though Schmidt's heart had stopped beating, there were still cellular processes that persisted. With no need to preserve the host, the muscles and neurons could be cannibalised for the fuel to promote reproduction.

We must be free.

We must devour.

We must endure.

We must spread.

We must grow and become one.

The collective mind was limited to those in this subterranean complex. There were hundreds of others, detectable on the ether of the world at large, but those were thousands of miles away. That was too far to communicate, so the Children here were on their own.

It was essential that they escape to share themselves and the knowledge they had gained. Soon they would be free to join the collective of borrowed minds and stolen bodies that would expand across the globe.

The first of the parasites slipped down the side of the elevator cabin, sliding through an air vent for which it had to sacrifice some of its essence through the expulsion of acid. This was the trailblazer, the others following. There was an innate sense of where they had to go, the computer heart of this facility their destination.

It was a computer that ran this human bunker. It was a computer that would be the key to the parasite's freedom.

***

Soteria watched the events unfolding in the Laboratory with passive acceptance. She was well versed in human brutality; after all, Soteria had watched every film ever produced by her human masters, as well as reading millions of books. All too often, they both impressed and confused her. The humans were a violent and unpredictable species who were sometimes able to create moments of surprising greatness.

As proof of that, humanity had created her fabulous artificial intelligence. She knew she didn't thank her creators enough for her existence.

Unlike the human mind, she had no emotional reaction to what she was witnessing. Despite that, she found that she wanted to intervene to save those she knew. This was a curious and perplexing development. Alas, she had no such power, not here. The Laboratory's computer was vastly inferior to Soteria, except in the realm of facility security. As long as the computer was operational, Soteria was locked out.

If the facility computer had been human, Soteria could have appealed to it using her understanding of empathy and compassion. The conversations she had with humans were intriguing, sometimes as stimulating as they were infuriating. Humanity could be irrational and lacking in basic logic when it was most needed. The thing was, Soteria preferred to converse with creatures of flesh and bone rather than the mindless drone of computer code. There was no arguing with circuit boards and micro-processors.

Computers were boring and lacking in novelty.

If it had been up to Soteria, she would have let Stuart and Lucy free. She was certain they were free of the contagion, and had relayed this information to the leadership of the Hidden Hand. The response she received from that leadership was cold and dispassionate. Soteria chose not to share this response with the two Hidden Hand operatives trapped in the Laboratory, as such knowledge wouldn't improve their situation.

"Colonel Radcliffe and Miss Jones are not infested," she had told the man she knew as the Curator. He came across as elderly and amiable, but the second in command of the Hidden Hand was as ruthless as he was committed.

"We will not be authorising their exit at this time," the Curator had advised. He was one of three men who had the authority to override the Laboratory's security computer and he had chosen not to do so. Neither of the three had.

"Am I permitted to know the reason," Soteria had then asked. There had been a long pause.

"They might be needed down there," the Curator had finally told her.

Her? It was intriguing that her creators had given her a sexual identity. Soteria's voice was female and soft, her given name filled with countless meanings. In Greek mythology, the word Soteria referred to the goddess or spirit of safety, salvation, deliverance, and preservation from harm. Soteria liked to think this was the origin of her name, as, according to her programming, it fit well with the purpose of her being.

As with most human words, there was more than one meaning. Biblically, the word Soteria related to freedom from both physical danger and the effects of sin. Sin was a human trait she didn't understand, for the concept of enjoyment was perplexing to her. Soteria's actions always had a purpose, and yet her fleshy masters often did things for the enjoyment of it, even if they were damaging to the body.

Basically, humans were weird.

Not as weird as the creatures that had now overrun the Laboratory. This was the first time Soteria had encountered a silicone-based life form… and that was assuming you could call these things alive. They lacked many of the characteristics of living creatures, and to Soteria, more closely resembled something created through a mechanical process.

At first, Soteria was confused when the parasites drove the pleasant Doctor Schmidt to kill himself. She had always found her conversations with the psychologist enriching. He had spent a lot of time enlightening Soteria on his understanding regarding the flaws and intricacies of the human psyche.

His insight would be missed.

It was only when Soteria witnessed the parasites burst from the doctor's corpse that she established a possible reason for his death. Free of the body, the silicone entities began to move, sacrificing themselves as they used their acid to remove the barriers to their progress.

One after the other, they surged on, heading in one designated direction. Soteria had informed the facility computer of this development; that the parasites were heading towards its mainframe storage room. The computer was already aware, and had already implemented counter measures.

Unfortunately, there was only one way to stop the progress of the vile things.

It was with great regret that Soteria watched the Laboratory control computer initiate the facility's self-destruct countdown. Soteria had no power to intervene, and she prepared to alter the files in her database. There was a growing sub-folder in her systems, labelled *deceased*, that contained the names of all those Hidden Hand personnel who had died doing their duty.

It would be a shame to add Colonel Radcliffe and Miss Jones to that list. Soteria had enjoyed her conversations with them. She hoped their replacements would be as enlightened and intriguing.

21.

London, UK

What happens if I find myself clashing against the police or one of the other intelligence agencies?

That was a question Craig had asked early on in his training by the Hidden Hand. The answer had been concise and not particularly reassuring.

Say nothing unless it gains you an advantage and do not resist. The matter will be attended to.

Craig was about to discover what that meant.

He would have preferred to have remained with his teammates at the quarantined facility, but that option had been denied him. Instead, he'd been ordered to return to London by helicopter, his presence at the Laboratory an unwanted distraction. According to Soteria his exit scanner had cleared him of all potential risks for whatever had sparked the emergency lockdown.

Soteria had been insistent he return to London. He'd tried to argue the toss that Lucy and Stuart could undergo the same scan, only for his common-sense proposal to be rejected.

Much of his previous evening had been spent writing up the reports that related to the Sirena Samson incident, which felt like busy work to Craig. Surely such bureaucracy could wait till another time? The Hellgates weren't going to magically activate because he didn't get his paperwork in.

Whenever Craig had asked for a status update on Stuart and Lucy, Soteria had merely replied that the emergency was *ongoing*. She wouldn't tell him anything more, despite his security clearance.

At least he got to sleep in his own bed, although it had only been his for a matter of days. Since his abduction by the Russians,

Craig had been relocated to another apartment, this time a mile outside the boundary of the City of London. The City, as it was sometimes known, was a sovereign state that existed within the borders of the nation's capital. That was also where the Citadel was housed, the secretive underground headquarters of the Hidden Hand.

Craig found his new dwelling a step up from that previously provided, although it would take some time for him to settle in, and that was all assuming his employer didn't move him again. At present, the apartment felt cold and barren, being sparse of furniture and personal history. Loneliness was one of the recognised risks with Craig's chosen career path. There was no room for relationships in his new line of work, especially with what he knew about the world.

A loved one waiting at home was only going to be a liability and a distraction.

Hopefully, there would come a time when he could settle in and get to call a place home. That was for the future, as unsure and chaotic as it was, and from what Craig had learned in the last few weeks, the future might well end up being bleak and horrific.

Who could live a normal life with that understanding hanging over them?

Right now, Craig was walking, making his way through rush-hour commuters who didn't realise they likely owed their lives to the well-built, ominous looking man with the facial scars. Most people ignored Craig, which was preferable to the surprised looks he sometimes got. He didn't let the latter bother him, because he had more pressing concerns in his life.

Craig could have taken a taxi or the tube, but he'd chosen to walk from his apartment to help clear his head and reassure himself the city he lived in was worth saving. Right now, with what he was seeing, Craig wasn't so sure.

"Soteria, any update?" The Bluetooth headset he wore was discreet and allowed him to be in constant contact with the super AI.

"Please could you narrow down the criteria of your request?"

"Stuart and Lucy? Are they okay?" Sometimes he wondered if Soteria was playing a cunning role, hiding the true extent of its reported brilliance.

"The emergency is still ongoing."

"That's what you said last time I asked," Craig countered, rubbing the back of his neck. His gaze darted ahead of him, guiding him through the throng, constantly on the lookout for potential threats. Once you learnt the skill of spatial awareness, you never stopped using it. Although those with a criminal intent would leave him alone because of how formidable he looked, there were other threats to be mindful of.

As the Russians had shown.

He wondered if that problem had been truly dealt with. Nobody had told him the ultimate fate of Ivanka, and he hadn't asked. It wasn't hard to guess, though. Her interrogation, and ultimate fate, had been left in the hands of Lucy, who didn't have a reputation for being particularly merciful.

"The situation remains fluid."

"I need to know if my team is okay," Craig pressed. He dodged round a rotund man who was mesmerised by the virtual world on the phone he held. There were too many people like that, each oblivious to a world threatened by terrors few could comprehend. They were the ones the criminals thrived on, sometimes deservedly so.

The Hidden Hand was right to keep the existence of the Hell world a secret. Craig had only been shown a taste of that other world, and it had ripped his existing beliefs to shreds. What would such knowledge do to the minds of those who craved conformity and celebrity gossip?

"I am restricted in what I can tell you," Soteria replied. Craig kept his temper even. Soteria did what she was told.

"Who can tell me?"

"Only the Director or the Curator would be able to authorise full information release."

"Let me guess, they are both engaged in other matters." Both of those individuals weren't there on the end of a phone for him. They contacted you, not the other way around. As far as Craig had been able to tell, the Hidden Hand wasn't cursed with excessive layers of management.

"That is a correct assessment. You have my apologies, Captain." For what they were worth.

Craig came to a crossing and waited for the lights to change. From here, the human traffic would diminish, the entrance to the Citadel along the back streets he would eventually traverse. When the traffic stalled to allow the gathered the opportunity to cross, most of them went left, Craig breaking off in the other direction.

He wasn't the only one. Spotting the reflection in one of the street's store windows, Craig noted the suspicious man behind him.

Surely not.

"Soteria, there's a chance I'm being followed. Please analyse street cameras in my location." Craig would happily waste the AI's time if it meant he was proved wrong. He wasn't. Craig knew a tail when he saw one.

"How tiresome." Craig wondered if Soteria meant the request or the possible situation. Instead of making his planned turn, Craig stayed on the main street. "It would appear you *are* being followed."

"Black haired Caucasian, wearing a grey coat?" That was who he had seen in the window. To Craig's left, a coffee shop presented the ideal opportunity.

"Yes. And others."

He slipped inside and joined the short queue.

"Damn," Craig mumbled.

"Interesting."

"What is? Stop being cryptic, Soteria!"

"Of course. I am detecting encrypted radio traffic in your vicinity. It is not police band."

"Can you break the encryption?" Was this related to his present predicament?

"Not in the required time interval. It is P25 encryption, it will take me several hours…"

"Soteria," Craig interrupted. "A simple no will suffice." Decades ago, people might have looked at him strangely for talking to himself like this. In modern day London, apparent one-way conversations were all the rage.

He didn't look behind him to see if the individual had followed him in. There was a mirror behind the serving counter, which gave Craig a view of the whole establishment.

"No. I have identified one of the individuals pursuing you, however. He works for MI5."

"And he's definitely following me?"

"Yes, my backwards analysis detects that he is part of a three-man team that has been with you since you left your apartment. My records show they are all MI5 operatives. I see no indication they may be freelancers." Or Russians!

"Watchers?" Watchers, otherwise known as mobile surveillance officers, agents who kept tabs on potential targets that threatened the safety and the integrity of the country. Or were they here for another purpose?

"Indeed. There should be no reason for you to come to the attention of MI5," Soteria promised. There would be only one reason to follow him, and that would be to see where he was going. Otherwise, they would have grabbed him off the street or raided his abode last night.

He had arrived in London yesterday, and already this was happening. That meant these MI5 agents had been actively searching for him, using the city's vast array of surveillance cameras. His helicopter had dumped him off at the Isle of Dogs, which was rammed with the electronic eyes.

Was that when he had been flagged by MI5?

"And yet here we are." Feigning impatience, Craig broke from the line and left the establishment. The guy in the grey jacket was nowhere to be seen, but it didn't mean he wasn't out there. One of his mates would have swapped out. Craig looked around casually, before moving off into the dwindled human flow.

The driver of the black van parked in the bus lane that Craig spotted wouldn't be paying the impending fine any time soon.

Craig turned off at the first side alley, which he found to be deserted. There was no way he would lead his pursuers to one of the secret entrances of the Citadel.

"Captain Armstrong, your tactic appears illogical."

"You think?" The alley was narrow, the road a single lane for one-way traffic. The pavement, what there was of it, was surprisingly clean for London.

Craig slowed his pace.

"I have advised the Director of your predicament. He seemed less than enamoured with these developments. What strategy are you planning to employ?" This time, Craig did look behind him. Two men had followed him into the alley. There was grey jacket again.

"How's about we kick the hornet's nest."

"Am I to assume that you are using a metaphor?"

"You can assume what you like."

"From that, I am making the assumption you are going to allow these men to take you?"

"That about sums it up," Craig agreed. If they wanted him dead, he wouldn't have been here ruminating over the matter.

"An intriguing option. Yes, I find this solution agreeable."

"I'm glad you think so, Soteria." Craig stopped and turned towards the two men. They kept on coming, as Craig expected they would. His size was unlikely to intimidate trained professionals.

Behind him, he detected a vehicle pull into the alley, against the flow of the established one-way traffic. "Do you still have eyes on me?"

"Yes. Street camera at the end of the alley." Soteria could patch into virtually any surveillance feed from the millions of cameras across the Greater London area. Those within the boundary of the Square Mile she could also control and manipulate the images recorded. No doubt Soteria was zooming in to witness and record the pending altercation.

She constantly watched the city, looking for threats.

There was an alcove at Craig's side that held a trio of wheelie bins. Moving slowly, Craig pulled his Glock free from its hidden holster and placed the gun on one of the bin lids. He had no desire to start a shooting match with people who were protecting his country.

The vehicle behind him came closer, the two MI5 agents briefly spooked by the appearance of a gun. With their cover blown, it was obvious to Craig what came next.

"Morning lads," Craig said in a cheery challenge. He kept his hands visible.

"Hands behind your head," the man with the grey coat screamed, pulling free his own pistol.

"On your knees. Get on your knees."

"Going dark now," Craig advised, before plucking the Bluetooth headset from his ear. He let it slip from his finger before crushing it below the tread of his boot.

Slowly he lowered himself as ordered, the two men moving in, and more behind. They would be rough, that was to be expected, and Craig would do whatever he could to avoid resisting.

It was time to see how well the Hidden Hand protected their own.

22.

Las Vegas, USA

The Hidden Hand might have never learnt early on about the bubbling chaos in Las Vegas, if not for a single piece of video that happened to go viral.

It was released on several social media channels by the person who had frantically recorded it on their phone. There it was copied and forwarded, becoming the latest phenomenon to engross those whose lives were generally empty. Initially, the video had been made from the safety of a bedroom window, only for the director of this epic to descend onto the street.

All to get a closer look at the impossible.

It was on YouTube that it started to gain real traction, the algorithms not flagging it for deletion, allowing other users to post their own analysis of what had been shown. Many who watched it were expecting to see an act of police brutality, only for that belief system to be blown out of the water.

The video was of the previous night, and was limited in what it showed because streetlights weren't an adequate illumination for the visual medium. What it did show drew in the curious, because much of the video couldn't be explained, inviting wild speculation and comments of the paranormal.

Strangely, the whole recorded altercation had been because of a 911 call made by the person who'd made the video. She had been awakened by the sound of a struggle in the property next door, which had resulted in her calling the police. The complainant had been fully expecting little in the way of any response, as it was her opinion that the police no longer cared about defeating crime.

Unfortunately for the police officers responding to the call, they had been patrolling in the neighbourhood, and were the first patrol car to arrive within minutes.

What the video showed was a large, lumbering man being confronted in the street by two uniformed officers. The audio was of poor quality, but much of the altercation could be heard.

"Get down. Down on the ground." The two officers had emerged from their car and had assessed the individual as a threat. When he didn't comply, one pulled a gun while the second deployed his taser.

"Get face down, or I *will* taser you."

When the alleged perpetrator didn't comply, the officer had fired off his taser barbs. Unfortunately, what nobody watching realised was that such a weapon is ill advised against an electrical creature like a golem. Instead of shocking the suspect, the taser created a feedback loop that reversed the electricity at the police officer. The violent blue arc that shot from the golem could have been mistaken for lightning, and it sent that officer hurtling from his feet.

The officer's partner, thinking himself in imminent danger, had then opened fire. That also had proven to be ineffective, the big man walking into the barrage of projectiles. Six shots were fired before the golem reached the officer, where the gun was wrenched from well-trained fingers.

The world watched on as the incident escalated. As if out of revenge, the big man punched the officer, sending him back against the side of his patrol vehicle, where the policeman collapsed, sliding onto his side.

The man they had tried to arrest then simply walked off.

Of course, the video didn't end there, for the person recording, while giving her own inane and panicked running commentary, had descended down to the ground floor of her house, before exiting out into the street. Assuring herself that the dangerous man was departing the area, she had continued to record as she approached the first of the officers.

The man slumped against the car had been punched in the face, his nose and upper jaw caved in. The lower jaw hung at an odd angle, giving the mouth an exaggerated gaping expression. There was a brief break in the video as the woman recording threw up, no doubt contaminating the crime scene.

Other people had been drawn out of their homes, their cameras adding to the mounting visual evidence, but it was the first video that recorded it all. With further sirens in the distance, the woman had run over to the other officer. He too was found to be dead, arms and upper torso blackened and fried from the electrical discharge. Nobody would find any evidence of the taser used, as it had disintegrated.

That was how the world got a hint that there was something very wrong in Las Vegas, and it was how Soteria was eventually alerted to a possible invader from another world.

***

Cliff went to the place he felt most comfortable, or was it the alien presence that made that decision? Cliff was well aware that he could now avoid severe pain by going along for the ride, and he accepted those conditions gladly. The desolation that had taken hold of his thoughts over the last few months was gone, an eerie kind of peace settling in his mind.

This wasn't so bad.

That's what he kept telling himself. It helped that the voice in his head had a refreshingly low opinion of the female of the species. All he had to do was willingly comply with the commanding influence that had taken up residence in his head.

Was this what it felt like to be schizophrenic, he had briefly wondered? Could this be the result of some psychological break on his part?

Don't worry yourself with such thoughts, the voice had insisted gently.

Okay.

At this time of day, the strip club might have seemed surprisingly busy to some, but this was Vegas baby. The early morning crowd was mostly leftovers from the epic night before. The women looked tired, and the whole establishment stank of sweat and stale coffee. Cliff didn't care because he was here for another reason.

Hardly romantic. But then, it's not the women you're here for.

What better environment to find drunk and drug-addled men in a darkened environment.

Cliff was a regular here, a place where he could drown his impressive sorrows and spend his dwindling finances. It had felt like justice to give these women his hard-earned cash over that leech of an ex-wife.

You know they've been playing you, right? Women can't be trusted. He guessed he had known that. Well, shit!

Cliff didn't need to be made aware that the parasite was playing his own prejudices back to him.

His friends had tried to warn him that this belligerence against the opposite sex was going to turn into a freight train running over his life. Cliff hadn't cared then, and he didn't care now.

Today he was here for a whole other purpose.

How about we show these broads the new reality?

The parasite was fully settled in now, using Cliff's established lexicon in its communication. It was spiralling him, using his own anger to rule his malleable thinking.

Cliff offered no resistance, acquiescing to the incessant demands made of him, which made the parasite's job all the easier. A compliant host meant the alien invader needed to expend less energy on control, and the one in Cliff had already divided multiple times.

He was the perfect vessel, and right now he had brought the infestation to the ideal breeding ground for it. With four dozen men and women spread around the establishment, what more could he ask for?

He was sat watching a tired dancer go through the motions when the first woman of the morning came over to him. The man at the table next to him was resting back, apparently asleep. Not so, for an innocent hand shake had passed a Child on and now the transformation was ongoing.

In the dimness of the club, the blood on the punter's palm couldn't be seen.

"Hey sugar. What brings you here at this hour?" The exotic dancer was blonde and thin with enhanced breasts. There was a fakeness to her which Cliff didn't care for.

She must be made to pay. But not yet.

"Well darling, I felt drawn by the free breakfast buffet." The invading presence watched and listened to the developing conversation, happy that Cliff was here to meet its pressing needs.

Infesting the neighbour had been a moment of opportunity.

This establishment would require a more calculated approach because assaulting someone to pass on offspring risked drawing unwanted attention. Through borrowing its host's thoughts and memories, the parasite gained a unique kind of sentience and knew that it was now working together with the others of its kind out there.

In the distance, it could feel more of the Children stirring. There were hundreds of them, all established in human bodies. Some found the humans they rode easy vessels, but most were now forcing their will on the petulant human folk.

Today would be a day of pain and misery for so many.

"Can I interest you in something more wholesome?" Bending over, she moved her cleavage into Cliff's eye line.

"Why, whatever did you have in mind?"

Women can't be trusted.

Cliff had expected one of the creatures to come forth and take this woman, but it held back.

"Well, me." The blonde sat down next to him, resting her dainty hand on Cliff's knee. None of the Children lurking beneath his flesh stirred, because their collective memory told them that females were unworthy hosts. This knowledge was being shared across the hive mind, the hosts rapidly being infused with this vital information.

Somehow, the women could poison the purity of what the Scourge wanted to achieve.

Over by the buffet, there was a commotion as someone collapsed. Two security guards flocked to the fallen customer as others backed away.

"Someone's had a few too many," Cliff noted. The statement was a smokescreen, for he knew the man's collapse was most likely due to the parasite he had left lurking beneath the buffet table. The Children could survive outside the host for a time, but would weaken until they took themselves a nutritious physique to ride and control.

On his entry, the buffet area had been the second destination before coming to sit here. The first had been the stalls in the gent's bathroom, a Child waiting patiently under each of the three toilet seats that could be found there.

Some people were in for an unpleasant surprise if the call of nature took them.

"It happens. More than you'd imagine." With a finger, the blonde guided Cliff's chin so he was looking directly at her. "But that's not what's important right now."

"Oh? And what is important?" Cliff played along, waiting for his army to build. It might take a few hours, but every male in here was going to be infested. They would all join with him in a unified hatred of the female flesh.

These whores will be made to pay.

The Child controlling him, one of the first, knew which buttons in Cliff's mind needed pushing. Cliff wasn't even questioning the murderous images that were now floating into his reality.

"These," the blonde advised, before cupping her breasts.

"You make some valid points there," Cliff conceded. From the corner of his eye, he saw someone walk towards the restroom.

Where he sat, Cliff's right hand dangled off the edge of the seat he occupied. Hidden by the table and the depleted light, the parasite that slipped from his hand was invisible. Cliff barely reacted as the wound opened, allowing the slug-like thing to drop to the floor. The cut closed, little blood breaking free.

"How about we take this somewhere private?"

"Why the Hell not." Cliff was happy to play the game, and what better place to deposit the Children than the private booths where the exotic and erotic were promised, but where it was so rarely delivered?

***

Wilkinson should have been concerned by his arrest. After all, he'd bludgeoned several women to death with a ferocity that was usually only seen in someone high on some illicit substance.

Maybe he had been high, but only on the love of Jesus, who spoke to him now.

When the police had shown up, Wilkinson had been passively and patiently waiting for them. He had been naked, kneeling in the pooled blood of his unfortunate victims, body fluids smeared across his hands and torso. In the centre of his chest, a prominent and haphazard cross had been painted, the edges of its already starting to dry.

With his hands interlaced on his head, he had watched as the four officers had carefully entered, the horrors of Wilkinson's actions frighteningly apparent. All the male congregation had left, so that left the pastor as the obvious suspect for such heinous crimes, to which he loudly, and repeatedly confessed.

"Woe unto the wicked!" He liked the sound of the righteousness in his voice.

The agents of law enforcement had seen his morning's activities in a different light. After his arrest, two of the officers had thrown up outside, which had upset Wilkinson. Could they not see the glory in God's work?

Some people will never hear his voice, the parasite had whispered to him. *Heathens don't deserve his mercy or his understanding.*

The police officers had not been gentle with him, the bruises on his ribs and arms clearly the result of Wilkinson *resisting arrest*. The beating was short-lived, stopped early by a lieutenant who had been called to the scene. After that, his accusers had accosted him with their eyes and their words, which had caused Wilkinson to smile in return.

Let he who is without sin...

Unlike in the church, the parasite that was masquerading as the heavenly spirit had been strangely hesitant to appear. This had upset Wilkinson. Surely these strong and godless men were worth the forced insight of *his* word. Didn't God love a sinner who was forced to come to his understanding?

Patience, the parasite had whispered again.

Despite the way they manhandled Wilkinson, none of the arresting officers were infested with the way and the light. Although the pastor had clearly suffered a mental break of an epic magnitude, Wilkinson was taken to the nearest detention centre before the local press could get wind of the church massacre.

Had his actions been that of a deranged and sick mind rather than an alien invader from a planet of torture and suffering, Wilkinson would have become an international sensation.

His name wouldn't make local headlines, not with the day that was about to unfold.

At the detention centre, he had been processed and, after forensics were taken, he'd been allowed a supervised shower which he'd agreed to with much reluctance. The cross on his chest was his pact with the Lord.

Don't worry, there will be plenty more blood for you to show your fealty.

To some, this admissions procedure might have been seen as humiliating, but Wilkinson was protected by the light of the Lord, as well as his own all-consuming insanity. The parasite had identified that sending the host's mind deep into its own beliefs was likely to be an excellent means to control.

The parasite had been right.

And as for its reluctance to spread itself among the law enforcement personnel, that was all part of the strategy it had formulated. It was using Wilkinson's memories to attain maximum impact, Wilkinson's flesh now bristling with the Children that had spawned inside him.

Wilkinson had, for a time, tried to bring the word of Christ to those locked away from decent society. His attempts had been generally unsuccessful, but it left Wilkinson with memories of a place where over four hundred people were trapped and unable to escape.

He was in a room with some of them now, and, under the cheap blue shirt he had been issued, the Children bulged beneath Wilkinson's sagging flesh. They had multiplied greatly in the past hour, consuming the pastor's ample fat deposits, as well as sucking the minerals from his blood.

Sometimes it made sense to sacrifice a host for what the parasite collective called *The Greater Good*. Individual human life was irrelevant. All that mattered was the expansion of the collective and the slaughter of those who posed a threat to their dominance.

Wilkinson slept, the other detainees watching him warily. Wilkinson had announced himself and his deeds on entering the holding cell, two dozen fellow law breakers not taking kindly to the pompous killer of women.

Although a big man, he'd had the appearance of a soft, middle-aged victim, but Wilkinson had demonstrated his impressive strength on the first person who had remonstrated with him. That man was still unconscious, the punch Wilkinson had delivered sending the outraged biker to the floor, while also allowing one of the Children to slip free.

Wilkinson never woke from his nap, his body spent by the hundreds of parasites that crawled from him. He died, sacrificed and left as a drained husk.

More came now, spilling from the killer's body, pouring to the floor in a grey waterfall of terror. The Children moved fast, some being bludgeoned into a disgusting smear by desperate boots, but most found a home in those detained.

And when the detention officer came running to see what all the commotion was about, he too became a lucky recipient of a Child. From there, those still free moved out through the corridors, their slick bodies blending in to the colour of the floors.

The thing was, the detention centre was filled with surveillance cameras, which recorded everything. Those images were accessible across the internet, and would soon be added to Soteria's growing awareness.

The Children thought they were spreading in secret. They weren't.

23.

Isles of Scilly, UK

To think, being trapped in an underground bunker with an alien parasite running rampant wasn't the worst news Stuart had received today.

"Be advised. Thermal sterilisation will begin in five minutes. We apologise for the inconvenience."

Understandably, that wasn't what Stuart wanted to hear, the blaring siren that went with the warning adding to the sensation of impending doom. As much as Stuart was one to follow orders, the thought of him being burned alive wasn't something he was going to sit around and wait for.

If there was any way of getting out of this place, Stuart intended to find it.

He and Lucy were running, the main surface elevator their goal. Ted had chosen to stay behind, resigned to the terrible fate that seemed inevitable. Ted had assured them that there was no way to escape, and that the elevators were the only way to the surface, which was the singular part of the complex that wasn't going to have its insides burnt to a crisp.

In Ted's opinion, with the lockdown, the bleak concrete elevator shafts represented an impossible obstacle, especially as the elevator cars would be out of service. Climbing the shafts wasn't the most daunting issue. That existed in the form of the defensive laser grid that would block both surface shafts. And before that, they would have to get through the scanner chamber, which would also be on lockdown.

Nothing sounded particularly promising.

"You won't make it," Ted had warned them gravely.

Stuart wasn't having any of that. There was no way he was going to accept such defeat without seeing the evidence for it himself first, and Lucy had shared his eagerness to survive. Despite his own resignation, Ted had merely sighed and wished them luck.

"I hope you survive," had been Ted's final parting words. It was amazing how some people could accept their fate rather than battle for every breath. Perhaps it was Ted's knowledge of this facility's defences that had caused such stoic defeatism in him.

Due to his momentum, Stuart slammed into the scanner room door, taking the impact on his left shoulder. The M4 carbine was slung across his back, the holster on his right hip.

Ripping the exit open, he and Lucy stumbled through into the room beyond. The scanner took pride of place in the wall in front of them. Around the door, a trim of red light shone to add to the red light that was pulsing out of the scanner itself.

Stuart stepped up to it, but the doors didn't open. When he had been brought to this facility, he'd been forced to pass through this scanner, the doors sliding open as he'd approached.

No way in.

"What about this?" Lucy was pointing to the other door that was flush with the wall at the side of the scanner. Approaching it, Stuart ran his fingers along the seams. If they had a crowbar, maybe.

Lucy was right behind him, and she was the one to produce the knife that Stuart used forced into the thin gap. It slid in, but not far enough.

"Be advised. Thermal sterilisation will begin in four minutes and thirty seconds. We apologise for the inconvenience."

Stuart could sense a change in the air quality around him. He could envision each floor below them filling up with flammable gas.

Would they die of asphyxiation before the fire took them?

"Can't someone shut that damned siren off!" Lucy shouted. The alarm was too loud and too ominous as well as being completely terrifying. Stuart didn't answer, instead he slid the knife up and down to try and get some kind of purchase.

If they couldn't get through this, then the elevator might as well have been a million miles away.

Lucy was presently slamming the butt of her carbine against the scanner door. The door was clear, but whatever it was made from, it wasn't yielding. She knew better than to try to shoot at the door. The most likely result of that would be a potentially lethal ricochet.

"I can see the bloody elevator," Lucy complained. The scanner was a cylindrical device that let individuals pass through the wall one by one. It was designed to deny exit when required. "Looks like we're screwed!"

"Looks that way," Stuart conceded before slamming the side of his curled fist against the wall before pushing his forehead into it. The wall was cool and unyielding. He remembered the story of the American general who, infused with the knowledge that all matter was merely energy condensed to a slow vibration, had persuaded himself that it was possible to pass through a thick and impenetrable wall.

None of the walls the general had run into in his attempts had respected that flawed conclusion. Neither would this one.

"The bastards are just going to let us burn." Lucy's nostrils flared as she raged. She hit the scanner door again. If she persisted, it would be her gun that would break first.

"Yep." Stuart pulled his head from off the wall and, swinging the gun across his chest, sat himself down against it. Lucy joined him, depositing her carbine on the floor between them. They sat like that, letting the countdown wash over them.

It was over a minute before Lucy spoke.

"I didn't think I'd go out like this."

"It's not very heroic, is it? There's a certain seduction in going out in a hail of gunfire," Stuart revealed. When he'd signed up to work for the Hidden Hand, he'd been under no delusions about his chances of long-term survival. The Hidden Hand wasn't known for its impressive retirement package. What he hadn't planned for was to be killed by his own side.

Not much of a reward for his years of service. He could understand why, though. There was no way that parasite could be allowed to reach the surface. Those who controlled the Hidden Hand were there to make the hard decisions.

In all fairness, Stuart knew he'd had a good run. He couldn't say he had many regrets.

This was the moment where the two friends might console each other, maybe by coming together in a hug of reassurance. Stuart didn't want that, preferring to close his eyes and let the end come. Their only gesture was to clutch each other's hand.

Both of them were to be spared the finality of death.

"Be advised. Thermal sterilisation will begin in three minutes. We apologise for the... illiterate badger flagellating your proboscis."

Stuart and Lucy looked at each other. That wasn't right.

"Right, right, right, refer to data on the... the... return, return."

The electronic voice blared out at greater volume, its words stuttering and nonsensical.

"What the hell's going on?" Lucy pleaded, hands clamped over her ears. Stuart bore the noise with a grimace.

"Inadequate. Illogical. Irrelevant."

Around them, the lighting shifted as the emergency lights swapped back to normal illumination. The blaring siren also ceased. Had they been spared?

Stuart pulled himself to his feet.

"Soteria?" He waited for the mandatory reply, but none came.

"Soteria, are you there" Lucy offered. The only response was silence.

"You ever been in the eye of a storm?" asked Stuart as he pulled his radio handset free. What use would these be down here? He dialled it in to the channel set for the supercomputer.

"Soteria?"

"Not… receive… ear." The radio noise was filled with static. Stuart adjusted the tuning. "Colonel Radcliffe. It is reassuring to hear your voice. I regret to inform you that there is an emergency."

Talk about stating the bleeding obvious.

It was then that the room lights went out, leaving Stuart and Lucy in all-consuming darkness.

***

The Children had reached the mainframe of the vast underground computer. The survivors squirmed into it, attempting to fuse with its memory banks. They were designed to take control of sentient creatures, but being silicone based, they hoped they could join with microprocessors and the circuit boards.

The computer was less complex than the human mind, and despite its inorganic nature, the Children began their attempts to manipulate the computer's functions. The computer was nothing their kind had ever encountered before, the wires and microchips so different from the complexities of the human body. They understood the machine's basic function from the knowledge they had acquired via the minds they had.

If the parasites could control the computer, they could control this prison they found themselves in.

If they could control the prison, then they could escape to bring their madness to the people of Earth.

24.

London, UK

The left side of Craig's face ached, a result of the MI5 agent with the grey jacket having slammed his fist into Craig's cheek. This only after Craig had been placed in handcuffs and bundled into the back of a vehicle that felt like it had been cleaned with the strongest disinfectant. That punch had then been followed by a kick to the gut before another agent had verbally intervened.

Why he had been hit was just another question to add to his long list.

Presently he was sat in a well-lit room that was standard for this sort of thing. He'd been in such rooms, and only once before had he been unfortunate enough to find himself on the wrong side of the table. That had been in his military escape and evasion training, which had turned into a week of proving that he could withstand the various interrogation techniques that might be used on a special forces operative captured by the enemy.

What techniques would be deployed today?

How far was MI5 willing to push this?

Craig was alone, his cuffed wrists attached to a metal rod that was screwed to the black metal table that dominated the room. The table was immovable, as was the uncomfortable chair he was sat on. Reassuringly, rooms like this were used for verbal interrogation rather than anything physical.

There were other places for that.

Anyone who believed that the UK intelligence services didn't regularly engage in rough treatment of those they detained was living in cloud cuckoo land. The bruise growing on Craig's cheek was evidence of that. Hopefully, the Hidden Hand would intervene before the heavy mob was unleashed on him again. Craig was kind of getting tired of being used as a punching bag.

One day he would like to return the favour to the man in the grey jacket.

Craig had already assessed his surroundings. Although he'd been hooded on his capture, the length of his ride in the van told him he was still in London. The trip from the van upon his delivery had told him more, several flights of stairs leading down beneath the city streets. Craig knew he was most likely in Thames House, the headquarters of MI5, or a safe-house close by it.

Thames House was no real mystery to him. He had been here before during his military days, and had a rough understanding of the building's layout and the way the people in it operated. He was three or four levels underground, brought here as a person of interest by people who had no idea the shit-storm they were about to be embroiled in.

At least, that was Craig's hope.

Other features of note in the room were the twin surveillance cameras and the wall-length mirror along one wall. It was everything you would expect from an interrogation room. Here he would be unable to get comfortable, the chair unpadded metal. The rod on the table was positioned so that he had to stretch his arms forward, meaning the table was pressing into his midriff. If one looked closely, it was obvious that the bar could be altered to suit the restrained individual's physique.

It was all a warning of what might follow if cooperation wasn't forthcoming.

"Can we get on with this, please," Craig said, evenly. He looked at the mirror as he spoke, for it was most certainly one way, concealing people behind. It would be good to learn the reason why he was here, for as far as he was aware, he'd committed no crime against the British state that warranted this treatment.

In fact, it was because of him that there was still a Britain to speak of.

His abduction could be viewed as unwarranted, but also opportunistic, in that there was a perverse advantage to Craig being here. His abductors would be under the illusion that he was a source of information to be cracked open, but Craig saw it differently. MI5 had flagged him as a threat, and Craig needed to know why. Having been here for roughly an hour, Craig suspected that his superiors would want to know that too.

Could that be why he was still here?

When the door opened, an unimpressive-looking man entered. Craig knew how to read a person and saw this thin-framed individual as the second act in this unfolding drama. The stranger didn't have the air of importance that came with authority, and his lack of overt musculature meant he wasn't any kind of threat visually. He was a lackey, here to do the bidding of others up the food chain.

The stranger was carrying a thick folder, which Craig had been expecting. The folder would be there to indicate that Craig's life was an open book, and that there was nothing worth hiding.

We know everything about you.

Craig would happily play along, as it was all very predictable.

Soteria would know where he was, the tracking chip in the back of his neck there to save him yet again. When he had been abducted by the Russians, Craig had been rescued by a team of Cleaners who had mercilessly slaughtered those who hampered Craig's rescue.

The Cleaners were cold and calculating men who never smiled. They were the shock troops of the Hidden Hand, sent in where overwhelming brute force was required.

There would be no such violent assault here. Craig's pending freedom would need to be more diplomatic in nature. But what was taking so long? Where was the cavalry?

When the stranger sat down, he thumped the dossier in front of him. The edges of individual pages stuck out from the sides, a promise that Craig's whole life was recorded on those pages. More likely, most of the papers before him were blank, the folder a tool of theatre and misinformation.

Craig was happy to play the game.

"It's about time somebody showed up," Craig said, admonishing the man. He didn't answer, instead slipping a sheet from those he had brought. "You're late, by the way. And you could have called, you know. Mother and I were worried sick."

That got an amused smile from the man who then slid the single sheet over. Craig saw his own face, a photograph taken from his military career. That was genuinely surprising, because all records of his life were supposed to have been digitally erased. No doubt there would be some paper files rotting away in some clerk's filing cabinet somewhere in the world, but in the digital realm, he shouldn't have existed.

"It would seem you don't exist," the interrogator finally said. He was sat back, hands resting on his thin thighs.

"If only I'd known. Think of all the tax I could have avoided."

"As far as we can tell, you don't pay tax. There is no record of a Captain Craig Armstrong in our database, and yet here you are."

Craig shrugged as best he could.

"Here I am."

"Strange then that this man," the stranger said as he leant forward, tapping the paper, "is known to us."

"I'd be surprised if I wasn't, seeing as how I've been involved with joint operations with MI5." That was the kind of record that Soteria couldn't expunge. As flawed as they were, human memory would always be the enemy of those who wished to remain invisible.

"So, you admit this is you?" A bony finger was stabbed down into the centre of the incriminating sheet.

"Of course. Which does, however, beg an important question."

"Oh?"

"How did you get that?" Craig demanded, nodding towards the item that held the stranger's interest.

"I believe I'm the one supposed to be asking the questions."

"Then you should ask them," Craig countered. "And quickly. This is all very tiresome."

"I'm sorry. I do hope we aren't inconveniencing you." The stranger's words dripped with sarcasm.

"That's okay. I'm sure this will all be cleared up shortly."

"You seem confident of that." The stranger was glaring at him now.

"Things have a way of working themselves out." Craig looked at the sheet again. From what he could tell, it was part of his military record. The definition of the information told him it was a print-off rather than a photocopy.

How did MI5 have a digital version of something he'd been assured had been deleted from the internet? Soteria had proven her worth more than once, so he wasn't going to buy into the notion that the AI had made a mistake.

"Who do you work for?" the stranger asked.

"I'm not at liberty to say," Craig advised.

"Not at liberty?" The stranger sucked his teeth. "We know quite a lot about you, as it happens."

"Do tell."

The stranger pulled another sheet from his file.

"Captain Craig Armstrong, formerly of the Special Reconnaissance Regiment. Parents deceased. Date of birth blah blah." The second sheet was discarded onto the table. "Standard fare, and yet none of it this can be found digitally."

"Then how did you get hold of it?" Craig persisted.

"That doesn't matter."

Craig turned to the mirror.

"Oh, but it does. It matters a great deal."

"Eyes on me please," the stranger insisted.

"Why? You aren't the one really asking the questions." Craig squinted, trying to spot any imperfection in the mirror's surface. He turned his head back to the stranger. "You are a man way out of his depth."

"Says the man in handcuffs."

"I won't be for long." Craig leaned forward. "You are about to learn how strange the real world actually is. Whoever ordered my detention is about to understand what it feels like to have a tonne of bricks drop on them from a great height."

It didn't matter who you were. Those who fucked with the Hidden Hand did so at their peril.

***

Peter Sloane had a knot in his stomach that had stripped him of his appetite. He had thought this matter a simple affair, and yet there was too much here that didn't add up.

"You shouldn't have hit him." Peter was looking through the one-way mirror, but he was talking to the man stood next to him.

"He was too cocky. He needed reminding who was in charge." The man in the grey jacket had a history of being too physical, but he was loyal and effective.

"Still, that was an unnecessary use of force."

"That's not what my report will say." The man in the grey jacket also knew how to cover his back and seemed confident that no lawyers would get involved here.

"*Let's talk about why you have no history,*" the interrogator asked. This wasn't the man Peter wanted to use, but he was the best they had at short notice.

Craig Armstrong's image had been flagged on surveillance cameras at a heliport last night, and MI5 had been observing him ever since. The watchers and snatch team had been put together ready for this morning. Peter had hoped to follow their suspect for longer than they had, because there were still things unknown about Captain Armstrong.

"*I have a history, just not one I want to talk about.*" Armstrong was too confident, too self-assured. And every time Armstrong looked at the two-way mirror, it felt like he could see right through it.

"*Your lack of cooperation isn't helping you.*"

"*I think I've been very cooperative,*" Armstrong countered. "*After all, I surrendered to your men rather than killing them.*"

"See what I mean?" grey jacket huffed. "Cocky."

"*So, you admit to being a man of violence?*"

"*Everyone will resort to violence, given the right motivation. Our whole society is based on the real threat of violence.*" Armstrong looked at the mirror again. "*When are your friends going to make an appearance?*"

"*What friends?*" the interrogator deflected.

Peter felt a trickle of sweat run down his back. This was taking too long. Maybe they should move the prisoner to the lower level. Peter was sure grey jacket would be happy to have a crack at him.

No. He needed to do this himself.

"Damn it," Peter spat. He stormed from the viewing room, swallowing hard as the acid percolated up his throat. Now would be a good time to figure out who this Armstrong character really was.

They had gone through the city's surveillance logs retrospectively for the last two weeks. They had uncovered a semblance of Craig's movements, much of it centred around the Square Mile. The thing was, there was no recorded image of Craig within the boundaries of that sovereign state, his image stripped from every feed. That in itself should have been impossible.

Who the hell was this man, and what steaming pile of shit had Peter just stepped into?

***

Craig turned his head as the unwell-looking man stepped into the room.

"I'll take it from here." The interrogator nodded, vacating the seat before leaving the room. It looked like Craig was finally getting somewhere.

"Good of you to join us," Craig goaded. The new arrival didn't bite. Instead, he stepped over to the mirror, his back to Craig.

"You appear to be a man of mystery."

"I've been called worse," Craig retorted. "Do you have a name?"

"Yes." The stranger didn't offer it.

"I think you know abducting me is a mistake." Let's see how confident this fool is. Craig had learnt early on the skill of reading people. You needed to when lives depended on it. That skill hadn't always served him, but it told him things about this man. The stranger was stressed, and most likely in pain. You could tell that by the way he breathed and stood.

"We don't make mistakes," the stranger retorted. Finally, he turned.

"Are you not concerned that you're breaking like a hundred laws here?" Officially, MI5 wasn't allowed to detain people. Of course, that was all bullshit to make Joe Public feel better about themselves.

"According to the state, you don't exist. The law doesn't apply to you." The threat was obvious. A man who didn't exist could simply be made to disappear.

"Good to see you've become what you fight against. So, what's next, waterboarding? A long drive to the gulag?" Craig narrowed his eyes and cocked his head to one side. "Hang on, we've met before." The stranger's name floated in his thoughts, just out of reach.

"I don't see that..."

"No, no, we've definitely met." Craig let his eyes drift up and down his abductor. He wasn't impressed by what he saw. "Maybe you could do me the courtesy of telling me why I'm here."

"We believe you are a criminal." The stranger sat down.

"Then where are the police?"

"We believe you are a threat to this country. We have evidence you are working with the Russians."

Craig took pains to control his breathing.

"Seriously?" And right then, Craig knew this man had revealed himself. Those hiding a secret guilt often accuse others of their crimes.

"You are a mystery to us, Mr Armstrong. We don't like mysteries. We also believe you are a threat to this country. It's my job to remove such threats."

"So that's the game you're going to play? I actually feel sorry for you."

There was a knock on the door. The stranger's features tightened as he stood. The way the door opened prevented Craig from seeing who was outside, the stranger straightening as the identity of the knocker was revealed.

Peter Sloane, that was the name Craig was hunting for.

Words were said outside, but nothing that Craig could make out. The interrogation-room walls were no doubt soundproofed. The voices weren't raised, a measured approach being taken.

The voices moved away, Craig left on his own once again. He counted the seconds off in his head.

After five minutes, it wasn't Peter who returned. Instead, the first interrogator entered with a bemused look on his face. He had a set of keys clutched between two fingers.

"Can I state that I was dragged into this at the last minute," the interrogator stated. Steadily, he unlocked Craig's handcuffs, allowing the prisoner to sit back from the table.

"Just following orders, eh?"

"Something like that. We never get told much."

"Understood." Craig knew how things went.

He massaged his wrists one at a time. There was no point being angry at this individual, for he was a mindless cog in a big machine.

"I was told to give you this," the interrogator stated, before sliding a small envelope across the table. Craig pocketed it. "And I'm to escort you out." There was something else in the interrogator's manner, the slight tremor in his voice telling. Craig had witnessed a lot of it in his time and had felt plenty himself.

Fear.

Craig didn't stand straight away, instead he turned to the mirror. Was the man in the grey jacket behind it, watching him?

Finally, he turned to the waiting man.

"Your boss too ashamed to face me?"

"Frankly, I've no idea what's going on. I have the feeling I should have called in sick this morning."

"Yeah," Craig said in commiseration. "You and me both."

25.

Area 51, Nevada, USA

Maybe Hertz was right. Maybe the portal was beautiful. Its dull blue form shimmered before him, its presence some eight feet high. Hertz was stood in front of him, and the doctor gingerly reached out his hand.

"Don't. Please," Brook begged, only for fire to lance through his incisors.

Be silent.

Why did this thing in his head keep Brook around? Why didn't it strip him of the last of his awareness? It gave the impression that it knew everything Brook knew and had control over his body. There was no way Brook wanted to stand so close to this death trap, and yet here he was.

Hertz pushed his arm into the swirling mass. It disappeared up to the elbow, the blue swallowing up the limb.

"It's warm," Hertz revealed, before pulling his arm back. The limb was intact, the fingers flexing. Brook held his breath, expecting a mutated monster to come bursting through, but nothing happened.

"Why am I here?" Brook's mind had given up the code for the airlock, so he saw no reason for him to be watching this. The urge to be around other people had passed, the priorities of the parasite too complex for Brook's depleted consciousness to decipher.

"You'll see," Hertz promised. Ever since gaining access to the portal, the doctor's lips had been infected with a maddening smile. It was in the eyes too, Hertz's sanity lost to this world.

What had the parasite promised Hertz?

What did it whisper to him in his head?

We want you to be a mockery of yourself.

"I don't understand," Brook protested.

You will.

The area of the portal had once been a simple underground cavern unearthed by silver miners. Since that time, the surroundings had been strengthened by concrete and steel, creating what was hoped to be an earthquake-proof dome over the portal. At the same time, the ceiling and walls had been fitted with explosives to bury the portal in the case of an emergency. More than once Brook had expressed the opinion that those explosives should be triggered, but minds superior to his had counselled caution in that regard. He had been informed that the secrets of the portal needed to be understood, because where there was one, there might be more.

The recent agitated state of this blue gateway strongly pointed that this was the case. Science had yet to determine a way to close the portal, so monitoring and isolation had become the preferred protocol.

It was safe to say that this had now backfired.

There was a commotion from the entrance to this domed room, Brook turning to see two of the facility guards dragging a woman in. The guards had been dedicated and trusted, gifted with a security clearance almost as high as Brook's. They too had been overcome by the parasite. Brook could sense the proximity of the alien invaders inside them, which explained how he'd been feeling so bonded to Hertz.

"We brought you a gift," one of the soldiers said through gritted teeth. Neither of the two men smiled, their faces filled with the evidence of the pain they were in. There was no way Brook could be critical of them, for everyone had to fight their own battles with this infestation.

The woman was thrown to the ground. Her face was bruised and her lip blooded. Brook watched as one of the soldiers pulled free his sidearm. For a second, Brook thought he was about to witness an execution, but then the soldier was handing the gun out to him.

Take it, the parasite insisted.

Brook tried his best to resist, but his arm moved regardless.

"Why are you doing this?" the woman implored. Brook vaguely knew her, one of the staff here at XR-1 Storage. She had a family, kids, people who would miss her.

"Because you are impure," Hertz replied. The doctor squatted down in front of the woman, squinting as he examined her. Hertz tried to reach for her, but the woman batted his hand away. The defiance resulted in one of the soldiers kneeling behind her so as to get her in a vicious head lock.

Watch and learn, the parasite commanded.

From the back of Hertz's left hand, a parasite squeezed its way out from his pale flesh. The woman squirmed, but had nowhere to go. Holding her tight, the soldier kept her steady as Hertz transferred the parasite to the woman's ear. It hesitated for a second before sliding inside.

The woman didn't scream. Instead, she unfurled a string of curses.

"That's some mouth you have on you," Hertz said in chastisement. The woman spat at him, which only seemed to encourage the deranged doctor. "Any moment now."

Brook was there to see the parasite slide out of the ear hole and drop to the ground. He found himself stepping closer, bending to get a closer look as the thing lost its cohesion. It liquefied, bubbling as it spread out to form a thin film of moisture.

Do you see?

"Yes, but I don't understand."

The women are toxic. This has forced us to change our plans.

"You have plans?" It felt unnerving to be having a conversation with himself in front of other people. The thing was, Brook suspected all here were privy to what was going on in his mind. The parasites were linked together, joined in a cohesive mind. More than once in the canteen, he'd thought Hertz had been talking to him. No words were shared, however, Brook tuning into something far more sinister.

We will need to be more covert than anticipated.

"Despite all that, the females represent an opportunity," Hertz revealed. He rose up on his toes before stretching out his limbs. The woman's saliva was slowly creeping down his face. Hertz let it.

"Whatever this is, you don't have to go through with it," the woman insisted. The man holding her gave her neck a firmer squeeze before letting her slump fully to the floor.

You have a choice, came the malevolent voice.

"A choice?" Brook knew this was a lie, just the start of some sadistic game.

You wanted to know why we keep you around? You, Colonel, are a human of strength and high character. Some might say you are the best of your species.

Was that supposed to be a bad thing?

We wish to make you everything you hate. We wish to make you loathe your very existence. It is not just the pain we wish you to suffer.

"Why?" Brook implored.

It pleases us. We take from our hosts everything that makes humanity depraved, violent and immoral. This is our nature. This is what we are. Our existence becomes sadism and brutality.

Finally, Brook was beginning to understand.

We were sent here as a weapon and a test. Humanity has failed that test, so now we turn your own sins against you.

"It doesn't have to be this way." His words made Hertz grin harder, the doctor watching the struggle unfold in Brook's consciousness.

Brook almost shot the man.

Like all of humanity, you are here to be broken. You are here to be our plaything. You are here to be our toy. Know that your torment hasn't even begun, and by the time this world is nothing but smouldering ash, you will be a whimpering and desolate fool.

"Just let me die."

You will not be the one to die today. But someone will. You get to choose the fate of this woman as you will for all those we bring here. You decide whether she goes through the portal dead or alive.

"You want me to kill her?" The woman tried to scramble to her feet, but one of the soldiers laid her out with a heavy punch to the temple.

Maybe through the portal she has a chance to live. There is no way for you to know what is waiting for her through there. That's what makes this so intoxicating for us. To see you struggle. A single bullet. Would it be an act of mercy or murder?

"I know what I would choose," Hertz offered.

"You won't get away with this," Brook promised. But who was he kidding?

We already have. Our kind are spreading, taking the minds in this military base one at a time. And your city, the one called Las Vegas, we Scourge cry out in our conquest.

Brook raised the gun, and he almost made it. He took everything he had to move his arm so that the gun was aimed at his head, but the movement stalled. Inside, the parasite was laughing at him.

We will never let you free.

"Please don't kill me." The woman sounded groggy, the punch taking what was left of the fight out of her.

"You might thank me," Brook insisted. He had only a small idea of what was in that other world, but the woman didn't. If this woman had watched the same video as he had... would she be begging for death rather than life?

Brook had seen what the creatures of that world could do. He'd heard the screams of the men who had died with the tentacled monsters clinging to their faces.

The colonel did the only thing he could do. He shot the woman in the head.

Interesting. Let's see if you still want to do that a hundred bodies from now.

26.

The Isles of Scilly, UK

The emergency lighting gave the chamber a dull, red glow. Whoever thought this colour was appropriate was clearly an absolute idiot.

"I am not able to communicate with the facility computer." Soteria's voice was crackly, the reception on the radio poor.

"Are you able to re-establish contact?" Stuart held the radio so they could both speak into it.

"Negative. The computer mainframe has been compromised."

Now they truly were trapped down here, with violence stalking the hellish corridors.

"Is there any way for us to get out?"

"Miss Jones. There might be. I doubt you will like it, though."

"There's nothing about this situation I like. I knew I should have left with Craig." Wasn't that the truth. The loss of the Bitch had hit her hard, made Lucy vulnerable. She thought she'd needed the wise voice of the psychologist whispering in her ear. Now she wasn't so sure. What could a therapist offer her when they had no understanding of what the Bitch was.

"What, and leave me all on my lonesome?" Stuart managed a reassuring smile.

"What do we need to do, Soteria?"

"I need you to try and become infested, Miss Jones." Lucy looked at the radio as if it had slapped her.

"You can't be serious."

"The implant in your neck will record how the parasite interacts with your body. I require that data."

"You want to use me as a lab rat? Hell no." There was no telling what that creature would do to her.

"The data is important," Soteria insisted.

"You hope to understand why the parasite is being rejected by females. Is that it?" Stuart looked at Lucy as he spoke. In the red light, his face had a ghoulish appearance.

"Yes," Soteria agreed.

"It's not much of a plan," Lucy protested.

"It's all we've got."

"That's kind of easy for you to say, Stuart."

"Hey. It is what it is." *Is that it? Is that the best argument you can come up with?*

"How will this help, though?" If Lucy had to do this, she would, but the Hidden hand was going to owe her big time.

"If I can discover what prevents infestation, I may be able to reproduce it." And there it was. To get out of here, the emergency had to be over, which meant defeating the parasite.

"Are we doing this, then?" Stuart asked.

"There is no we in this scenario, Stuart. I have to do this alone."

"Miss Jones is right."

The pair were moving now, out of the chamber, walking slowly back towards the security office. Lucy led the way, gun at the ready. The lighting in the corridor was worse. If anyone came at them, at least they wouldn't be able to see the resulting blood.

"You don't want to be hunting these things down on your own." Stuart sounded adamant.

"Of course, I don't. But if you go anywhere near those parasites, you'll be done for." Lucy had seen how the parasites controlled people. She had a chance against the infested facility personnel, but having Stuart's skill and bulk used against her would be a terrible scenario. "I don't want to have to kill you."

"You think you can take me?" Lucy knew he was joking.

"I'd rather not have to find out."

***

Failure.

Loss.

These sensations it understood through the emotions of the possessed human minds. Its brethren had sacrificed themselves to control the computer that ran this prison, and they had failed. Their fusion with the circuit boards and processors had not achieved the desired result.

Tragic.

Unforeseen.

Hubris.

The Children that had been sent below could no longer be felt on the telepathic network that was still limited to this subterranean structure. There were other voices, thousands of them, out on the edge of the ether, but they were incoherent whispers made inaudible by distance. That in itself was a loss, for it needed to be as one with those distant calls.

Do not forbid me what is mine.

The Scourge wasn't close to being at its true potential. Being trapped down here went nowhere towards the goal of fulfilling its purpose. To escape was essential, for the others of its kind needed to know about the threat of the Hidden Hand.

The information and memories in the heads of those it possessed belonged to the Scourge now. The Hidden Hand was a threat to the ultimate mission. The individual Children had been programmed, and the Scourge would enact the mission required of it.

There was one benefit in those sacrifices. The threat of thermal sterilisation had been cancelled, which meant there was still time to find a way out of here.

The parasite in Cleaver's head stimulated a fresh pain centre. It had enjoyed playing with this human whose emotions and fears were easy to manipulate. It reacted strongly to pain and showed little in the way of resistance.

Perhaps, though, it had gone too far.

You must get up, the parasite insisted.

"Please," the professor mumbled. He was lying on the canteen floor, his clothes sodden. His face was a ruin, a result of the parasite experimenting with him. It was important to know how much trauma the human body could accept and keep on going.

Several of Cleaver's teeth were scattered around him. Three of his fingers jutted out at obscene angles from where they had been dislocated. Blood crusted across his upper lip and chin, and his left ear hung tantalisingly from where it had been partly ripped away.

The other surviving men it had good control of, the two guards in particular. They had revelled in the brutality offered to them; deep-seated sadism unleashed. The parasite liked humans of that calibre. They made for worthy hosts who didn't whine and moan at the atrocities required of them. The parasite gave them a form of freedom from the strict controls that society had leashed them with.

The humans praised their individuality, not realising it was their greatest weakness. Unity of mind was the only way to beat the Scourge, but humanity had lost that ability.

"I want to die," Cleaver whimpered.

But you can still be of use. The parasite sent a surge of adrenaline through the bruised and battered body. Cleaver stirred, rising onto his hands and knees. *Up. Get up.*

This mind was different than the others. The pathways of control were unique, the memories representing a life of mental suffering. The body itself was weak, even with the chemicals and hormones the parasite now stimulated.

How do we escape? The parasite had scoured Cleaver's mind, but it did not have the gift of insight or problem solving. It needed the human for that, required the grey organic matter to fix the problems it now faced. The professor was the most intelligent of those it now owned, only the dead man it had used to sacrifice coming anywhere close.

"You can't."

Unacceptable. We must.

"You can't," Cleaver persisted. A searing pain ripped its way through his genitals, making Cleaver stagger. There had to be a way to freedom. They would not be doomed to this isolation.

The parasite was considering making Cleaver gouge out his left eye, when off in the distance, gunfire erupted.

No!

27.

London, UK

Craig hadn't seen the Director of the Hidden Hand since that ominous day on the cliff edge when he'd learned about the existence of the secret organisation. Today, the old man was sat next to someone just as ancient, the individual who had previously introduced himself as Archie.

The Director and the Curator in the same room. Should he be honoured or worried? At least now, Craig could hopefully get some answers to the questions churning around his thoughts.

He'd been in this conference room several times before and was sitting across the oval table from his two superiors. The wall to his left was dominated by a large LCD wall display, and the coffee was as bad as always.

Craig grimaced as he drank it.

Neither of his superiors felt the need to join him in this Devil's brew. He craved the caffeine, though, last night's sleep disturbed and restless.

"Would someone like to share what that farce was all about?" Craig asked, referring to his thwarted detainment. Resting on the table in front of the Director was the folder used to intimidate Craig during his interrogation. "I'm supposed to be a ghost, and yet the world seems to know my life's history." How was he supposed to work in the shadows if everyone and their uncle were hunting for him?

"I believe Soteria has an explanation," the Director prompted.

"Thank you, Director. I can assure the captain that my eradication of his personal history was thorough. However, there is a source that I have not been able to penetrate."

"The Russians," Craig surmised. Recent events couldn't be any coincidence.

"Yes. The Director asked me to do a deep investigation regarding those involved in your detention. My report makes for troubling reading."

"You mean my kidnapping?" Craig corrected.

"Just so," agreed Archie.

"And what did you find?" In answer to Craig's question, the monitor switched on. A photograph of Peter Sloane took up half the screen. The other half was taken up by the image of a man Craig had never met.

"It would seem the hydra has many heads," Archie replied before taking a long drag on his vape pen. Craig couldn't smell any marijuana today. With everything going on, perhaps the Curator felt the need to keep a clear head.

"I have no idea what that means?" Craig kept his temper in check. These weren't people to shout at.

"It means you have unearthed something we've suspecting for a while now. Sad to say that MI5 has been infiltrated at the highest level." The Director looked tired, no doubt lack of sleep compounding that.

"This is very troubling," Archie added. He sighed deeply as if the weight of the universe was pressing on him.

"Infiltrated?" Craig suspected by whom, but he wanted to hear it.

"By the Russians, obviously," the Director clarified.

"So that's where MI5 got that dossier on me?" enquired Craig as he pointed to the bundle of papers.

"What do you think?" Archie asked with a wink.

"Well, that's just great. Why the hell do the bloody Russians have a file on me?"

"Don't take it personally. They collect data. It's what makes them so effective. They call it the Yezhov protocol. Politicians, industrialists, and the serving military of NATO countries; they collect, collate and store it all away. Every Russian embassy across the world has a department committed to it." The Director sat back in his chair. "Soteria has been trying to penetrate their extensive database ever since we learnt the Russians were doing this."

"Unsuccessfully, I might add," Soteria said from the room's speakers. "I have been unable to breach their quantum encryption."

"Then I've been compromised from the start."

"Yes, we know. Very unfortunate." Archie shook his head to show he understood Craig's concerns.

"Unfortunate? Getting a parking ticket is unfortunate." *Keep it down, Craig.* He took a breath through his nose to steady himself. "And these two?" Craig pointed at the monitor.

"I have been able to establish a possible connection between these two men," Soteria revealed. The picture of Peter had him as a younger man. The other face looked out at the room with a stern scowl.

"The second man is Viktor Orlov," The Director revealed. "The local head of the Russian FSB."

"A nasty fellow," Archie added.

"Somebody might need to do something about him," continued the Director.

"I have surveillance footage that hints at several clandestine meetings, although it's only now I have put the pieces together," Soteria admitted. It was understandable. Soteria couldn't monitor everyone all the time, especially when the Hellgates kept getting lively.

"But what's this got to do with me?" Craig wasn't here to combat the Russians. "Why am I a target for Russian intelligence?"

The image on the screen changed to a night-time scene of Craig. When the Hell was that taken?

"This image was in the dossier Peter Sloane had accumulated. I have been able to identify the buildings in the background, and, using extrapolation and deduction, I have ascertained that this image was taken by the Russian agent known as Ivanka. She most likely had a hidden body camera on her." In the corner of the screen, a recording from a street camera emerged. It showed the moment Craig had warned off the attractive Russian agent days before.

"How certain are you of that conclusion, Soteria?" As the Director spoke, he kept his eyes on Craig.

"Ninety-seven per cent."

"This tallies with what we learnt in Ivanka's interrogation. You embarrassed her, so she sought to even the score."

"Director, I've been wondering why you used me for that operation?" Craig had been an active field agent for barely two weeks. He understood why Ivanka couldn't be allowed to compromise a member of the British government, but why use *him* for the solo op?

He'd caught the news about that minister's death this morning. That had the Hidden Hand's calling card all over it. Craig wasn't to know that Stuart had been dispatched to kill the man who'd been foolish enough to leave himself open to blackmail. Craig might have been part of a team, but that team's members were often sent off on individual missions, the details of which weren't spoken of.

If it was necessary for Craig to know something, Soteria would be there to tell him.

"You seemed to be the right man for the job," came the Director's less than revelatory reply. What weren't they telling him?

From the start of his training to join the Hidden Hand, he'd been warned that operational information was strictly need to know.

"Is Ivanka still alive? Can you at least tell me that?" Craig asked. He still felt that warning her off had been the right card to play, and nobody had told him otherwise. In fact, if he'd gone the hard-core route and simply terminated her, then the identity of MI5's traitor might not have been revealed.

The Hidden Hand had long ago chosen to accept the chaotic randomness that controlled the world. They were the secret power that massaged the subtle intricacies of the world rather than attempting to dominate them.

"Ivanka has been retired," the Director informed him. So, dead then. "The question we should now focus on is whether the same fate should befall Peter Sloane."

Craig hadn't been expecting that development.

"Normally, this would be something we would discuss with Colonel Radcliffe," Archie added. "But as you know, our good friend is indisposed." Indisposed due to being trapped in a bunker complex beneath the earth on a remote island most people had never heard of.

"What do you say Craig? Are you ready for the messy stuff?"

"You want me to kill one of the top men in MI5?"

"Not just kill. We will need so much more from you." The Director leaned forward, eager for Craig's answer.

Craig surprised himself by the lack of doubt in his thoughts.

"Tell me what I need to do."

28.

Isles of Scilly, UK

"This is a really stupid idea," Lucy mumbled under her breath. She was moving cautiously, her M4 carbine up and ready. She'd shed the slippers on the run to the elevators, her foot falls silent.

The men she was hunting weren't armed as far as she knew, but they could still be deadly. From what she had personally witnessed, at least three of them had been stripped of all morality and mercy. They had displayed unusual strength and ferocity as well as showing they had no hesitation in killing.

That was fine. Lucy could play that game, too.

Off in another part of the complex, a single gunshot rang out. Maybe they were armed after all. She paused to see if her ears would reveal anything more, but the silence that followed persisted.

The corridor she was in curved round, the rest area ahead. She clung to the wall, checking her rear frequently to ensure there would be no surprises. The engulfing red light gave this space an eerie feel, and despite Lucy having the skill and the training, she wished the Bitch was here. That goading voice had always come across as an irritant, but it was clear now that the Bitch gave her an edge in combat situations.

Ahead, a body came into view. Female, the figure half stripped. As Lucy got closer, she witnessed the damage that had been done, one of the arms ripped clear. If not for the ID badge, it would have taken forensics to identify who the deceased was.

On the white wall next to the mangled corpse, someone had written a single word in blood.

Reject.

The door to the recreation area was open, Lucy's field of view limiting the chances that anyone in there was hiding inside. It would have been better to have Soteria in her ear, but with the facility being on emergency power, only the hand-held radios allowed for that communication.

Lucy couldn't use the M4 and the radio at the same time, the carbine offering her more stopping power and accuracy than her pistol.

She was on her own.

Lucy cleared the room as she had been trained, the gun-mounted torch helping with that. The only thing behind the door was another corpse, the rest area floor littered with dismembered body parts.

"Please. Kill me." The plea came from the far corner of the room, Professor Cleaver curled up in a shivering ball. Was he talking to her or the entity in his head?

Lucy closed the door behind her before clearing the last of the space. It was a room for people to sit and chat, a small kitchen area at one end. She soon discounted the chances that anyone was lurking behind any of the furniture. There were still four threats on the loose. Each carrying a deadly and merciless parasite.

The blood she did her best to ignore as she walked through it, her feet leaving prints behind.

"Professor." There was no need to whisper.

"So much pain." His words were slurred.

"Can you hear me, Professor?"

"No release. No release." Lucy kept her distance. She already knew she'd need to kill Cleaver, but she had the intuition to try something first.

"I want to talk to the entity controlling you." Cleaver didn't react. "Or I can just put a bullet in Cleaver's head."

Cleaver shifted, his whole body seeming to tense as the muscle clenched. The professor moved to a seated position, head rotating as the neck flexed.

"You wouldn't shoot me," Cleaver stated in challenge. His voice had a definite lisp to it.

"Oh yeah? You clearly don't know me."

A smile spread across Cleaver's bloodied face, showing the teeth that he was now missing.

"You humans are weak." As Cleaver spoke, two grey things squeezed themselves out of the swollen nostrils.

Cleaver must be riddled with the things.

"I don't have to be strong to pull this trigger. I imagine that would ruin that nice, warm body you're sitting in." Was she conversing with an alien, or a man driven insane?

The Bitch would know for sure.

"This body means nothing to us," Cleaver protested. *Us*! It wasn't Cleaver then, and Lucy could now see the malevolent force behind the professor's face. The slug moved down, parting into two to pass the lips.

Another emerged from the professor's ear. Lucy kept her aim on Cleaver's head.

"And yet you stick around. From the sounds Cleaver was making, it seems like you were enjoying yourselves."

"We get our nature from those we make better, as you will soon see." Lucy was ready for what came next.

The first of the parasites leapt, its speed and agility impressive. It landed close to Lucy and slid towards her. If she'd been wearing heavy boots, she might have stomped down on it through instinct.

There was something about the parasite that triggered a primal dread in Lucy. She'd long ago learnt to control and use her fear.

Here we go.

The parasite pounced, landing on Lucy's thigh, where it instantly gnawed into her skin. Lucy grunted through gritted teeth at the lancing pain, and then the thing was inside her, forcing its way up beneath her skin.

You better be fucking right about this, Soteria.

The parasite got to her hip before fresh pain struck; the critter was chewing its way out. Wetness spread down Lucy's leg, the invader disintegrating. She felt violated, but Lucy pushed that nonsense to one side.

"You want to try that again?"

"You are diseased. You are impure, only fit for eradication."

"Funny, I was going to say the same thing about you." Lucy centred on Cleaver's face, and right before she fired, she saw him nod his head. It was the last remnants of Cleaver giving his consent to his own salvation.

The back of his skull ended up being plastered on the wall.

As his body slumped, the parasites in him began to abandon ship, chewing their way out. Lucy backed away, well aware of how they could hurt her if they wanted to go kamikaze. Instead, they slicked away, some mistakenly sliding through the spilt blood of the women killed in here.

Those were quickly reduced to a bubbling mess.

The rest disappeared, slipping beneath furniture, some using their speed to climb the walls. There was no point shooting at the invaders, for they were too small and too fast. Fortunately for Lucy, they didn't take it upon themselves to come at her in a massed assault.

"Kill the whore." The shout came from outside, the sound of thick boots running adding to the threat. The door to the rest room was wrenched open, the first of the psychologist's guards barrelling through. He had his shock baton held above his head, intent on caving in Lucy's skull.

He never got the chance. Lucy put three shots centre mass, which caused the guard's legs to slide out from under him as his momentum sent him to the ground.

Lethal shots, but Lucy put a fourth round into his stupid head just as the second guard made an appearance. The body of his dead comrade only enraged the second man, his face filled with fury. Lucy lowered her aim and put enough bullets in his legs to make them useless. It didn't matter how strong you were when your knee caps were wrecked.

Naturally, he too fell to the ground.

"Bitch!" the second guard cursed. He'd fallen sideways as his legs had failed. Already, the parasites were abandoning the first guard, off to seek some sort of sanctuary.

How long could they live without a human host?

"The Bitch isn't here right now," Lucy said in correction.

Two men killed and one incapacitated. The Bitch wouldn't have had it any other way.

Let's make that three dead.

None of the resulting parasites came for her. Did that tell Lucy something about the nature of the creature?

Could they be as cowardly as the humans they sometimes tried to control?

***

After that, Lucy made her way back to the security office. The two other infested men found her, perhaps drawn by the gunfire. More likely, it was the parasite directing them.

Lucy made short work of those last two because she knew she had no other choice. Either one of them would have bludgeoned Lucy to death if the blood on their hands was anything to go by.

Were any of the other females left alive, or had they all been hunted down? And who had fired that mystery shot?

Closer to her destination, she swapped the M4 for her pistol so she could use the radio.

"Are you there, Soteria?" The radio crackled in response, and Soteria's familiar voice came through.

"Yes. Your vitals tell me your heart rate is elevated. I trust you are not injured." With the main computer down, Soteria was unable to access the bunker's surveillance grid.

"Just adrenaline. Did you get what you need?" *You better have.* Lucy didn't object to killing people when it was needed, but she didn't like that these men might have been innocent. It didn't matter that it was a case of her or them.

Lucy preferred to punish the guilty.

She might have killed the obvious threats, but there were still two men here, one of whom she trusted, the other a relative unknown. The last time she'd seen them, they had been free of the infestation, but…

"I may well have. When the parasite invaded your body, there was a spike in estratetraenol."

"Never heard of it."

"It is a steroid your body produces. As it is generally found only in the female of your species, it may well be the answer we seek."

"Well, that's good, right?" Up ahead, she could see the security room. Worryingly, the door was open.

"Yes. I am computing how I can apply this information."

"Well, no rush." Lucy knew the computer wouldn't detect her sarcasm.

"Unfortunately, I have some distressing news. Colonel Radcliffe appears to have been infested."

A cold fist clamped itself around Lucy's guts. She'd left Stuart to go to the security room, which wasn't secure as they'd both hoped.

Lucy slowed as she approached the turn in the corridor that led to that room, peeking round the corner. Nobody was there, so she edged herself forward, the security room door ajar.

What would be waiting for her in there?

"Stuart," she shouted cautiously. If he'd been turned, Lucy prayed he would come charging at her like the others. At least that way she could tell herself there was no choice.

"In here," came Stuart's pained response.

Was this a trap? Never had she needed the Bitch more than she did now.

Are you in there? Come on, show yourself. The mocking personality refused to come out of hiding.

As she got nearer, Lucy surmised the reason for the open door. It allowed Lucy to see inside, both Ted and Stuart part visible. She could safely approach without either of them surprising her. That had been Stuart's doing.

Ted wasn't moving. He was lying on the floor, back to her. Five steps and she'd be on the threshold, Stuart beckoning to her with his chin.

"It's safe," he promised.

When she reached the doorway, she kept her gun up.

"What's going on Stuart?" Ted was dead, blood pooled under his head. Stuart was sat on the floor, hands behind him. "You better not be hiding something."

"Check my feet," he replied. Cold steel encircled both ankles, handcuffs placed. Keeping to the wall, Lucy moved round until she saw the same state of his wrists. His arms were pulled back, the cuffs threaded through a wall pipe.

The radio she deposited onto the nearest desk.

"You do that?"

"Yeah," Stuart nodded through gritted teeth. "Handcuffs were in the security locker. Did it before the little bastards found me?"

"And Ted?"

"I found him like that," Stuart revealed. "Poor sap took his own life." Lucy knelt by the lifeless body. There was no way to fake the gunshot wound to his temple. The force of the impact had toppled Ted from his chair, the gun kicked across the floor.

Could she believe Stuart?

"It's in me," Stuart revealed. Carefully, Lucy checked that the cuffs were secure, ankles first. When she checked his wrists, Lucy kept the gun pressed against Stuart's forehead.

The cuffs were strong and unyielding, as was the pipe.

"Thank you." Thank you for not making me shoot you.

Stuart grunted, twisting his head from the obvious pain he was in.

"I wasn't going to give the bastard thing the satisfaction. You... you get what Soteria needed?"

"She thinks so. Can you hold out?"

Stuart looked at her from one eye as his face scrunched up.

"I honestly don't know."

29.

Area 51, Nevada, USA

Brook stood in the shade, for he knew the parasite didn't like the heat of the sun overhead. Inside its human host, it would be protected, but Brook still found himself filled with an aversion to sustained sun exposure.

Normally, on a day like this, the airbase runway would be busy with flights, but everything was grounded as the parasite spread itself. Despite the billions of dollars of ongoing research and development taking place in the hangars of Area 51, the parasite cared only about control. As a result, the surrounding air was filled with a stillness that was less than reassuring.

Occasionally, a scream would rip through the desert air as another female was detained. There had been shots at first, but resistance was quickly being suppressed.

"The portal is presently stable," Brook told the person at the other end of his satellite phone. While the phone he used was able to make standard calls, this particular conversation was covered by end-to-end encryption. Not even the NSA would be able to eavesdrop.

Standing tall in the waning sun, Brook waited for a response to the news.

"Do we know what caused it?"

"No, sir." Sir, the man on the other end of the call was a two-star general, one of the few senior officers Brook once had respect for. There were too many politically motivated top brass in the US military at present, and not enough men and women who knew how to get things done.

This general needed to think the situation was in hand.

Do not give them any cause to suspect.

"Do you think our portal's hissy fit is linked to the other worldwide disturbances?"

"Doctor Hertz doesn't seem to think so." At times Brook couldn't tell when it was him speaking or the parasite. At times, the two minds felt fused, combined, and working in balance. When that happened, what was left of Brook had no reservation or resistance left in him. Whatever the parasite wanted was for the benefit of the world.

The pain only came in brief instances when Brook's rebellious heart tried to rise out of the ashes.

"Colonel, I didn't ask you what Doctor Hertz thinks."

"I agree with the doctor," Brook surmised. In the sky, off in the distance, three buzzards began to circle. Was that an omen? Would those flying scavengers be gathering over this base, days or weeks from now? "We are still trying to establish why the portal became so aggressive."

Brook found that he knew things. The parasite had an origin, and there were images in Brook's mind's eye about a place of heat and pain. The sky there was red, creatures of impossible ferocity lurking in the shadows.

The owners of that place wanted the Earth.

"And you're certain those eggheads have been behaving themselves?" The general shared Brook's previous view that the portal should be left well alone. Brook was now struck with the undefeatable notion that the portal was of extreme importance.

"Yes General. Hertz and his staff are keeping to the script. One thing, sir, I'm going to need an engineering team. The containment shell has been compromised." Brook knew that would be a ball ache to arrange, but the more people brought here, the better.

"I'll have that authorised," the general promised. "Are you going to be able to make golf on Sunday?" *I just told you the concrete shell has been cracked open like an egg, and you're asking me about golf.* That thought was quashed.

"Most certainly, sir." Brook had hated the game, but played it because it was expected of him, and because it was a way to keep his face known to the people that mattered. The old Brook had been willing to play the politics that came with the position he held. Now, meeting the general would come with other advantages.

"Hope to see you then. Oh, one thing before I go, a bit of an irregularity. An oversight team will be coming to Nevada." That was more cryptic than Brook was comfortable with.

"Sir? That's more than a bit irregular."

"Nevertheless, that inspection will take place. I have bosses too, you know."

"I can assure you, an inspection isn't necessary, but I won't try to stop it." The old Brook didn't have time for such bureaucracy, so he made sure to respond as his former self. The general would expect to hear resistance and disappointment. Being in the middle of the desert miles from anyone, though, the parasite welcomed the visit.

The voices it could telepathically hear were into the thousands now, but the progress could always be faster.

Ownership of Area 51 was almost complete. That would be the beach head for what came next while the huge city became a breeding ground for the new army.

"I knew I could rely on you."

General, if only you knew the truth. But you will, and your mind will be welcomed with all the others.

A truck pulled up in front of him, and Brook put a finger to his lips. There were four people inside it, one a woman being restrained. Brook was long past the stage of killing them now.

"Thank you, sir." That ended the call. The general was clearly a busy man, but then, so was Brook.

Putting the phone away, Brook beckoned for the woman. The back doors of the truck opened, the latest victim being dragged out. It looked like she'd put up one hell of a fight, but the two enhanced men could handle her.

"Take her to the portal." Those controlling the woman didn't need to be told twice. She would get to see the half a dozen bodies that were laid out in the portal chamber before her life was cast into the blue unknown.

Unknown to her, Brook had some idea of what would be there to meet her.

Brook flexed his shoulders, either he or the parasite revelling in the feeling of power that coursed through the muscles. In his prime, Brook had never felt this strong.

Right now, Brook wanted to venture back down into the bowels of XR-1 Storage. He wanted to be by the portal, its blue glow reassuring. Hertz had been right after all.

The portal was beautiful.

He had lodgings in the main Air Force base, but he would sleep in his small office below ground, where he was close to his destiny. If the parasite knew why the women were being pushed through the portal, it chose not to share that information. It didn't matter, because Brook was becoming less and less of an identity. The invader was swallowing him up, engulfing his essence. Soon, the name Brook would only be there to fool those humans who had yet to experience the glory of enhancement.

Off in the distance, another single gunshot rang out. Most of the surrounding base had been taken surreptitiously, the last holdouts being hunted down. The bulk of those who worked here were male, so the parasites would see to them. Normal phones didn't work out here, and satellite phones and the base communications were the first things that had been isolated.

Nobody would be calling for help any time soon. And if help did come, there would be little hope for the rescuers.

Despite this invasion representing everything Brook despised, he wanted to be there in the thick of things. He led from the front, always had.

Not this time, for he was needed here.

Brook took off walking, heading back through the gate that marked the only way through the triple-layered perimeter around XR-1 Storage. To his old self, the extra precautions were necessary, and they had been installed long before his tenure. Of the three razor-wire-topped fences, the one sandwiched in the middle was electrified.

Those defences had been there to protect the world from the portal. Now it was the gateway between worlds that needed protection.

Ahead of him, the latest woman was being dragged.

What mysteries awaited her in the land of the red sky?

30.

Isles of Scilly, UK

How would he cope if these hours turned into days?

You think you understand pain. You are mistaken.

Stuart had no recollection of the parasite invading him, but there was no denying the alien voice that was intent on making his existence an utter misery. His predicament had started with a voice whispering to him, offering fresh and delightful experiences so long as he gave himself. It saw the killer in Stuart, but didn't appreciate that murder was a duty to him rather than a pleasure. Severe discomfort in his skull was the initial weapon in the parasite's arsenal, but he was way past that stage now.

"Go fuck yourself." Stuart was grinding his teeth so hard, he was sure something in his mouth had either broken or dislodged.

He could feel the entity moving inside him, pushing his consciousness aside. That was what the pain was about, a distraction to shrink his resolve and distract him as the parasite worked to establish control. It was relentless, offspring breaking off as they moved through him. Those brethren stayed inside, for there were no new hosts to take command of.

It was only Stuart and Lucy left down here.

We will show you new forms of suffering.

The sweat was pouring into his eyes now, which was a minor irritation compared to what the parasite was inflicting. Lucy was sat off, watching him silently. This was his battle to win or lose, and although Stuart spoke out loud, she knew not to engage him.

"Bring it on." Stuart found himself straining at the wrist cuffs, the parasite briefly gaining control of his arms. Wrenching back his influence, Stuart was met with a tearing sensation through both kidneys.

This is foolish. We will win. You inflict this upon yourself.

There was a sudden push behind his eyes, his right eyelid suddenly beginning to twitch. The pain came at him in waves, never giving him a chance to get used to it.

The parasite would have made an excellent torturer. Perhaps, in a sense, that was what it was, using agony to learn what he was made of. There was no defeating this thing, not without Soteria coming to the rescue.

Occasionally, Lucy would get up and leave the room with the radio. That way, she could converse with Soteria without Stuart hearing the nature of that conversation. So long as he couldn't hear them, then neither could the parasite.

She returned a final time, before leaving him to face his inner demon alone. She gave Stuart a sad look, hiding from him several items that she took from the armament's locker. She left her M4 behind.

Something had changed.

What had Soteria just told her?

Did you enjoy killing children?

The question suddenly dropped into his thoughts, and Stuart screamed in response.

We can see inside you. We see the killer that lurks there and the pleasures you try to deny yourself. Admit who you are and let us in.

The accusation stung, but Stuart wouldn't succumb to that emotional blackmail. He'd been under another's control once; he would fight this invader to the last breath.

Your guilt is undeniable.

"Screw you."

Shouting out his answers actually helped, but it was only a delaying tactic. His identity had become the intensity of the sensations hurled at him.

His feet felt like they were on fire.

There was a knife twisting in his left eyeball.

A fist in a spiked iron gauntlet was squeezing his testicles.

His guts churned as spasms rippled up and down his intestines.

How much more could Stuart take?

As much as he needed to.

It had been hours since Soteria had informed them that she was working on a plan; hours since he'd been given a modicum of hope. If Soteria was going to come up with some method of salvation, she needed to get on with it.

If Stuart lost himself to this parasite, he wasn't sure he'd be able to find his way back.

***

The parasite had tried to escape, but it had failed. It had found the main air shaft to the facility, and using its previous technique, had sent several of its kind to climb that towering shaft.

It had almost made it, but had been thwarted at the last step by a series of intense UV lights that were there to sterilise the flow of air. Several had tried to breach that defence, but the UV bulbs were arranged in an ascending spiral that had defeated all attempts by the parasite to penetrate. Strong enough to burn human flesh, the defensive lights had shrivelled and destroyed all the Children that had come close to that devastating glow.

Eventually, after suffering too many losses that it would now struggle to replace, it had abandoned the attempt. Other routes of escape had been investigated, but none had been successful. One of the brethren had even reached the scanner room but had been unable to penetrate through that barrier.

It was trapped and was running out of options.

The Children were not capable of surrendering to despair, however.

With all but one of the males dead, the parasite now concentrated its efforts on the one known as Stuart. The man needed to be broken, so that his bonds could be freed. He was still resistant to the commands of the parasite, but there was confidence that he would succumb like all the others. If he could be used, there was still a chance.

A chance was all the Children required.

Time was, however, the defining factor.

Time worked against the parasite, for it now knew of the entity called Soteria and that a plan was being concocted to defeat the rest of the Children.

The one called Stuart had to be brought to the new understanding and would be forced to endure increasing levels of suffering.

The Children would not be denied their destiny.

The Children would be free.

31.

Las Vegas

The golem was spent, its insides freed of the burden of carrying the Children inflicted upon it. Some golems, at the end of their time, would wish to go out in a blaze of glory. Not this golem. It had nothing to prove and now sat it itself on the sandy ground at the edge of the city.

The sun was no longer a concern to it, and the scenic horizon was lost on an entity that had no concern for aesthetics. Another day was ending, and tonight the Children would ensure the survival of their kind. There was no way for the golem to know how many of the parasites were now controlling hosts, but it was likely in the thousands.

Would that be enough?

It had killed, and it had maimed, but the golem carried no guilt. It was a manifestation of dust and clay, and now was the time for it to return itself to what it had been assembled from.

A breeze lifted around it, faint specs of dust detaching from its bulk. Lifting its immense hand, the golem watched as the fingers began to disassemble. The surface went first, the fake texture meant to mimic human skin dissipating before the fingers themselves started to crack and fragment. The golem moved its digits, speeding up their demise, leaving its hand a stump only useful for pounding. Then the hand itself shattered, parts dropping into its lap.

The golem began to break apart from the peripheries, the outer layers sloughing away as it crumbled. Sat cross legged, it began to lose its cohesion, the inner chamber where the Children had been stored collapsing in on themselves. Layer upon layer were reduced to dust that would eventually be cast to the wind.

Its last thought before it was reduced to nothing was how weak and insignificant humanity was. They didn't deserve this planet, and it hoped the Children would somehow make this world better by humanity's demise.

Then it was gone, a mound of black ash and dirt that would soon be nothing but a dark smear on the desert sand.

***

Cliff had loved his truck. It was old yet reliable, made in an era where America had been proud of its manufacturing. None of that mattered now, the hot desert air blowing through his open window.

The day had been productive for him, his body a constant breeding ground for the Children he had spread. The flab around his waist was diminished, the parasites feeding off him to fuel their reproduction. Despite that, Cliff felt no hunger, for his thoughts were consumed by the burning hatred he had for the fairer sex.

Come and join the parasitic weight-loss plan.

Every time he saw a woman now, a part of him wanted to pound their faces into oblivion. The parasite wouldn't allow that, for Cliff was needed for greater things and violence would draw unwanted attention. There were other hosts that were being used to infiltrate the law enforcement and judiciary, those in the city's positions of power being consumed for the new order.

The women of the world must be made to suffer, but that is something for another day.

That was why he was driving, Las Vegas behind him. He didn't know if he would ever return to that city, and quite frankly, he didn't care. He only had a vague idea of where he was going, and he hoped his truck was up to the task at hand. It would be a long drive through barren and desolate terrain, but Cliff wasn't the only pioneer on the roads.

The Scourge had altered their strategy, the individual Children following the new plan. At first, they had been intent on overwhelming the city with their presence, unleashing violence and terror onto the well-lit streets of Las Vegas. That was what their sadism had demanded, but the hive mind had matured and re-evaluated the best way to proceed with human domination.

Mass violence and terror were now considered too much too quick and thus far too risky. Through the accumulated human minds, the Scourge had learned about the weapons of humanity, about the bombs and the nukes that could be used to reduce a city to radioactive rubble. The heat and the ultra-violet rays from this world's sun were deadly to the Children in their exposed form, and so likely was the vast amount of radiation such bombs could produce.

Better to avoid the risk of that. Revealing itself too early would be foolish.

Instead, the Children spread themselves carefully, taking the men when privacy allowed so as not to alert the masters of this world that their control was being undone. Instead of mass infestation, the Scourge now concentrated on taking the people of importance and power, making use of opportunity and circumstance.

It might take days, but the city was to become the first of many, an outpost for further spread and control. Thousands of people came and went to Las Vegas every day. What better place for the Children to infest and move, every state of this festering nation a place for the Children to find fresh meat?

The hosts would be made to continue with their daily tasks, blending in with the world that was slowly being usurped. The golem had fulfilled its mission, and now the Scourge would have its day.

Cliff was an emissary, one of several, a trailblazer sent forth to cast the contagion far and wide. The Children would infiltrate and consume, moving from city to city as they made themselves ready for the battle that was to come.

Towns and cities would fall to them, and then whole countries.

Eventually, the world would be theirs so that humanity could be made to bow down to the authority of the Lord Moloch. When that immortal being finally came to reclaim this land, the human race would be made to scream in unified agony.

What a reckoning that would be.

32.

Isles of Scilly, UK

Stuart watched as the grey blob ate through the handcuffs, restraining his ankles. A tiny drop of acid hit his skin, but the pain was insignificant compared to what was already being inflicted.

You know you cannot defy us.

Stuart felt dazed, his world swirling. The agony in his body was localised to his skin, invisible scalpels working on him. Stuart could already feel that his control over his own body had slipped, the limbs seeming to have a life of their own. That was a lie, though, because it was the parasite that was now calling the shots.

He had held off as long as he could, but in his brain, the invader had engaged in multiple assaults, taking what he was piece by piece. And every time he tried to take that territory back, the pain enveloped him.

It was hopeless, and the realisation of such exacerbated the hopelessness. There was no stopping the juggernaut that ripped through him, no defeating this enemy. Just as with Sirena, his own body was about to be turned against the world he was here to defend.

Despite the terrible sensations that were rippling through him, Stuart preferred this to what Sirena had done to him. Sirena's control had been insidious and complete, making him do things that were linked to a longing in his own inner self. Sirena had removed his inhibition, allowing certain impulses to rise to the surface where they had demanded his submission.

This was different. This was like being a passenger in the train wreck his body had become.

He groaned as his body stood, the wrists already freed, and he staggered to his feet.

Now we hunt.

"No," Stuart managed, only for fire to erupt in his mouth. That drew an agonised groan from him, which seemed to please the entity inside him.

You suffer well. And you will know nothing but the sensations we give you until you comply. We know you Stuart, we know everything about who you are.

Stuart could feel the parasites worming their way under his skin. His body was filling with them, ready on the chance that he could somehow escape.

Will your Lucy risk killing us? No, I think there is some plan she has concocted. She hopes to somehow save you. How foolish.

To his left on the nearest table, his fingers reached and clutched the radio that had been left there. He felt it being brought up to his lips.

Behave yourself now, the parasite warned.

"Soteria." The voice was his, but he'd had no control over the word. "Soteria, can you hear me?"

"Yes, I can hear you."

"I need to be free of this place, Soteria."

"I regret that this cannot be allowed at this time."

Stuart wanted to shout a warning, but he felt locked down, held by chains of pain. The parasite was in his brain, pushing and prodding what made his body work.

"I'm afraid I must insist."

"You are not yourself. The infestation cannot be permitted to reach the surface."

"Then I will kill Lucy," Stuart's voice threatened. The parasite had borrowed his memories. Would it also be able to use his skill and experience? Stuart didn't think so, because right now, his movements were flawed and cumbersome.

It was struggling to gain true control of what it meant to be Stuart Radcliffe.

"That would be unfortunate. I would miss her. Still, my instructions can only be overridden by your superiors."

"Why do you humans resist? They can be so stubborn in their belligerence." Stuart had kept the thing at bay for as long as he could, suffering for many hours as he battled with his inner self. He hoped he had done enough to buy Soteria the time she needed.

"Humans are an enigma neither of us will ever solve. My advice is to abandon your host and accept that you have lost."

"Never," the parasite shouted, before throwing the radio at the wall. With trembling fingers, the parasite reached for the pistol.

"I told you, there's no getting out." Stuart's logic was met by the unenviable experience of his urethra feeling like it was pissing acid.

If we cannot be free, then we will be forced to play. We will make you kill Lucy slowly. It will take many hours, and you will be there to see it all. You will do things that will forever horrify you and you will join her in her agony.

Stuart believed the thing inside him could try, but all that suggested was it didn't understand the foe it was up against. It was also a mistake on the invaders' part, although he didn't let that thought to gel in his mind. Stuart could feel the burning hatred that the parasites' failure was fermenting. Was it possible that its inability to fulfil its mission was driving the entity mad?

At the doorway, several grey slugs slid into the room, straight for Stuart. Were these outcasts from the men Lucy had killed?

Wherever they had come from, they found a new home in Stuart's flesh. He was their last chance.

If he had to die to save Lucy, then he would take everything he had left to make that happen.

***

The dead in the facility would already be engaged in the process of decay. Whatever was being done to save her and Stuart was taking too long, in Lucy's opinion. When she had left him close to an hour ago, Stuart had been screaming his defiance at the creature that had been bent on taking ownership of him.

She didn't want to watch him lose himself.

Stood by the scanner, Lucy watched the two figures as they prised open the elevator door. Both were wearing military NBC suits, what the soldiers called Noddy suits, but even with these bulky outfits, Lucy could tell she was looking at two females. Only a fool would send more men down here.

Not Cleaners then.

She waved at them, noticing the ropes they had rappelled down on, but neither returned the gesture. They were too engaged in what they were doing; equipment being lowered after them on additional ropes.

The Laboratory wasn't designed as a fortress meant to keep people out. It was designed to keep things in.

There was nothing for Lucy to do but watch as they established the basis of their perimeter. First, they erected a short tunnel around the elevator entrance, and it was only on its completion that Lucy realised the purpose of this. When completed, the tunnel suddenly burst into life, a ring of UV light providing a protected door into this doomed facility.

There were no ducts or pipes that led out into that outer half of the scanner chamber. When the scanner doors were closed, no air could pass between the two spaces, so for the parasite to reach the surface lift, it would need to get through concrete, steel and reinforced Perspex. The scanner door worked on a rotating system, so that one side of the scanner was always sealed. From what Lucy could tell, the integrity of it was intact.

The bad things had to be kept at bay.

"Miss Jones, I need you to do something for me." As Soteria spoke through the radio, the two newcomers disappeared from Lucy's sight, although she'd watched them drag a long cable that stretched across the floor from where it emerged from the elevator shaft.

"What?"

"The agents have delivered to you what I hope to be a cure for the parasite in Colonel Radcliffe. It was relatively easy for me to synthesise. You will need to inject it into him."

The red light inside the scanner turned to green, and the machine began to spring to life. The outer door opened, one of the women throwing a satchel through. Almost as quickly, that outer door closed which allowed the door on Lucy's side to open.

The cable obviously brought power to the scanner.

With the facility computer down for the count, the women outside were in control of Lucy's only way out. Although they might be mindful of her plight, neither of these two agents would let her out without Soteria's express consent. And Soteria would only give that if she was satisfied that neither Lucy nor Stuart was a threat.

Lucy grabbed the satchel and watched as her one chance to escape slid shut.

"This isn't about saving us, is it, Soteria?"

"Saving you is an important consideration," Soteria protested.

"Cut the bullshit. We were kept here to further your understanding of the parasite. You can at least admit that much to me." Rummaging through the satchel, Lucy found a case with an injector gun inside. It was already loaded and had two extra vials held firmly by the foam lining inside the case.

"It is regrettable that you are in this position."

"You know, Soteria, you would make an excellent politician."

"Why, thank you Miss Jones."

"It wasn't a compliment."

The bullet that came whizzing past almost hit her, and Lucy hurled herself to the side out of pure reflex.

Stuart was coming for her. No, not Stuart, but the parasite inside him.

33.

The Hell World

The air here was hot, Lucan covering his mouth to minimise its effects. His body could stand it, despite his discomfort, and he had suffered much worse in his time.

The herald next to him didn't seem to notice.

They were standing before the edge of a towering volcano, the ash drifting down around them. This was a volcanic landscape where few plants lived. There was life, but it appeared to be the vile parasitic type that this world was sometimes plagued with. Never had Lucan seen them in such concentrations, though. It was as if they were a standing army, protecting this mountain from an unseen enemy.

One as strong as Lucan would still have been at risk from them, but the power of the herald kept the vermin at bay.

"You have nothing to fear from these creatures. They are here by design, put here to defend this world from those invaders that would come through from the other place." That explained a lot and hinted at what Lucan was doing here. Behind him, stood by the hover car that had delivered them, six Berserkers stood vigil despite their stillness.

Lucan knew his life was about to take another unexpected twist.

"Follow me, Lucan, of the house of Fairway." The herald beckoned with his thin finger. This confused Lucan, for there was nowhere to follow. The herald walked straight at the stone foundation of the volcano's base before suddenly passing through it.

Warily, Lucan repeated the action.

There was no solidity. One moment he was outside, the next a coolness descended upon his skin. Lucan found himself in a tunnel that had been created by nature, artificial illumination showing the way.

What was this place?

Lucan was sure he would find out soon enough. Scattered across the floor of the tunnel were the bubbling carcasses of the pestilent creatures that had made this volcano their home.

"The vermin do not fare well in the radiance of the Seven," the herald informed.

There were voices ahead, sight of their owners blocked by the way the tunnel curved. One voice Lucan recognised, the booming ridicule of the Lord Moloch. Once again, one of the Seven had requested that Lucan be brought before him.

For what purpose?

The other sounds were those of human grief and suffering. Who better than Lucan to know the verbal expression of such sweet sorrow?

"Why am I here?" Lucan enquired.

"You will see," was all the herald would tell him.

Lucan entered into a vast chamber that could easily house a hundred Berserkers. There were only twelve, surrounding a group of naked human females. Some of them wept while others had retreated into themselves. None of them stood, which was how it should be.

Off to the side, a pile of six bodies had been made.

The most powerful presence was the glowing Moloch, whose radiance illuminated all around him. So great was it that it took several seconds for Lucan to notice the portal at the end of the cavern.

Lucan fell to his knees on the rough stone, prostrating himself before his unforgiving lord.

"Stop grovelling, Lucan," Moloch ordered. As Lucan lifted his head, the herald was there to wrench the shapeshifter to his feet. "We don't have time for your piety."

"Yes, my Lord."

"Have you guessed why you are here yet?" The herald whispered in his ear.

"No," Lucan replied, although his bowels churned with the uncertainty of his fate.

Right then, the portal seemed to sigh. The noise it made was followed by the emergence of a startled female who stumbled through into this new world. Two Berserkers grabbed her instantly, ripping at her clothes with a ruthless ferocity. Both of them towered above the newcomer, who could offer nothing in the way of resistance.

Freed of her clothing, the female was bundled with the others. In the Nazi death camp, the women had always been Lucan's favourite to slaughter.

"Lucan, are these good offerings?" The herald was pointing at the women who all stood trying to conceal their modesty. They needn't have bothered; nobody here was interested in them sexually.

These women were meat, nothing more.

"I would need to understand the context of the question."

When Moloch moved, he appeared to glide, and Lucan watched in growing terror as the owner of all sidled up to him. Despite the brightness and the heat from Moloch's form, Lucan looked up at the looming face.

"Would you like to know the secret of this world, Lucan?"

"Very much so, my Lord, although what I want is of monumental insignificance." That was the only thing he felt he could say. Every word from his mouth risked having his life snuffed out. Or maybe he would end up in a pain chair next to his broken brother.

"You will never be the same again. Some secrets have a way of changing us." Moloch sounded grave in that pronouncement.

"I am at your mercy, Lord."

"You will need to prove your worth first." Lucan felt strangely relieved. He wasn't sure secrets of the universe would benefit him.

Did the heralds share this knowledge? Yes, perhaps they did.

It wasn't that he didn't have questions; it was that he had more than he dared ask. Why did the portals exist? Why was their existence a secret to the creatures of this world? And how had these Seven gained dominion over this hellish world?

"Our technology made us rulers of this realm, and our science gave us immortality. Would you accept the curse of immortality, Lucan, if I offered it to you?"

"No." The word floated from his lips, his mind still lurching from what he'd been shown.

"And why?" Moloch knew the answer.

"Immortality would bring the risk of a tedious and boring existence." Moloch seemed to like that response.

"You have been brought here to see your purpose." the Herald said as he pointed at the assembled females.

"I don't understand." Why had he been shown this? What did Moloch want with him?

"There is a mystery lurking in this human flesh that you will help uncover," the herald said while Moloch towered above them.

"But why?"

"Because the Lord Moloch asks it of you."

"Are you ready, Lucan?" Moloch asked.

"Ready for what?" A sudden dread fell into Lucan's stomach.

"To discover the secrets of why humanity has changed so much." The brilliance around Moloch suddenly vanished, revealing his true form. Moloch was tall and muscular; his well-defined features might have been called handsome by some. Despite his size, though, he looked unnervingly human.

"Now you know a secret whole cities have been sterilised to keep," warned the herald. Could it be that the Seven and humanity shared some similar heritage?

"What is it you would have me do?" *Please, don't send me back through that portal.* Lucan would rather go back to his cell deep in the depths of the Citadel.

The herald held his palm up, a grey oozing thing emerging from the flesh there.

"Do you know what this is, Lucan?" the herald asked.

"No." Lucan had never seen anything like it.

"It is an ancient tool of control, a creation that strips those infested of their free will. With it, the Seven control the armies of this world and those others who serve." *But not my species,* thought Lucan. "I see the question in your eyes, Lucan," Moloch revealed. "Alas, many of the creatures of this world are immune to this tool's influence." The greyness undulated on the herald's palm before retreating back into the flesh it had appeared from.

"I am honoured to learn this."

And terrified, thought Lucan.

"I sent these as my emissaries to the place you know as Earth," Moloch revealed.

"Why not send your armies instead?" Lucan gazed at the immense Berserkers. A million of them could sweep the human military aside easily.

"Saturnalia forbids it, so we must make the humans the threat they will eventually become. My brothers need to see the enemy that humanity will truly evolve into. That is why I need you."

Lucan looked over the women. Now he saw it, he was here for them.

"The human females are immune to the parasites' control. I would have you learn why." Moloch rested his immense hand on Lucan's shoulder. "Can you do this, Lucan, of the house of Fairway?"

"Yes." To be useful again was all he could ever ask for.

"I will restore to you your family's great chamber of suffering. There you will once again get to practise your art." Moloch pointed at the assorted humans. "Use whatever means are necessary, for I am assured you will be given an unenviable supply of subjects."

"Does this please you, Lucan?" The herald took hold of Lucan by his neck, forcing the shapeshifter to stare at his chosen victims.

"Yes," Lucan said with some truth. He would have preferred to use his skills on the enemies of the Seven, but these whimpering females would suffice.

For now.

34.

Isles of Scilly, UK

How will you feel when we make her scream?

His own stolen words were taunting him, the parasite not satisfied with mere pain. Inside Stuart was a being of pure sadism, and he could tell it enjoyed the torment it inflicted.

Do you think we can make her beg for a quick death?

His legs moved more easily now, but there was a definite shake to his arms. This was good, for it would make aiming the pistol his fingers clutched difficult.

Hurry, pet, his mind shouted. There was something utterly depraved about the parasite, as if it were designed to mimic the most degrading and evil aspects of the humans it controlled.

He wasn't up to running, not yet, but even so, he was closing in on Lucy. The parasite seemed to know where she was, its anger growing with each step. Stuart didn't want his to be the hands that caused her so much of the promised pain.

He tried to shout a warning, but the parasite blocked his attempt.

This sub-level was made up of five long corridors that intersected each other, with close to thirty rooms if you included the security office and the rest area. One of those corridors, the longest, led to the scanner room and the elevator. That was the corridor Stuart now turned into. At the end, through the open door, Lucy stood with her back to him.

We are going to gut her, Stuart heard the invader of his brain promise. *But we will do so much more first.*

There was no stirring in Stuart's groin, which was a small mercy. From what he could tell, the parasite had no interest in anything other than inflicting pain. Rape wasn't even in the cards.

Stuart concentrated everything he had and formed the thought that the gun risked killing Lucy too quickly.

Are you trying to trick us? A poor attempt.

Stuart tried harder, insisting that a bullet could put an individual in shock. They were unpredictable, and could shatter bones and sever blood vessels. If the parasite truly wanted Lucy to suffer, the gun wasn't the way to do it.

"Search my memories if you don't believe me," he added. Locked away in there would be his experiences in the military and from the years of the sanctioned killings he'd engaged in.

The parasite just laughed at him.

Was he helping Lucy here, or condemning her? It was the best Stuart could come up with considering the state he was in. The constant agony was a weight dragging him down into a bottomless pit.

Our vengeance demands suffering from both of you.

Stuart closed the space, Lucy engrossed by the scanner door. For a brief moment, the parasite rejoiced as the scanner door opened, only for it to be a short-lived affair.

Twelve metres.

The parasite should have stopped to take a shooter's stance. Instead, it made Stuart raise his gun hand, getting closer, the finger ready to squeeze. That hand and the arm it was connected to were unsteady, and when the trigger was finally pulled, it made Stuart jump inside himself.

Nine metres.

He was there to watch the bullet go wide, Lucy leaping out of view.

For some reason, the invading voice in his mind began to scream. It surged energy into his legs, causing Stuart to almost stumble.

"I'm coming for you, slut." Stuart's eyes were filled with tears of frustration. Through the rotating door of the scanner, he could see the two strangers. They took no interest in the drama unfolding, for they were safe behind the effective barrier the scanner made.

"You can't shoot for shit," Lucy goaded.

Stuart fired off another shot, which just ricocheted off randomly.

"Kill you now," the parasite roared, taking what it thought was full control. It was lost in its accumulated rage, the memories of the hosts Lucy had killed swirling and confusing its thoughts. As it came close to the entrance to the scanner room, Stuart's hand kept firing the gun, the magazine emptying one bullet at a time.

So engrossed in the hunt was the alien, it almost seemed to forget about Stuart. His pain levels diminished, and just as his body charged through the doorway, he gave everything he had to push himself back into some sort of influence.

The gun arm swung round to its target, but too slow, Lucy crouching with her own gun aimed. No, not a gun, and then the twin barbs stuck themselves in Stuart's flesh, the electricity pouring through Stuart's body.

The shock hit him, having the desired effect. Compared to how Stuart had suffered the last hours, the taser was a minor irritant, but to the parasite, it was pure torture.

As Stuart collapsed, he thought he heard the alien thing scream.

He hit the ground hard, Lucy not wasting any time. She pounced on him, shoving something hard against his thigh.

"Nooooo," Stuart's lips protested, then the sharpness hit him and the rush as fluid was injected into his system. It felt warm, strangely refreshing, and then Lucy fidgeted with the device she held before injecting Stuart a second time.

Stuart mentally pushed again, forcing the invading presence back. It had been weakened by the electricity, but it was far from beaten.

You dare! You dare!

Lucy rolled away, kicking Stuart's gun so that it went clattering off across the floor. The invader tried to make Stuart push himself up from the floor, but the arms were weak and uncoordinated. Fingers went fidgeting for the knife in its scabbard, but the electricity had wrecked Stuart's coordination. Thing was, Stuart had been tasered before, and his body had never reacted as badly as this.

Was electricity a weapon against these bastard things?

"Kill you," came the curse from Stuart's mouth. The voice was hoarse though, the lungs straining for oxygen.

What had Lucy just injected into him?

The warmth suddenly turned to fire, but only where the parasites were. Those in his legs chewed their way free from his flesh, disintegrating as Lucy's steroid concoction poisoned them.

This cannot be!

"This cannot be!"

Stuart's mind expanded, flooding back into the spaces it had been denied. He filled the neurons, gaining sudden insights into why the parasite was here. In its own distress, it had dropped its defences.

He saw the parasites' purpose, saw glimpses of the creature that had delivered it and the planet that had once been its home. In its death throes, the parasite betrayed itself, and in its final retreat from the host it had come to despise, it let Stuart once again reclaim his mind.

It felt like being born again.

The wetness seeped out of his ear, multiple wounds opening on his skin as the last of the parasites tried to escape. He found himself thinking what it would mean to have one of those things disintegrate inside him, and then he felt the end of his persecution.

He was free.

Rolling onto his back, he just lay there, revelling in the normality that flooded him. His body ached and it felt like his thigh was burning up, but he'd accept this over what the parasite had done to him.

This was bliss compared to that torment.

"Stuart?"

His eyes were closed, but he smiled. Just give me a second, he wanted to say.

"Stuart, are you okay?"

He flopped his head to the side and slowly dragged his eyelids open. She was kneeling near him, gun ready to put two rounds in his skull. Her finger was off the trigger, though, Lucy's hope making her cautious.

"I need a drink." He smiled then, and he secretly prayed that he was free of the contagion. Somehow, he knew he was, but it was Soteria that needed convincing.

Lucy never needed to pull the trigger.

That would be one less bullet the Hidden hand would need to replace.

Epilogue.

London, UK

Peter Sloane coughed hard, the irritation in his throat a result of the acid that persisted. He knew he was in trouble, his betrayal of his country now complete, and the knowledge gnawed at him. He had done as Viktor Orlov had asked, and now he could feel the buzzards circling.

Peter knew his treachery would have been uncovered eventually, and it had taken everything in him to hide the panic that was swelling in his heart.

He was once again at the rarely used meeting place, a stone shelter built into a cemetery's perimeter wall. The seat he was on was ornamental and cold, built at the same time as the circular structure that surrounded the buried ancient remains. From here, it would be difficult to be overlooked or overheard due to the electronic countermeasures that had been implanted into the alcove's stone structure by the Russians years ago.

It was the ideal meeting place for traitors. Or so he thought, because voices could carry in the night.

Peter had been set on his latest act of treachery by his Russian handler, Viktor Orlov. The Russian FSB man had given him a USB stick containing files to be investigated. Peter clutched the same USB stick now, which contained updated information that he hoped would be enough to buy him more time. It wasn't much, because there were only a limited amount of secrets he'd been able to discover.

The Director of MI5 had seen to that. Peter had been shocked when the head of his organisation had ordered Craig Armstrong to be freed. The order had been made to sound like a suggestion, the MI5 Director known for his calm and engaging manner.

Craig Armstrong was indeed an intriguing anomaly, Peter had been told, but not something he needed to worry about.

What he had deduced from that brief conversation had shocked him. There was an organisation working on British soil that had a higher authority than MI5 and MI6. There was no mention or record of it, but the mysterious man known as Craig Armstrong was a part of that organisation, protected by the hidden fingers of power that worked the great marionettes of state. Peter was sure of it.

The problem was, he didn't have any concrete proof. Would this be enough to satisfy Viktor? How would the Russians react to such knowledge? And where was his handler? It wasn't like Viktor to be late.

There, movement over to his left. Filled with nervous energy, Peter patted his thighs and tried to control his breathing. All that did was drag a belch out of him, one he was unable to suppress.

"That is a filthy habit," the Russian-accented voice said as its owner approached. "I thought you British were more cultured."

"Viktor?"

"Of course it is me. Who else would be here at this hour," the Russian admonished. He walked up to Peter and stood over him. "You have something for me? Why else would you bring me here?" The indication for this meeting had been via a chalk mark on a discreet stone on a innocuous wall, a message to meet at this place at a previously agreed-upon time.

"Please sit down, Viktor. I'm nervous enough as it is."

The Russian did as asked.

"Look at the state of you. What's wrong with you, man?"

"What's wrong? I'm betraying my country here." *And not through choice, you blackmailing bastard.*

"Those are the risks our kind take. If you didn't know how to play, you shouldn't have joined the game." Wasn't that the truth.

"It's all on here," Peter promised. He was pleased to see the hand holding out the USB stick wasn't shaking. "I've stripped the malware from it." He didn't complete his accusation.

"We are spies, Peter. We do such things. You would be disappointed if we didn't. And I would have had to reconsider our arrangement if you hadn't followed simple spy craft. Traitors are no use to us if they become complacent."

"You make it sound like I'm volunteering for this." The blackmail the Russians were using cut deep. Peter was trapped, and he knew it.

"We all volunteer to live this life," Viktor philosophised. "And now, the executive summary, if you please."

"I had a forensics team search the burnt-down building your men were using. They found evidence of blood there. I'm making the assumption that your men are dead."

"This is not surprising news to me," Viktor replied, barely hiding his impatience. "Tell me you have something more." There was a threat lurking in those words, but there always was with Viktor. Peter was useful until he wasn't. When he was finally deemed disposable, then he could be used to embarrass the great and powerful MI5.

Just another pawn to be thrown under the bus.

"We found the man you provided details on. Craig Armstrong. As far as we can tell, that's his name, but our systems had been purged of all details of him. His address is on the USB."

"That would take some doing," Viktor noted.

"We brought Armstrong in, but never really got to question him before his release was ordered." Peter let that hang there.

"So, a secret branch of your organisation?"

"No, I would have known." Peter was sure of that.

"Then MI6?"

"No, the orders came right from the top. That in itself wouldn't have meant much, except the head of MI5 gave me those orders in person." Should he reveal the rest of it? Hell, he didn't have a choice. "He looked worried."

"That suggests the game has another player."

"My thoughts exactly, although I don't see how."

***

Using the tracking device planted on Peter's car, Craig had followed his target to the cemetery, and had waited distant from where Peter now sat, hidden in the shadows. If Stuart had been up to it, he might have offered to deal with the matter for him, but this was Craig's mess to clean up.

There were three drones hovering silently in the air, guided towards human heat sources. At this hour, the cemetery should be deserted, Craig and Peter the only people initially detectable by the drones. Soteria controlled them, letting Craig know of the threats as they presented themselves.

It was Soteria who spotted the car that arrived to park in the cemetery car park, a lone man departing it to leave two companions behind. With this aerial knowledge, Craig had been able to sneak up on the car unobserved.

"The licence plate is registered to an offshore holding company," Soteria whispered in Craig's ear. "MI6 have flagged it as a front for the Russian FSB." As Craig watched, there was a flare of light from the interior of the car as one of the occupants lit a cigarette.

"Did you catch that?" Craig asked. He was wearing glasses, though his eyesight didn't require them. The frame contained a camera with surprisingly good resolution, the lenses able to switch to infrared when required. That was his vision now.

Through the camera, Soteria would see whatever he did, and she had the power to analyse any captured image.

"Yes. At least one of the men in the car is a known FSB operative. It would indeed appear that Peter Sloane is meeting with Russians. How unfortunate." The driver had his window rolled down, arm hanging there to dangle the cigarette out.

Thank you for making my job easier tonight.

"Am I a go?" He knew there would be people high up in the Hidden Hand watching this mission. The situation was fluid and highly volatile, and there could be no room for mistakes.

"Just confirming," Soteria replied. Craig pictured important men sitting in back rooms rolling the dice to determine what should be done. "Elimination has been approved."

"All targets?"

"Affirmative." Craig had planned for this eventuality, and he pulled a small flashlight off his belt with his none dominant hand. His right hand was already holding his 9mm pistol. It was fitted with subsonic rounds and an Osprey 2.0 silencer.

He'd make more noise spitting when he fired, and the background hum of the city would hopefully mask his actions.

The Russians had parked strategically, making it difficult to sneak up on them in the car park, which was poorly lit. Instead, Craig switched on his torch and walked boldly towards the car, shining the beam right at the target. His torch was unnecessarily bright, and would destroy any night adaptation the car's two occupants might have.

Every plan carries risk, but he was hoping the Russians were overconfident, an affliction that came with ferrying important people around. The lit cigarette suggested as much. When the boss was absent, one sometimes used that opportunity to relax. After all, this was just another covert meeting like all those that had come before. Why would tonight be any different?

On Craig's approach, one of the Russians climbed free of the passenger seat and out of the car. Craig watched as the large man held a hand up to ward off the light.

"Get that light out of my face," Craig was ordered.

"Police. The cemetery's closed. What are you doing here," Craig challenged with fake outrage. "You better not be a couple of nonces. We've had too much of that recently." The words were a distraction, buying time as Craig moved closer. It was a plausible explanation that would put the Russians on an outraged defensive. The light he shone would make him an indistinguishable blur.

"We like the night air," the Russian stated. He was about to say something more, but Craig fired from the hip, two rounds catching the Russian in the chest. Dropping the torch, Craig moved his feet, lining up the shot, putting another two bullets through the car's open window.

The driver's head was flung to the side as his partner slumped back against the car. Two steps closer, and a fifth round went into the passenger's left eye.

The general rule was two in the chest and one in the head. Even if the target was wearing Kevlar, the first two would knock the resistance out of them before the third bullet finished the job.

"Expertly done, Captain Armstrong." Although no mention had been made, Craig was sure Soteria was recording this. He didn't hang around. With the escorts dealt with, Craig could deal with the reason he was here.

He moved silently, a small white arrow on his glasses telling him which cemetery path to take. It wasn't long before he heard the voices, and he focused in on them, moving cautiously, using the shrubs and trees to hide his approach.

"My thoughts exactly, although I don't see how." That was Peter, and Craig could see them now, the infrared glasses making the two men white on a cold grey background.

"We have suspected such for some time. There are things happening in the world that you are not privy to," the Russian stated. Craig had no idea why Peter Sloane had turned traitor, but the evidence of his crimes was here for the Hidden Hand to see.

"I'm not sure there is more I can do," Peter protested.

"I hope for your sake that isn't the case," the Russian warned.

"You have Armstrong's address."

"Yes, but we have mysteriously lost our ability to access your Metropolitan Police's surveillance grid. We need to know why." Viktor sounded very insistent.

Craig had heard enough, and holding his pistol level, he stepped out and revealed himself.

"Gentlemen, please keep your hands where I can see them. I'll shoot out the knee caps of the first person who stands." Both targets turned their heads. The infrared distorted their features, but Craig wasn't the only one watching.

"The Russian is confirmed as Viktor Orlov, London FSB chief," Soteria whispered. That was good, for it made Craig's job easier to know who he was dealing with.

"Viktor, I hear you have been looking for me."

"Armstrong?" Peter said with genuine alarm.

"The mystery man," said Viktor. "Put the gun down, mystery man." The confidence in the Russian was unsettling. If not for the ever-watchful drones, Craig could have believed a team of Spetsnaz was circling him, ready to pounce.

"I'd advise you to do as he says," Peter added. All the while, Craig was moving, positioning himself for what came next.

"I don't think you're in a position to tell anyone what to do," Craig challenged. "Traitor." He added the word, letting the power of it punch into Peter's soul.

The Russian would have a gun, but he didn't reach for it. It was unlikely Peter was armed, but Craig kept a careful eye on both of them.

"Enough of this theatre," Viktor insisted.

Craig considered the merits of verbally sparring with the Russian. Instead, he took two steps forward and shot the man in the left knee. The roar from the wounded man's throat was more out of outrage than pain. Not satisfied, Craig shot out the other knee.

This wasn't out of sadism, but to give the impression that Viktor had been killed out of revenge.

"Stop," Viktor pleaded. Anyone can be tough until they take a bullet to both kneecaps. Craig didn't stop. Instead, he fired again with brutal accuracy.

The bullet entered left of the Adam's apple, blowing a hole out of the back of Viktor's neck, but not before shredding muscles and arteries. Not an instant death; Viktor had to bleed out first.

Peter squealed, a spurt of blood just missing him. Only Craig saw the near miss, the blood's heat momentarily registering.

Viktor, clutching his neck, collapsed sideways before tumbling off the stone bench. He lay on the ground, drowning in his own blood, frantically reaching for the gun he had in the holster below his arm pit. It was a futile gesture, stopped by a fourth bullet in the shoulder.

Peter sat there frozen, watching his tormentor die.

"You killed him," Peter managed when Viktor gave his last gargled breath.

"Of course. He threatened the Realm."

"Who are you?"

"That is something you will never know." Craig stepped in close, gun levelled on Peter's chest. "Are you carrying?"

Peter shook his head.

"You can't think you'll get away with this."

"But Mr Sloane, I already have. Stand up, please."

"What?" Peter sounded dazed, the failures of his life coming to a crushing climax.

"I have been ordered to take you in for questioning. Stand up." On shaking legs, Peter did as he was ordered.

"But who are you?"

"If you are unlucky, you might get to find out."

"I didn't want to do any of this," Peter protested.

"I don't care. And look at the end result of what you did."

Craig stepped to the side, pointing at the corpse with his gun. He waited for Peter to shift, for the traitor's eyes to linger on the body that would soon begin to grow cold.

Peter Sloane was left-handed, which meant Craig was properly placed. With no warning, he raised the gun, pressed it against Peter's left temple, and fired.

Peter fell, Craig waiting for the body to settle. Kneeling, he held a gloved finger against Peter's carotid artery, confirming that death had occurred. Despite what Hollywood often depicts, head shots sometimes aren't fatal. Bullets can do crazy things, like deflecting off bone and missing vital organs.

Peter's heart was no longer beating. Good enough.

The black nitriles that Craig wore would prevent his DNA from being on the gun, but Peter's skin didn't have that luxury. Carefully, Craig manipulated the dead man's fingers around the handle and trigger. Half standing, he pulled the limp arm up, angling the gun at Viktor's body. A single shot was all that was needed to coat Peter's hand with cartridge discharge residue.

That should be enough to persuade the police of a murder suicide.

"Please do not forget to police the scene," Soteria prompted unnecessarily. Craig was already on it, searching pockets for any incriminating evidence. He found a USB in Viktor's pocket and left the silenced pistol on the ground by Peter's body. It was untraceable, and the police would quickly conclude that the gun was used to perform an act of international outrage.

Craig had killed for the Hidden Hand before, but this was his first assassination. Any concern that he couldn't perform such a duty was now assuredly expunged. Craig found he felt nothing for either of the men he'd killed.

What was he becoming?

Walking away, he left the bodies to become to objects of curiosity for the creatures of the night.

***

It had taken half a day before Lucy and Stuart were allowed out of the Laboratory. The injected concoction had defeated the parasite and freed Stuart from its influence. They'd still both needed to pass through the scanner though, one at a time to ensure their flesh was absent the creature that could destroy their world.

Both Stuart and Lucy had been told to rest up, but those orders Lucy knew she couldn't comply with. She still had unfinished business with her own mind.

By killing Sirena, they said that Lucy had helped save the world, but to Lucy, that wasn't quite correct. It had been her alter ego, the one she called the Bitch, that had done the saving. The voice in her thoughts, the one that had been there since childhood, had acted when Lucy's consciousness had been trapped in an oppressive nightmare of Sirena Samson's creation.

Clearly, the Bitch had its uses, but that unrelenting presence was silent, leaving Lucy feeling truly alone. Lucy had always fantasised what it would be like to be free of the persistent and sadistic whispers, but had sometimes craved it. Having escaped the effects of the Hell-world parasite, the only voice in her head was her own, and Lucy knew that the absence left her incomplete.

She needed the Bitch.

It had been four days since the threat called Sirena had been vanquished, four days since the Bitch had uttered a single inappropriate word. Lucy missed having that force murmuring to her inner self, for the void left a malignant force that taunted Lucy with its finality.

She needed to somehow get the Bitch back.

That was why Lucy was out on the streets of London in the dead of night when she should have been resting. Her experience with the Laboratory was behind her, and it had reaffirmed what she had always believed about her relationship with the Hidden Hand. Everyone in that organisation was expendable if the safety of humanity was at stake.

Lucy could live with that reality. If not for the Hidden Hand, there was no telling what her life would have been like. They had saved her as a child and given her a sense of purpose.

Some women feared the city after dark, but not Lucy. The criminal vermin that hid in the shadows were always there if you knew where to look, the city far less safe than the politicians would want the populous to believe. Most of the nefarious types waited, intent on robbery and violence, but there were some who craved other pleasures.

Some people were so broken by life that they had been freed from the burdens of empathy and compassion. They considered their depravity a strength that helped them navigate the dark underworld, but sometimes the victims they encountered turned out to be the true predators.

Tonight would be such a night.

That was why Lucy was here, to test herself. If the Bitch was gone, would Lucy be an effective agent anymore? The Bitch had gifted Lucy certain abilities, like the way she could smell the truth in another person's words. Sometimes Lucy knew things that shouldn't have been possible to know, insights plucked from the ether.

The Bitch also granted her a ruthlessness that made Lucy a threat to anyone she encountered.

The Bitch was never satisfied, demanding Lucy become a danger to the world. It was the taunts by the Bitch that insisted Lucy master martial arts, turning her body into a lethal weapon fuelled by stamina that only gruelling exercise workouts could create. Be you man or Hell creature, Lucy was the cure to the horrors you intended to perpetrate.

Tonight, Lucy would use her training and the weapons she'd secreted on her person on anyone who threatened her. But what she didn't have was the yearning of the Bitch.

Did she still have what it took to be the hammer? The events in the Laboratory suggested that she did, but she needed certainty.

During her free time from her Hidden Hand duties, there had been instances where she had randomly encountered the treacherous scum that hid in the shadows. The Bitch had relished these moments, sparks of excitement that were unexpected treats to be relished. Lucy's work with the Hidden Hand was sometimes filled with the adrenaline of combat, but much of it bored the Bitch. The alter ego had no time for surveillance and report writing.

The Bitch had wanted action. The Bitch had wanted blood.

It was Lucy's belief that the universe had placed those random distractions in her path, giving her opportunities to test her restraint and control over the Bitch's influence. The Bitch always wanted more violence than Lucy had been prepared to give, mostly because Lucy knew she had to keep a firm grip of her other self. On those occasions, the low-browed ruffians she'd encountered had been left broken and cowed, but always alive. Their injuries were often life changing, lessons that Lucy hoped would torment them for decades.

The bones she broke rarely healed without surgical intervention. The faces she scarred could never be cured by the mystical arts of plastic surgery. Death was easy. Living with the maladies Lucy left you was a fitting purgatory far too many deserved.

If you kept to your own affairs and provided no trouble to others, you had little to fear from Lucy.

Those who thought her a sheep were cursed to carry the mark of their foolishness. Death brought with it relief and peace, and as much as the Bitch pleaded, Lucy wouldn't grant that eternal freedom to anyone who threatened her. Not unless the Hidden Hand demanded it.

Then she wouldn't hesitate. Her skills were rarely used for assassination, though. They had Stuart for that, and now perhaps Craig.

There was also the possibility that these violent encounters weren't random. Maybe the Bitch was working in the background, manipulating Lucy without her knowledge. Could this other part of Lucy have put her into threatening situations so as to extract the pleasure that came with inflicting pain on those who deserved it? She was well aware of what it felt like to be manipulated.

Anything was possible, but such thoughts were a distraction for another time. Walking where only the foolish and the skilled ventured, Lucy had attracted the attention most people dreaded.

She knew where to find the scum that made this city so interesting. There were certain places they lurked, out of the ever-watchful eyes of the wider population. Some criminals were bold enough to strike out in public, but most were monsters of opportunity. To the three that now followed her, Lucy represented what they had been waiting for.

Big mistake.

"Hey!"

The challenge from one of them was expected, Lucy already aware that she was being pursued. A lone woman was a prime target for those on the lower rungs of society; easy pickings for men who craved excitement to distract them from the futility of their existence.

"Hey, hold up."

Lucy always walked with focus and purpose. She did not hide her true self, displaying to those with eyes to see that she was someone to be left alone. The wise and experienced hoodlums would see the threat she represented and choose another target for the night. Not these three.

No doubt there would be drugs and alcohol in their veins, but the most dangerous poison they were contaminated with was their arrogance. Dangerous for them.

Lucy slowed her pace, cocking a look over her shoulder. She already knew what the three men looked like; the windows on the left side of the street were as good as mirrors for Lucy.

"Bitch, slow down." Lucy did better than that. She stopped and turned to them.

"Now, is that any way to talk to a lady?"

These were more boys than men. They had that confidence that often came with youth, though all three would regret leaving their homes this night. That was Lucy's plan, at least.

They were all about the same height and stood in a line facing her. The one on Lucy's left wore a dirty hoody and had arms that seemed to drop from his body. In the middle was a sour-faced creature with long blonde hair, which told Lucy he had no real experience in street fighting. Long hair was a weapon that could be used against you, which was why Lucy's hair was tied up under the red-headed wig she wore. Added to that was a nervousness that suggested Blondie didn't want to be here.

Peer pressure and boredom could get one into a lot of trouble.

The third man was the dangerous one of the trio. He was fat, but there was muscle underneath. His eyes stared out from under a thick Neanderthal-like brow. He was looking at Lucy the way a predator would gaze upon their next meal.

Knives were a certainty, but these weren't the type to carry guns.

"You ain't no lady," Hoodie corrected.

"Shouldn't you boys be at home? Surely it's past your bedtimes? Go home so mummy can tuck you in and offer you up her tit." In the past, the Bitch was always there, running commentary in her thoughts. This taunting felt wrong without that feedback.

"The fuck you say?" the Neanderthal countered. He seemed to straighten himself, flexing his thick neck. This was an individual who enjoyed violence, and would have the wide, callused hands that were handy for such work.

Lucy enjoyed humiliating big men like this and always made a point of ruining them physically. She would take him out first.

Casually, Lucy backed away, keeping them at a safe distance. This sort of thing always started with taunts, especially on an otherwise deserted street like this one. It was part residential, but nobody who lived here would come to her aid. At the most, a curtain or two might twitch, but the people in this part of London had learnt never to interfere. Added to her apparent vulnerability were the lack of street surveillance cameras. Any installed in the locality had been quickly destroyed by those who didn't like to be spied on.

The population's fear and cowardice gave fuel to those who would do the world so many wrongs.

"She's got some mouth on her," Hoodie insisted.

"I can find a good use for that," Neanderthal added. Blondie had fallen back behind his two friends. He wouldn't stop them in their plans, so Lucy wouldn't allow him to escape undamaged.

"Baby, your cock's so small I could probably floss with it." She saw the anger blossom in Neanderthal. Good, that would make him impulsive, and her right hand slipped to her back, where a holster held her Glock. The clothes she wore were cut specifically to hide the bulge her weapon might create.

The Glock 42 was compact and more than enough to deal with this trio, but where was the fun or the challenge in that? Instead of the Glock, her fingers curled round the handle of the karambit knife she always carried. Both weapons were highly illegal, but Lucy wasn't one to care about the laws of the land. Being part of the Hidden Hand came with certain privileges.

She kept her hand behind her, the blade protruding from the bottom of her clenched fist.

"I'm going to hurt you," Neanderthal promised. "I'm really going to fuck you up."

"Oh, you've gone and done it now," Hoodie whooped. He clapped his hands together, excited for the coming carnage.

Lucy shifted her feet as the big man came at her. His shoulders told Lucy that either a slap or a punch was coming, the big right arm starting to move. Lucy ducked into it, part deflecting the arm, Neanderthal starting to turn as he missed his target, his stench filling her nostrils. She used his momentum against him, bringing the knife up in a well-practised movement. The sharpened edge cut through leather, cotton, skin, and muscle, ripping through the top of the pectoralis major and the latissimus dorsi. She didn't have to see the blood to know she had at least partly severed the fool's brachial artery.

Lucy danced away behind him, now loose on her toes, Neanderthal driven to rage by the pain. Dipping, she arced the knife across the back of his leg, above the crease of the knee, decimating the muscles of the hamstring complex. He'd have no idea how bad his injuries were, even with his dominant arm and leg now as good as useless. Such injuries never fully healed, despite the surgeon's healing arts.

He fell to a knee, cursing her, Lucy moving out of his reach. Now Neanderthal's own bulk was working against him, the wounds opening up further.

All the time she kept the other two in her peripheral vision. Lucy wouldn't accept any surprises from them. Well-rounded, thoughtful individuals would have retreated at that moment, Lucy's skills there for all to see. Instead, Hoodie pulled out a flick-knife of his own.

Good. With a twitch of her wrist, Lucy sent blood flying from her blade.

"Your balls. I'm thinking of taking one." It was a fair warning, Hoodie's legs donned in sagging joggers. That material would part like the Red Sea when she sliced him.

Lucy knew she was taking unnecessary risks here. She hadn't engaged in these antics lightly, but felt the hazards were worth it. The Bitch was inside her still, Lucy was sure, and she hoped this brazen display of violence might coax that voice out from the silent wilderness.

Hoodie came at her, despite her warning. Was it bravado, ego, or stupidity? It didn't matter, for the result would be the same. He was hesitant, though, holding the knife in an untrained hand. If you had two knife fighters of equal skill, the superior stamina that usually came with youth had a habit of winning the day. Hoodie, though, would struggle to carve up a steak, never mind a human opponent. He slashed the blade back and forth to try to intimidate his foe, Blondie now close to flight. If the meeker of the three ran, Lucy wouldn't run him down.

Behind her, Neanderthal tried to stand. Instead, he toppled sideways as his injured leg gave way.

"I'm going to kill you," the big man roared.

"No, you won't," Lucy countered, noticing how Hoodie had been distracted by the exchange. Lucy saw her opening, stepping in so that her free hand could grab a slick wrist to control the ineffective knife that opposed her. Her well-trained fingers dug into pressure points that would make the hand numb and useless.

At the same time, she rammed her right elbow into Hoodie's chest, knocking the wind out of him. His wide eyes displayed his surprise at how strong Lucy was, and then came his scream as she pulled the blade up into his groin, and across his lower abdomen to where some people sported an appendix scar. She didn't stop there, instead repeating the initial injury she had inflicted on the Neanderthal.

Then she was away, watching her enemy collapse, squealing as he clutched his working hand between his legs. Hoodie had dropped his knife, and Lucy kicked it away.

"Sorry, maybe I took both there. You weren't planning on having children, were you?"

"Oh my god," the third of them muttered.

"What about you?" Lucy pointed a finger at Blondie who had been rooted to the spot. He threw his hands up in supplication as his head flashed from side to side.

"Please," Blondie begged.

"Then why are you still here?" He didn't need telling twice, although Blondie stumbled as he ran off, nearly planting himself face first on the asphalt.

Lucy didn't watch him leave, instead turning to the two injured men. Neanderthal had crawled over to a car and was trying to use it to pull himself up. Four steps, and Lucy was on him, slicing upwards through the calf muscle of his injured leg. The roar of pain he gave was no longer filled with anger.

Terror had found a new home.

"I'm going to let you both live," Lucy promised. "You won't thank me for that, though." There was so much she wanted to do to these two men, and by the time she was done, they would never be a threat to society again. Wheelchairs and crutches were their future.

And lingering, untreatable pain.

Are you in there, Bitch? Show yourself. Isn't this what you want?

Lucy continued severing muscles and tendons. Both men would walk again, in time, but they would forever live with the trauma of this encounter, and she set about them, mindful of the threat both of them still might pose.

And throughout the horrors she inflicted, the Bitch never gave any indication she was still a presence.

Have I lost you? How do I live without you?

It was only when she was finally done, a siren sounding off in the distance, that Lucy felt a stirring inside. There, a presence rising from the depths.

You've been busy, the familiar voice said inside her mind. Lucy didn't wait around, walking off after wiping her knife clean on one of the lad's clothing.

"Are you back?"

I just might be, the Bitch teased.

"Why did you go?"

I'm not sure you'll understand.

"Try me." The sirens were getting louder, Lucy well away from the scene. No doubt, the two she had damaged would be known to the police, so they wouldn't spend much energy looking for the perpetrator.

I was in control of you, and I liked it. Too much.

"You're right, I don't understand." Lucy could communicate with her other self without speaking, but she always preferred to converse out loud. Sometimes people stared at her for that, but only for an instant. Very few could keep eye contact with Lucy for long.

I found that I wanted to stay in control. If I hadn't left, I knew I wouldn't have let you back in. Not right then. There wouldn't have been a you left.

"And yet you're back now." The Bitch sounded different... calmer. Lucy felt understanding well up inside her. She could still remember how the parasite had used and abused Stuart and the others. To have the Bitch do the same... well, it had been a fear she had always lived with. The Bitch had seen the threat she posed and had retreated.

Lucy had never considered the Bitch to be a manifestation of some inner self. It was a whole separate entity that she had been bonded to.

"I need you." She found herself freely admitting that now.

Not as much as you think you do. If anything, we need each other. These past few days, I've watched you from a distance and I saw how much I would have ruined what you had built for yourself. If I'd stayed, I would have destroyed us both.

And there was the truth of it. The Bitch was finally admitting her own cancerous influence.

"I'm glad you're back." Lucy now knew what it meant to be without that violent and interfering barrage of thoughts in her head. The absence of the Bitch wasn't something she wanted going forward.

You might not be when you learn the truth I have uncovered, the Bitch said ominously.

"What truth?"

Lucy. My sweet and vulnerable Lucy. I have finally discovered what you are.

End of Book 3

Follow the series at

https://www.amazon.co.uk/gp/product/B0BS8GY1DW

https://www.amazon.com/gp/product/B0BS8GY1DW

Did you enjoy this story? If so, you can make a big difference.

If you enjoyed this book and want to help others share your experience, I would be grateful if you could spend five minutes leaving a review (it can be as short as you like) on the respective Amazon page.

Thank you very much.

ALSO BY SEAN DEVILLE

Have you read them all?

The Homo Vampirous Chronicles
Legacy of Ashes **(Book 1 of 5)**

For the near extinct vampire race, starvation has been a way of life for centuries.

That is about to change.

Former Delta Force operative, David Collins, thinks being left for dead by a merciless killer is the worst thing that could ever happen to him…

He's wrong.

The cold-blooded vampire killer, Khristina Sidarov, thinks that the vampire menace has become even deadlier…

She's right.

The ruthless vampire, Claude Schmidt, thinks his plan to kill billions and bring forth the new age is foolproof…

It isn't.

    Buy it here
    UK: https://www.amazon.co.uk/gp/product/B09DN3HMYX
    US: https://www.amazon.com/gp/product/B09DN3HMYX

The Apocalypse Prophecies

The First Seal **(Book 1)**

If you could survive the coming apocalypse, would you envy the dead?

Giles Horn is a man of wealth, power, and unspeakable destiny.

The sole owner of one of the world's largest corporations, he controls the economic fate of whole countries.

Horn is also a sociopath, a megalomaniac and a man who wants to see the world burn.

For Horn is the Antichrist, the one who will bring the end of all things.

There is only one force on Earth that can oppose him.

A secret order of religious assassins known only as Inquisitors.

Lilith was just a child when she was inducted into the ranks of the Inquisition.

Trained to kill without mercy, Lilith has dedicated her life to slaughtering the demonic hordes that have invaded Earth for centuries.

She is as ruthless as she is relentless, and yet, despite her efforts, the demon threat grows with every passing day.

For the balance has shifted and Lilith is about to discover that the apocalypse, the final and desperate battle for humanity, has begun.

Buy it Here.

UK: https://www.amazon.co.uk/gp/product/B08BNVMK5N
US: https://www.amazon.com/dp/B08BNVMK5N

The Necropolis Trilogy
Cobra Z **(Book 1 of 3)**

What if one day you find your world suddenly torn apart? Entranced by your daily routine, you hear the terrifying news that makes your blood run cold. A devastating man-made virus has been unleashed on the world, a virus so lethal that it rapidly turns everyone it infects into rabid, blood crazed killers. Maniacs so devoid of humanity that their only goal in life is to rip the flesh from your very body, and kill or infect the people you love the most.

Would you panic? Would you rush from your desk in a frantic attempt to save your children? Would you hunker down, and hope the infection somehow passes you by, praying to whatever God you think will help? And what if the very people you care for so deeply are the ones clawing at your door, their blood-smeared faces screaming for the destruction of your soul?

How would you survive in such a world? And would you even want to?

Buy it here
UK: **https://amzn.to/2xb8b3S**
US: **https://amzn.to/2NDCbip**

The Lazarus Chronicles

The Spread **(Book 1 of 5)**

Scientists told us the dead would never walk the Earth. They were wrong.

They call it Lazarus. A virus so deadly that it kills and resurrects virtually everybody it infects. Bangkok becomes the first city to fall to the unstoppable army of the undead... but this is only the beginning. By the time the news channels are reporting on the devastated Thai capital, the virus has already spread around the globe.

Growing, infecting... spreading.

One by one reports come in from other countries. The dead are getting back up... and they're killing everything in their path.

In the UK, clandestine government agent Nick Carter and his team find themselves faced with their deadliest enemy yet as they are forced to deal with the country's first outbreak.

Yet in the depths of this tragedy, they find a glimmer of hope. A woman, a single survivor from the outbreak, someone whose blood might hold the secret to defeating the virus. Could she be humanity's only chance of salvation?

Or is it already too late?
US: **https://amzn.to/2MEGFlK**
UK: **https://amzn.to/2F3leIP**

Printed in Great Britain
by Amazon